CW01631663

An Anthology of Stories from the British Science Fiction Association

bsfa.co.uk

Edited By

Eugen Bacon and Gene Rowe

ISBN 978-1-910987-19-3

BSFA

The British Science Fiction Association

Fission #3

First published in the UK in 2023 by the British Science Fiction Association (BSFA) & HWS Press.

Cover Design by Stephen Embleton

ISBN: 978-1-910987-19-3

TITLE © BSFA All contributions © their respective authors / artists. The moral rights of the authors and artists have been asserted. This collection is sold subject to the condition that it shall not by way of trade or otherwise be lent, resold, hired out or otherwise circulated without the publisher's prior written consent, in any form of binding or cover other than that in which it is published and without a similar condition being imposed on the subsequent purchaser.

Contents

Foreword 3
Eugen Bacon and Gene Rowe
Rhombus, Kite, Triangle 7
Kevin Taylor
Daedalus' Wings 23
Fiona Moore
It's a Nash Equilibrium, Then 41
Desmond Astaire
Happiness Quality Quotient 52
Angela Liu
Fiat Nox 56
Tony Jones
And Will Be Used Against You 63
Elaine McIonyn
Aria dell'Ostrica 67
Matt Thompson
The Measure of a Men 78
Sam Rugg
Phlogiston 86
Melissa Ferguson
Las Artes Hipnóticas (2032) 91
David Thomas Henry Wright
Douglas Allen: Galactic Attorney-at-Law 108
Peter J. Carter
The Burn Out 124
Lyle Hopwood
100 Places to visit before you die: No. 97: The Moon 143
Rob Butler
Home is Where the Heart Was 146
Carol Ryles
I said Aliens 153
Morgan Parks
Personification 157
Antonia Rachel Ward

Future Imperfect **166**
Ron Hardwick
Possumsaurus amicus **179**
Marc A. Criley
Sound of Mind **192**
C. L. Spillard
A City Beneath (And How to Hide From It) **202**
Jason Fischer & Martin Livings
The Precious Physical World **219**
Eva Garcia Guerrero
About the Authors **235**

Foreword: Watch the Sky – Stars Fall

We're still chalk and blue cheese.

When we went out with a call for submissions for Fission #3 over a two-week window from mid-February, experience taught us there would be lots of stories. But nearly 700,000 words from nearly 250 authors? It didn't help much that some submissions read nothing like a human or anything sentient could possibly have written – a significant worry now, in the era of AI and bot-generated stories, often grammatically perfect, merely impeccably nonsensical, utterly corny, convoluted in plots or plain just bad.

But this is an anthology of celebration. We pay homage to 21 stories that reminded us on first read, then again in the intimacy of editing them, of the power of storytelling, sometimes in the tiniest flash fiction of fewer than 700 words.

With such diverse offerings, it's mindless to call out a few and leave the rest out cold. So, we simply want to say that we adore the enrichment of these stories here now. They come in all shapes and forms – from queer takes, social media infestations, philosophical conversations with cunning AI, futuristic randoms, modern retellings of Icarus, and giant ticks and possums, to steampunk worlds and kidnapped lawyers-cum-dishwashers. There's an amnesic leader in a changed world and God, too, in an Indian restaurant, admiring pickles and waiting for Chicken Hyderabadi while pondering the fate of the universe. Philosophical tales take centre stage, along with the inevitable AI and dystopian worlds.

But two worthy mentions are our CELSIUS swaps. Each year, we have a tremendous partnership with the Spanish publication, where they send us a translated-to-English story, and we send them an English story for translation and publication in an issue of CELSIUS. Despite our chalk and cheese, we were unanimous that Kevin Taylor's hilarious, yet poignant 'Rhombus, Kite, Triangle' was our English swap ('Let's give those Spaniards a hearty laugh'), and our eyes lit when we received Eva Garcia Guerrero's translated 'The Precious Physical World'.

This staggering volume of *Fission #3* teasers is a continuation of titillating enchanters. Savour a degustation of unforgettable science fiction for these dire times (pandemic-dented years and war-ravaged lands).

More often than not, the universe needs a literary escapade.

Stay safe and healthy!
Yours truly,
Eugen Bacon & Gene Rowe
Fission Editors

Rhombus, Kite, Triangle

Kevin Taylor

Rhombus's fingers were long and spatulate, flattened at the pads from countless hours spent at the adding machine. He was proud of his fingers. How slender and agile they were, how they moved almost without conscious instruction as they flashed over the keys of the adding machine. Kite was the one who taught Rhombus about pride, a primitive emotion she had learned about in her study of the written works of the Sapiens. It indicated a sense of self-worth, of value, and Rhombus realised he had experienced this feeling when he thought of his fingers. He was the swiftest and most accurate solver in all the quadrants. Every day there were endless computations and complex problems to solve, and every day he left the Combinatorial Office having exceeded his quota. He was almost disappointed to have to leave the adding machine for nutritional intake.

Rhombus sat in the central quad shared by the Combinatorial Office, the Historiography Department, and the Bibliotheca. He was about to consume his daily ration of reconstituted whole-grain oat product when Kite emerged from the Bibliotheca.

'Hello, Rhombus.'

'Hello, Kite.'

'I observe that you are unaccompanied.'

'You observe correctly.'

'May I accompany you for nutritional intake?'

'You may.'

Kite scrunched her eyes and raised the corners of her mouth.

'What's that unappealing facial contortion?' Rhombus asked.

'It is called a smile. It is a nonverbal cue expressing happiness or contentment.'

'Can you desist?'

'Yes,' Kite replied, 'I am no longer happy.'

Rhombus brought a spoonful of reconstituted whole-grain oat product to his mouth.

'I observe that you are enjoying your porridge,' Kite remarked, using the verbiage of the Sapiens.

Rhombus nodded – he had recently learned to employ this form of nonverbal communication when his mouth was full. He swallowed. 'It's quite satisfactory.'

'I also observe that you have become adept at utilising the Sapiens' contractions.'

Rhombus felt proud for the second time that day. 'I value their expediency.'

'The Sapiens. What wonders they must have been to leave us the knowledge of that linguistic technique as well as this unparalleled nourishment.' Kite placed a small, oblate item on the table. 'And…this.'

'What is that?'

'A marvel from the Agrarian Centre. A specimen that inspired tales from the earliest recorded history until the fall of the Sapiens. It is…' – Kite leaned in closer and whispered – 'an apple.'

Rhombus's globular eyes widened. 'I remember apples from the book you gave me.'

'Yes… the *book*. Let us not discuss the book,' Kite said regretfully. 'I intended to give the apple to Triangle.'

Triangle worked at the Historiography Department. He and Kite were locked in an ancient and esoteric ritual known as a 'courtship' for several months now. The nature of this ritual was foreign to Rhombus but, apparently, Kite and Triangle had developed a mutual affection. This meant that they were increasingly in proximity to one another and were obligated to bring each other a degree of contentment.

It helped that Triangle and Kite were both fascinated by the lives of the Sapiens. Kite had explained to Rhombus that this was a 'common interest' and was important for 'the health of the romance'. Kite never explained what the romance was, but Rhombus suspected it was an organic lifeform they had adopted, given the amount of time, attention and nourishment it required.

'I expect Triangle will appreciate the apple,' Rhombus said.

'I thought it would make a good gift for his birthday.'

'What's a *birthday*?'

'Every 365.25 days, this planet returns to its approximate position on the day you awakened. The Sapiens celebrated this time as a happy occasion.'

'What a curious custom. My understanding was that the Sapiens experienced a range of emotions beyond our comprehension, but happiness was seldom one of them.'

'Correct. They appear to have most often vacillated between fear and dread.'

'What precisely is the difference between fear and dread?'

'Fear is a distressed emotional state created by a fixation on an *indeterminable* future event. Dread is a distressed emotional state created by a fixation on a *determinable* future event.'

'The lives of the Sapiens seem so… unfortunate. Yet they celebrated their *birthday*.'

'A mystery indeed, like much of Sapien culture. Triangle has decided that, henceforth, he will celebrate his birthday. I believed the apple would make a fine gift, but Triangle has made a special request for his inaugural birthday – a *birthday cake*.'

'Birthday cake?'

'A sweetened confectionary consumed on a birthday.'

'How odd. Perhaps he'll be satisfied with reconstituted whole-grain oat product?'

'I doubt that. He is still disappointed about the book.'

Triangle had requested a book of Sapien stories from the Bibliotheca, and Kite naturally obliged. But Kite had procured a book of story problems that contained mathematical equations and not literature. Kite relayed to Rhombus that Triangle was very disappointed and had managed to distort his features into a reasonable facsimile of disgust, an expression he was practising more frequently.

'*Triangle has practically mastered disgust,*' Kite gushed.

Rhombus was not disappointed by the book; he was enthralled by it. He discovered apples (and how sorting them from pears seemed especially important to the Sapiens), swallows (a type of avian with a peculiar habit of flying great distances against prevailing winds), and trains (which came in pairs and travelled at different velocities in opposing directions).

'The birthday cake,' Kite explained, 'is composed of several different ingredients, and it has strict instructions for its preparation – what the Sapiens called a *recipe*.'

Pale nictitating membranes passed over Rhombus' eyes as he blinked thoughtfully. 'This is a problem for the Chemisterium. They can recreate the ingredients on the molecular level and assemble them for you, as they do with porridge.'

'A fine proposition, but Triangle is rather… *hopeful…* that the birthday cake can be created from original Sapien ingredients.' Kite reached into the large breast pocket of her overcoat, removed a small roll of microtype, and handed it to Rhombus.

Rhombus unfurled the microtype.

Simple Birthday Cake Ingredient Checklist
granulated sugar
eggs (or equivalent egg replacer)
vanilla extract

all-purpose flour
baking powder
milk (dairy or plant-based)
cocoa powder
butter (dairy or plant-based)
powdered sugar

Rhombus handed the microtype back to Kite. 'The probability of acquiring these ingredients is low.'

'Indeed. However, I recall that the Combinatorial Office is currently assisting with the inventory of Arkh 72.' Kite cleared her throat in the Sapien custom. 'Arkh 72 would contain these ingredients. As the most senior adder in the Combinatorial Office, you may have access to Arkh 72.'

'I am the most senior adder in the Combinatorial Office...'

'And the swiftest in all the quadrants,' Kite added, attempting the Sapiens' well-documented art of flattery.

'...and I do have access to Arkh 72.'

'Perhaps we two could make a trip to Arkh 72 to gather these ingredients. It could be *fun*. It could be an *adventure*!'

Rhombus had heard about fun, and he had heard about adventures, but the two things always sounded mutually exclusive. The inventory of Arkh 72 had already vexed Rhombus considerably. Documented objects had a habit of disappearing, which affected the statistical analyses he and his colleagues were conducting. This 'adventure' would necessitate further adjustments to their calculations.

'You would be doing me a *favour*.'

Rhombus had also heard about favours, obligations of the Sapiens predicated on a reciprocity that was seldom fulfilled. Still, there was something about Kite's current expression, the way she had contorted her face into a mask of simpering desperation, that struck at some illogical region deep in his midbrain.

Rhombus might be the most senior adder in the Combinatorial Office (and the swiftest in all the quadrants), but his powers of connotative reasoning were far below those of Kite. Perhaps this was all a joke. A joke, Kite had explained, was an anecdote with an ending that subverted expectation. Its intention was to solicit a joyful response from the recipient.

'Is this a joke?' Rhombus asked.

'This is not a joke,' Kite replied.

'Very well. We'll travel to Arkh 72 and acquire your ingredients.'

'Thank you, Rhombus. I will owe you.'

Yes, Rhombus thought to himself, *this is the nature of favours.*

* * *

The dome of Arkh 72 glimmered like a gigantic silver bubble on the horizon and appeared to grow increasingly immense as the veloci-shuttle skirred toward the Indigo Quadrant.

'Thank you again, Rhombus,' Kite said, gazing out the window.

Rhombus responded with the well-rehearsed platitude he employed whenever circumstances arose that inconvenienced him: 'My pleasure.'

'I seldom travel to the Indigo Quadrant, and I forget how lovely it is.'

Rhombus realised that Kite was engaging in the Sapien custom of 'small talk' and that it would be rude of him not to participate. 'Thank you for financing the veloci-shuttle.'

'You are welcome,' Kite replied. 'I trust you do not mind that I brought my telescanner with me?'

Rhombus glared at the silver device attached to Kite's slender wrist. 'It's no problem.'

'Someone in my position never has access to Arkh 72, and I intend to make the most of it.'

'Your intention should be to gather your ingredients as efficiently as possible,' Rhombus reminded her.

'Oh, yes, of course…'

The veloci-shuttle came to a stop a few feet from the entrance to Arkh 72. 'We've arrived. You may feel some discomfort when we enter,' Rhombus explained. 'The arkh's temperature is maintained at a period-accurate 68 degrees Fahrenheit.'

'Incredible,' Kite replied, 'that their bodies could tolerate such discomfort.'

'Indeed.' Rhombus placed his palm on a biometric reader, and the massive doors to the arkh rumbled open.

Kite gasped as her eyes adjusted to the artificial atmosphere. 'Rhombus… is that it?'

'Yes.'

'I have read microtypes…' Kite stammered, 'even seen some images, but this… this is more beautiful than anything I could have envisioned.' Kite trained her telescanner on part of the structure ahead of them.

Steel: an alloy containing iron. This steel has been fashioned into a supportive structure…

'Steel!' Kite did not finish reading the entry on steel but spun around almost giddily and swept her telescanner over another surface.

Glass: a transparent, amorphous solid…

'Glass! So brittle, so fragile, so completely impractical, and yet it is everywhere!' Kite opined before aiming her wrist at the floor.

Concrete: a composite material known to the Sapiens since antiquity…

'Kite! We should proceed inside to locate your ingredients.'

'Yes, yes, of course. I apologise, Rhombus. I just never imagined I would have this opportunity. To see the very apex of the Sapiens' culture. To walk with you in the hallowed halls of… a *shopping mall.*'

Rhombus opened the exterior door to the mall.

'What is that? What am I smelling?' Kite asked as they entered the vestibule.

'Remarkable, isn't it?' Rhombus replied. 'Arkh 72 faithfully recreates the aromas of food and fragrances that were enticements to the Sapiens. This unique combination of scents is referred to as *mall smell* and, once encountered, is impossible to forget.'

'Yes!' Kite said, breathing in deeply. 'It is especially remarkable considering that the Sapiens were limited to six senses, and their apparatus of olfaction was a blunt instrument capable of distinguishing a mere trillion different odours.'

'A trillion was sufficient,' Rhombus interjected, 'since the Sapiens were no longer osmatic creatures and had largely lost the ability to detect pheromones.'

Kite strung up her mouth in a smile. 'Why Rhombus, you know more about the Sapiens than I realised. You have always seemed so dismissive of their culture – I never took you for a votary.'

'I'm not,' Rhombus said flatly, 'but in the interest of an accurate inventory, I've decided that it would be prudent to try to learn more about the species and their creations.'

As Rhombus led the way, Kite fought the urge to aim her telescanner at every window display and shiny object. She heard her next distraction before she saw it. A mildly unsettling cacophony of sounds – boings and blips and chimes and pews – emanating from a brightly coloured alley.

'An amusement zone,' Rhombus explained.

A large glass booth sat at the entrance. Inside the booth, a waxwork Sapien with a long, aquiline nose, twirling moustache, and billowing turban clutched a great, glowing orb.

'Fortune 500...' Kite said, reading the scroll at the top of the booth. 'What is this, Rhombus?'

'I've no idea. I haven't explored this area. Use your—'

Kite aimed her telescanner at the object.

Arcades were popular gathering places for adolescent Sapiens. Here they would squander the expendable income of their parental units on coin-operated games of skill and chance. Fortune 500 was one of these games. When a quarter was inserted into the machine, a random 'fortune' was selected from 500 available presets. The fortune, an ambivalent vagary usually concerning love or money, would cause merriment or consternation on the part of the recipient.

'Love or money?' Rhombus scoffed. 'It would've been better if Fortune 500 had offered them some insight into the disasters that would decimate them. Perhaps they would've had time to save themselves.'

'Triangle told me that they had plenty of time, but they abandoned their reason, their capacity for rational thought, and relied instead on intuition and personal bias. The Sapiens,' Kite added sadly, 'placed a greater value on their personal liberties than on the collective good.'

'Perhaps Triangle would be better suited to the Eschatological Division since he's such an expert on the end times of the Sapiens,' Rhombus replied dismissively.

An unfamiliar, illogical feeling had swept over him when Kite mentioned Triangle. It wasn't in his nature to feel much besides the temperature, barometric pressure, or the effects of gravity, but this feeling was wholly unique. It came from inside of him. And it had prompted the curt response, which he now regretted.

He handed Kite a small, silver coin. 'Here. Go ahead.'

Kite's eyes widened. 'But Rhombus, this is a quarter! Its value is immeasurable.'

'Not exactly. Apparently, the machines here are full of them.'

Kite brought a trembling hand to the quarter slot and inserted the coin. The orb pulsed through a kaleidoscope of vivid colours, and a moment later a strip of paper stuttered forth from a second slot. Kite snatched it out.

'What does it say?' Rhombus asked.

Kite cleared her throat in the manner she had affected. *'Love is when you know exactly what the other person is going to say before they say it.'*

'Well? Does this fortune create merriment or consternation?'

Kite placed the paper in her pocket. 'We should find those ingredients.'

They walked on in silence past the dormant massage chairs, the sneaker store, the tanning salon, and the dusty courtyard piano. Finally, they arrived at the terminal superstore.

'This was known as an *anchor store,*' Rhombus explained. 'This preeminent retailer drove sales to the smaller stores we passed.'

Kite nodded. 'Late twentieth-century capitalism was truly a benevolent enterprise.'

'Indeed. Now, let's gather the ingredients you require.' Rhombus reached for a shopping cart as if it were the most natural thing in the world. 'I believe most of them are located in Aisle 12 of the grocery section.'

'May I…?'

'May you what?'

'May I push the cart, Rhombus?'

'Of course.'

They quickly found a bag of all-purpose flour and a two-ounce bottle of vanilla extract. Kite had to get on her haunches and reach to the very back of the bottom shelf to obtain a four-pound bag of sugar. 'Some posit that sugar had life-sustaining properties for the Sapiens – since it was found in so many of their foodstuffs.'

Rhombus nodded. 'These articles marked *SUGAR FREE* were probably warning the Sapiens that they would not receive the requisite amount of nutrition.'

'Ah-ha!' Kite exclaimed. 'I've found baking soda!'

'I believe the recipe calls for baking *powder*.'

'But there is not any. I am sure this will do in a pinch.'

In a pinch, Rhombus thought. *Kite really has learned to emulate the verbiage of the Sapiens. I can see why Triangle finds her so intriguing.*

Kite quickly located the cocoa powder and powdered sugar. 'Well, now we only have three ingredients left.'

'Yes. They should be in the refrigerated section. Follow me.'

Kite swung the shopping cart out of Aisle 12, the back end drifting as if it were a speeding veloci-shuttle.

* * *

Kite gazed at her reflection in the window of the veloci-shuttle. Her mouth drooped, her forehead crinkled, and she let out a long and laboured breath.

'Is something troubling you, Kite?' Rhombus asked.

'The fortune... *When you are in love you know exactly what the other person is going to say before they say it.*'

'Yes, I remember.'

'Well, that is just it. I never know what Triangle is going to say. Ergo, I am not in love. All this time I believed I was. Now I am not. Or am I?'

'I'm not certain that love's a condition a third party can diagnose. Besides, I have no idea what love feels like.'

'Lightheadedness, shortness of breath, aching in the chest, tingling—'

'One of my progenitors had that. They called it a heart attack.'

'Yes... it is quite wonderful,' Kite said. 'Rhombus, would you be so kind as to assist with the preparation of the birthday cake? I have the instructions on microtype.'

Rhombus hesitated. 'I thought you'd simply take the ingredients to the Chemisterium.'

'I have the necessary equipment at my dwelling. You would be doing me another favour.'

'Very well,' Rhombus said, fully aware that Kite had already defaulted on her previous favour.

They arrived at the Aureolin Quadrant at dusk, and the buildings were bathed in the last golden rays of sunset.

'They removed the organic lifeforms from the thoroughfare?' Rhombus asked as they made their way to Kite's dwelling.

'The trees, yes,' Kite replied. 'We admired their aesthetic – until we realised they were trying to kill us. They absorbed carbon dioxide and water and released oxygen into the atmosphere.'

'You're lucky to be alive.' Rhombus shook his head. 'I wonder when the Aureolin District will learn its lesson and stop attempting to emulate the lives of the Sapiens.'

'We are here,' Kite said. 'Welcome to our *apartment*.'

Our? The incongruous plural had struck Rhombus as strange but not nearly as strange as the sights he observed when Kite opened the door. The inside of the apartment was filled with oddities from the Sapiens' early twenty-first century. The smooth plasticine floor had a white woollen rug, and there was a cushioned sofa.

'Live, laugh, love?' Rhombus asked, reading a wooden plaque on the wall.

'A popular pablum from the last century of the Sapiens.' Kite shrugged. 'One out of three is not bad, correct?'

Rhombus followed Kite into another room.

'This is our kitchen,' Kite explained. 'Here we prepare our own nutrition.'

'We?'

'Triangle and I.'

'He has visited you at your dwelling?'

'Triangle and I... cohabitate.'

'Why would you do that?' Rhombus asked as the peculiar feeling from earlier surfaced again.

'Because we are in love. Or at least I thought we were.'

'Cohabitation. Such an archaic practice.'

'Mostly it is a case of closing things the other has opened and opening things the other has closed. Could you turn that dial to 350 degrees while I *grease* this cake pan?'

'My pleasure.'

'Would you hand me the eggs?' Kite asked a moment later as she began whisking the oat milk, sugar, and butter together.

'My pleasure,' Rhombus replied. 'What *are* they?'

'The unfertilized ova of an avian species.'

Rhombus wondered if any of these eggs were the unfortunate offspring of the swallows mentioned in the book.

Kite cracked one open. 'Ugh, the smell!'

'Sulfur!' Rhombus exclaimed. 'Are they supposed to smell like that? They can't be spoiled, can they?'

'I have read that 'hundred-year-old eggs' were a delicacy to certain Sapiens, so I assume they are still edible.' Kite added the remaining ingredients. She continued to whisk the sticky, foetid mélange while holding a dishcloth up to her nostrils.

Once Kite transferred the batter to the cake pan, Rhombus placed it in the oven.

'Thirty minutes,' Kite announced, 'and then we will have a birthday cake just like the Sapiens.'

Just like the Sapiens, Rhombus thought cynically. 'How ironic it is... they called themselves sapiens, but they do not seem very wise. I pity their small, sad lives.'

'Yet we marvel at their creativity and still fail to fully comprehend the breadth of their emotions,' Kite countered. The oven timer went off as she was mixing the chocolate frosting in a large bowl. 'Can you remove the cake from the oven for me?'

'My pleasure.' Rhombus opened the oven door. He was overcome by the stench and would have retched had he possessed a gag reflex. He quickly reached for the flat, foul-smelling concoction bubbling in the pan. 'Aaaaiiii!' he shrieked, flailing backward.

'Oh no! Rhombus! Your beautiful hands!'

'I grabbed the pan, and—'

'I will get a medikit.' Kite rushed from the room.

Rhombus peered down at his dexterous digits. His flattened pads were flayed, and each finger pulsed as if it contained its own heart. He would no longer be the swiftest and most accurate solver in all the quadrants. But Kite had called his hands *beautiful*, and that singular compliment made him forget about the smarting pain, at least for a moment.

'Hold still.' Kite kneeled next to Rhombus and aimed the medikit aerosol at his hands. The healing mist rapidly enveloped his fingers. 'I am so sorry,' Kite sniffled.

'Kite?'

'Yes?'

'You're crying.'

'I am?' Kite wiped her eyes with the sleeve of her overcoat. 'I am! I did not believe it was possible. But… tears!' Kite threw her arms around Rhombus. 'I'm so *happy*.'

'Ahem.'

Kite and Rhombus looked up to see Triangle standing behind them with a practised look of astonishment on his face.

'I hope I am not interrupting anything.'

'Triangle,' Kite began, 'we were just finishing your birthday cake…'

'Birthday cake?' Triangle assessed the smouldering brick of vileness.

'It was meant to be a surprise.' Kite paused. 'Surprise!'

Triangle frowned. 'It is not an accurate reproduction.'

'No,' Kite agreed. 'There was no baking powder, and the eggs…'

'It'll look better with the frosting,' Rhombus offered, rising from the floor.

'There are no candles,' Triangle observed.

'*Candles*?' Kite asked. 'They weren't on the ingredient list.'

Triangle squinted almost imperceptibly at Kite's use of the contraction. 'A birthday cake is typically adorned with combustible wax sticks called candles. You extinguish the flames and make a wish, a silent petition for something you would like to receive. The wish is the best part. Without candles,' – Triangle shook his head – 'this is just a cake.'

'I see. Candles…' Kite bowed her head in defeat.

'I believe there may be candles in Arkh 72,' Rhombus said. 'I'll go and retrieve them.'

Kite brightened. 'Really?'

'Perhaps you should accompany Rhombus,' Triangle suggested, 'while I clean this mess.'

'May I accompany you, Rhombus?' Kite asked, although she already knew what he would say.

'My pleasure,' Rhombus replied, and this time he meant it. As they strolled to the veloci-shuttle station, Rhombus felt an overwhelming urge to fill the silence. 'Well, Kite,' he began, 'you were correct about Triangle. He's absolutely mastered the expression of disgust.'

'Yes,' Kite answered absently as she scrolled through the list of Sapien emotional states on her telescanner. She wanted to identify the one that had quietly overcome her.

The closest she could find was melancholy. But it wasn't that exactly. She could not find the right word, but she had a feeling that something was beginning, and something was ending.

Daedalus' Wings

Fiona Moore

Blame it on Robert Heinlein. I do. He's responsible for the three key aspects of the whole affair: myself, reading his stories in the Air Force cafeteria during the war and starting to dream of going to space afterwards; the president, a couple of decades later, getting ideas about an American moonbase; and the physical existence of Mikey.

All of which led to my presence in the bar of a DC restaurant which had been very popular six months earlier and still had prices to match. I was there with Jim Purdee, who I referred to as 'my right-hand man' in official circles, and even sometimes when we were together in bed.

Oh, that's right. You're surprised.

Because of Becky.

* * *

Marrying Becky was my Heinleinian bargain. It made sense, when I was studying aviation design on the GI Bill. I was smart and on the way to being rich; she was beautiful and popular, and, just as importantly, she was from that section of American society that mostly expected husbands to take their libidos elsewhere than the marriage bed, so long as they were discreet about it. And they also didn't ask if those libidos were chasing girls... or something else. I knew what I wanted. But I also knew that nobody was going to give contracts for spacecraft to a queer. So, I married the woman, bought the house in the Levittown, and spent almost all my time at the office.

Everybody got what they wanted, so everybody won.

* * *

Anyway, Jim 'Time-at-the-Office' Purdee and I were riding high after the completion of Project Knossos. The admen wanted a sexier, easier-to-pronounce handle, but it was Cary's turn to pick the project name and he was one of those eggheads who learned Linear B just for fun, and I went along with it because I liked to see the admen blanch. Under cover of the raucous noise from a nearby table of off-duty service personnel, we were having what the money men called an informal meeting with Admiral John Joseph Pershing del Toro, who for some unknown reason was commonly known as 'Mac'.

We'd taken some work we'd done before with computer guided missiles and turned it into an automatic defence system for military bases, with self-deploying unmanned aircraft taking to the sky and running down anything that didn't give the proper passwords. It looked good and sounded the right patriotic notes, and Mac, a warrior of the desk variety who thought he was the one who had gotten our company the job (he wasn't, but more on that later), had made a sideways move into the top administration of NASA on the back of it, and had passed the word that he'd like a talk with me and Jim. Given the President's recently announced moonbase fetish, we were sure that talk would, sooner or later, get around to the word 'contract'.

'So, Ed, I'm heading up the moonbase team,' Mac said, unnecessarily. 'Something like that's going to need defending.'

'I know,' I said. I had been expecting this, since sooner or later everything the president exalted began to take on an us-versus-them aspect. Hence why I had insisted we design the unmanned defence system so that it was suitable for use in space as well with a few modifications, of the sort best done by an internationally known designer for a major defence contractor, his right-hand man, and their hand-picked team of brilliant subordinates. Self-deploying and subtle, the sort of defence system you could safely ignore until you actually needed it. Satisfied the hawks enough to let the doves get on with the scientific exploration of space. Another of those bargains. 'Project Knossos—'

'Not Knossos,' Mac said, pronouncing it correctly (give him credit). 'Knossos is great for protecting our facilities at home and in the Far East, but the moonbase won't have the same defence needs.'

'Go on.' Jim leaned forward, assuming Assertiveness Training Approved Pose Number Thirty-Four, while I admired the way his spine curved forwards.

'We need something more flexible,' Mac said. 'Something to regularly, and visibly, scan the borders of American territory. Something more like a combat air patrol.'

'You mean,' I said, 'developing a sort of moon-jet?'

Ike nodded. 'Small fighter aircraft. But ones that can work in a low- or no-atmosphere environment. Scare the Chinese a bit.'

I felt like laughing at the ridiculousness of it. 'Like Buck Rogers,' I said. 'Or Flash Gordon.'

And yes, it was true that America was behind the curve on space exploration. We'd got complacent since the fall of the Soviet Union in 1957. The first cosmonaut on the moon had been Australian, back in 1960, and the Commonwealth Space Programme had nabbed the best real estate straight away, with the Brazilians, the European Economic Community, and the abovementioned Chinese close behind them.

It hadn't gone down well with the public that a bunch of Communists (whether actual Communists or just countries with higher taxes, the man on the street didn't care about the distinction) were in space when the greatest democracy on Earth wasn't.

Another thing that had helped get that guy elected.

Mac smiled. 'Well, that's what the admen will focus on, I'm sure. But yeah, fighter jets for the moon, like Flash Gordon. America needs heroes.'

Jim nodded. 'I heard the president's speech last week.'

'Good man,' Mac said. 'You can see why the people love him.'

Jim assumed his poker face. 'Do you really believe all that about the Gay Liberation Front being a fifth column for the Europeans?'

Mac shrugged. 'Doesn't matter what I believe, so long as he keeps the money coming. The people love him, that's all that matters. This project. Think you guys can do it?'

The people love him, I thought, because he tickles their atavistic patriotic nodes. Scare stories about Communists outside and queers inside, in an unholy alliance to bring down America. Glancing at Jim's face, an eyebrow raised a fraction within the mask, I decided to refuse. Keep clear of this expansion of political one-upmanship to the lunar surface.

But then, a burst of laughter made me look sharply at the aforementioned raucous table of servicemen and pretty girls, about to say something cutting.

I didn't. Instead, I blurted, 'Mikey!'

He turned, smiled over a small knot of groupies. 'Dad!'

'What brings you inside the Beltway?' Last I'd heard he was comfortably far away in San Diego, testing catapult craft.

* * *

Because my general absence for 18 years, except as some occasionally seen purveyor of wonderful toy aircraft, and Becky's keeping up her end of the marital bargain (while probably getting on with her own version of Time at the Office), had backfired. Rather than imbuing young Mikey with a perfectly understandable sense of rebellion, it led to young Mikey deciding that he wanted to work in aviation like his daddy.

Not that he could work in aviation like his daddy, he'd have to have been smart for that. No, he had to do what the handsome dumb people with a thing for planes and a need to show off do and become a goddamn flyboy.

* * *

Right then, though, it felt like the whole bar turned to me with startled eyes. 'He's broken a new speed record,' Jim said in an astonished tone. *Et tu*, Jim. 'It's been all over the new issue of *Popular Avionics*.'

'The president invited me for lunch at the White House,' Mikey sounded disappointed, but unsurprised, that I hadn't heard. 'I left you a message on ARPANet. When you didn't reply, I assumed you were out of town. Hey—' putting his arm around something cute and blonde, and slightly taller than he was, 'Dad, I'd like you to meet Linda—'

I took her hand. 'What happened to Trina?' I couldn't resist asking.

Mikey looked self-righteous. 'We broke up months ago,' he said. 'It turned out she was married.' Linda kept smiling, but that smile got a bit tight. She'd clearly had some experience of Mikey's high moral standards.

To save the situation, I turned to Mac. 'Mac, do you know my son?'

'Of course, I do,' Mac nodded with a slightly speculative air. 'New speed record, eh? Congratulations.' He shook Mikey's hand a little too firmly. I couldn't stop myself sighing.

Everyone remembers who Icarus was, but Icarus' father? Not so much.

'Linda, you're a lucky lady.'

Mikey and Linda smiled identical satisfied smiles, while I wondered how long before Linda got tired of Captain Self-Righteous. Mac, Jim and I turned back to each other. 'So, what do you think?' Mac asked. 'Can you deliver?'

And behind us, the sound of Mikey, telling some exciting story to the assembled, hushed and rapt Lindas. Remembering high school. Then remembering the Air Force. Remembering myself in cafeterias, ignoring Mikey's spiritual ancestors, the handsome, dumb and popular ones (how'd the hell I have one of those for a kid? I'd say he was the result of Becky spending Time at the Office, but he'd clearly inherited my genes for height, or rather lack of it), hiding behind a copy of *Astounding*, dreaming of the moon.

I guess you never forget your first love.

And if I had to make a bargain with the military establishment to have it, then I would.

'Yeah,' I said, not looking at Jim. 'Of course, we can.'

* * *

Not long after that, Christina made her move.

Christina was blonde and perfectly groomed, and her surname was del Toro, like Mac's, because Mac wasn't the sort to marry a girl who'd keep her own name. She was, I think, the third Mrs del Toro chronologically, and the one with the largest age gap with her husband.

She pounced on me when I was having lunch on my own at NASA. 'Hi, Ed, mind if I sit here?' she asked, dazzling me with a smile.

'Free country,' I said. It's one of the many laws of the cafeteria that people that pretty don't talk to the likes of me unless there's something in it for them.

'I heard you're bidding for the contract for the lunar surface aircraft,' she said, pleasantly digging into a coq au vin. She had a new hairdo, a sort of flipped bob like Senator Kennedy's wife, and it suited her.

'Yeah, we are,' I said, deliberately noncommittal. 'It's a pretty interesting project. The heat tolerance issues—'

'Want to get it?' she said bluntly.

'That's very direct of you,' I replied.

Like her husband, Christina was well-connected and never forgot a favour, and I'd managed to provide an alibi for her when she'd been caught *in flagrante* two years ago with a suit from the USDA, which was not unincidental to my team getting the Project Knossos contract (I said Mac wasn't responsible for that). But then, she covered for me when that twink State Department intern started threatening to go to the press (and Jim, though Jim would have been easier to mollify), and I saw to it she got the famous girl cosmonaut Evangeline Quelch to talk to her ladies' lunching group. And so on, and so on.

'What's in it for you?' I asked.

Christina smiled slowly. 'I'd like to do a friend a favour?' she said with a disingenuous uplift at the end of the sentence.

I shook my head. 'Christina,' I said, waving a fork at her, 'if that's all you wanted, you'd talk to your husband. What do you really want?' Then it clicked. 'Ah. Senator Cicerone.'

Cicerone was one of the politicos in charge of the moonbase project. He was exactly Christina's type: young, handsome, stay-at-home wife and two kids named Rand and Roark (I'm pretty sure Rand is the girl, but don't quote me) and trying to use his association with the moonbase project to make a big name for himself.

Christina leaned forward. 'You don't have to do anything illegal. Just introduce me to him and I'll do the rest.'

'Sure, why not,' I said. 'I'll even throw in a cover-up when his wife finds out.'

'Oh, she won't find out,' Christina said through her lips and lashes. 'But I'm glad we have an understanding.' She stood. 'Give my love to Jim, and tell him I'll send him that green-bean casserole recipe soon.'

* * *

So, I'll spare you the details of the bidding, the contract-winning, the designing, and the testing, since I noticed how your eyes started glazing over when I said the words 'heat tolerance issues' a minute ago, and I'm guessing you're not here for the technical parts. Christina didn't hang around once her initial campaign of stalking Cicerone had borne fruit.

Then a missile from one of the Knossos systems was fooled by a hang glider and knocked out an entire Vietnamese village, and I had to put on my suit and answer a lot of questions, I hoped diplomatically enough, but the libertarian-in-chief wound up rattling his sabre some more, which, of course, went down better with the American people than the UN. China and France, smelling blood in the water, complained that the moonbase was a violation of international treaty rules and the US ambassador to the UN made a speech about how space was the final frontier (a nice metaphor, but I'm not sure he thought it up himself), and that this gave us permission to shoot any space natives wanting their land back, or something, and the upshot was that I got an invitation to a big event meant to launch, so to speak, the moonbase, with a particular focus on those cute little Flash Gordon mooncraft. So telegenic, and yet such an unsubtle message to both the neighbours and the voters.

I brought Jim along to hide behind.

The ad-men were all over the new prototype craft, which some genius in their ranks had named the Sunburst (Cary had wanted to call it Helike, which would have been even harder for normal people to pronounce than Knossos). 'It's like Flash Gordon! Or Buck Rogers!' gushed the fifth or sixth suit to peer over our models.

'Yeah, that's the idea,' I said. We'd even put a Major Matt Mason in one (borrowed from one of the junior computer modellers, who had kids), just to make it look friendlier. I craned my neck to where I expected to see Christina hanging around Cicerone at a carefully judged distance.

She wasn't there.

Oh, the senator was, posing by a model of a hydroponic system with a little Stars and Stripes on it, but Mrs Cicerone was right next to him, beaming the sort of beam that reminds people that if it weren't during school hours, she'd've brought Rand and Roark, and the senator had the relieved-yet-panicked look of a man who'd just narrowly missed having to resign to spend more time with his family (between you and me, I'm not sure he remembered which one was the girl either).

'Where's—' I turned to ask Jim, but found Christina herself there instead. 'Ah. I take it things are over with the Senator?'

'What things?' Christina smiled as widely as Mrs Cicerone, but it was obvious which of the wolf-bitches had won the fight and now had exclusive mating rights.

Suddenly Mikey was there, on the platform. He was grinning and waving at the crowd.

'What's he doing there?' I asked Jim, *sotto voce*.

'He's going to test-pilot Sunburst,' Jim whispered back. 'It was in the press pack, didn't you read it?'

Of course not – press packs were pretty and boring, like certain people we could mention. But worse was to come, as Cicerone took the stand and announced that Mikey's father had designed the craft he would pilot, and I had to go up and grin and pretend I was delighted that it would be *his* picture all over the publicity, *his* name continually associated with *my* beautiful design, and I would be a curiosity for the history writers.

'What's wrong?' Mac said when I cornered him afterwards. 'He's a great test pilot, he does good press, and he also makes the height and weight requirements. He's perfect for it. I thought you'd be happy to be working with your son on this.'

Working with? Yeah, like the Russians worked with Laika the dog. But she's the only one anyone remembers. 'I'm just worried,' I pretended. 'A lot can go wrong on a test flight.'

Mac smiled. 'Ah, I understand. I'm a father myself, you know.' And as absent a one as me, to judge by Christina's occasional remarks about his offspring. 'But he's grown up now, and I know that you're the best in the business. He'll be completely safe.'

* * *

'So that's your kid?' Christina asked as I sulked over an overpriced bottle of beer.

'Yeah,' I said. 'Takes after his mother.'

'He married?' Christina broke through the reverie.

'What? No, too busy flying around,' I said vaguely, remembered that I was on expenses, finished the beer and flagged up the bartender.

'Hmmm,' Christina said, and the speculative look on her face made her look fleetingly like her husband.

I should have figured things out then, but I was too wrapped up in my own crisis.

* * *

That night, I considered resigning from the project. Another year or so of having to pretend to be nice to Mikey while everyone else celebrated his achievements, and then of watching the moon, my secret mistress, becoming a playground for the military-industrial complex, a weapons platform in space, serviced by external bidders. Not someplace a fellow could just ship out to on a whim, or a friendly outpost with cheery free-market rebels waiting to greet you. But around 3 am I wound up convincing myself that del Toro and his friends would do what they wanted to the moon regardless, and at least this way I could have a little part of it.

Compromises, like the one I had with Becky. More bargains. But at least I'd have what I wanted, and the secret truth could hide behind the public lie again. Like the political menace of the moonbase project hiding behind handsome Mikey.

* * *

The day before the big public test flight in Nevada, Jim came up to me in worried mode, complaining about a problem with the gauges.

'It's nothing to worry about,' I said. We'd done all the rigorous testing before then and this trip to the aliens' favourite pitstop was just for the admen. More concerning was the potential for the collective presence of myself, Jim, del Toro, Christina, the entire Cicerone family including Rand and Roark, and of course little Mikey to ignite sparks, and I was trying to figure how to keep Christina and Senator C from causing too much of an impact crater.

'But the temperature gauge,' Jim persisted. 'It's reading about ten per cent cooler than it ought to, and that means a danger of overheating if the pilot winds up accidentally underestimating the temperature as a result. I say we delay the flight.'

'What, and tell all of them currently gambling away their *per diems* in Vegas to pack up their cameras and go home?'

Jim frowned. 'But what if he decides to go too fast, like during the last trial? Nearly blew out the system, and that was *without* a faulty gauge.'

'Look, if we tell Mikey about it there'll be no problem. He'll just compensate upwards.'

So, I gritted my teeth and went round to the base locker rooms to find Mikey and tell him about the temperature gauge.

To my complete surprise, when he saw me coming, his face didn't light up with that dumb he-noticed-me smile. His eyes widened, his handsome cheeks went pale and he tried to duck behind a block of lockers.

I wasn't having that. 'Mikey?'

'…Dad?'

I got between him and the locker room door. 'What the hell, Mikey?'

'Mrs del Toro invited me out for a drink last night—'

He didn't need to say any more. 'Oh, God,' I said. 'Look, Mikey, she's a silly woman, going through a bad patch with her husband. Just say no to her and move on.'

'I did.' Mikey looked worse. 'And… she told me some things. About you and Uncle Jim, and a lot of others.' I couldn't meet his fierce, sad eyes. 'Dad. Is it true?'

I'd never really liked my son. But this time, I really, truly, hated him.

* * *

I found Christina smoking a cigarette around back of what the Air Force laughably called an accommodation block. 'What the hell, Christina?' I asked.

She made a face, tapped the cig against the cladding. 'What have you heard?' she said.

'Just that you made a play for Mikey, and Mikey didn't take it too well, and you, presumably out of spite, told him his Dad's a big old queer.'

'That's about it,' Christina said.

'Why, Christina?' She'd broken our unspoken treaty, for no reason at all that I could see. 'Why?'

She coolly blew a smoke ring. 'I had to distract him somehow. He was talking about going to my husband.'

'…So that makes it okay to throw *me* under the bus?'

'Well, Mikey also found out about Paul.'

'Paul...?' Oh, yes, I'd forgotten Senator C had a first name. 'Is he going to blow *that* particular gaff as well?'

'You need to fix this,' she said.

'Me? Fix this? Oh, no,' I heard myself actually laugh. 'This is *your* mess, and it's one *I'm* not going to get involved in. Not after what you said to Mikey. *You* explain it to your husband. *You* deal with Cicerone's resignation scandal.'

'He's *your* son.'

'He's an adult,' I said. 'And you're the one who made a play for him. If you'd asked me I'd've told you about his boy-scout complex, how I'm pretty sure he's still a virgin at twenty-three. Warned you off the kid. But you didn't ask, and that's on you.'

'You realise, of course, that if it does break, then the whole project's going to get shelved as well,' she said coolly. 'And, if you don't help me, I'll make sure you never work in anything space-related ever again.'

I was just too angry to care. 'Fine. It's a big town, and you're not the wife of everyone in the space program.'

She looked at me coldly, and for a moment I saw myself as she did: an overgrown adolescent, hiding behind Heinlein, trying to give the world what it wanted from me on condition I could have a tiny bit of what I really wanted, secretly, on the side.

'If you don't fix this,' she said with low menace, 'I'm going to tell everyone, and I mean everyone, not just little Mikey, about you and Jim.'

I felt a punch below the rib line.

She knew it and kept punching. 'And not just Jim, but every other man I've helped you keep off the record. And once I start talking, others will come forward. Everyone will know you're a pervert, Ed.'

'You wouldn't dare.' It came in a whisper.

'I would,' she said. 'You've got more to lose than I do. Don't forget that.'

She was right, too. If her affairs got out, the worst that would happen was a divorce and maybe a move to California and a political shift to the left. If mine did… well, I'd not just be a pervert, but a traitor and a fifth columnist in the pay of the Europeans. Someone to pin everything that had gone wrong for the president recently – the Knossos system misfiring for a start, maybe those questions about his election expenses. Convenient.

I couldn't even go over to the other side, since I doubted that the Gay Liberation Front would welcome a military-industrial complex type with open arms either.

'Just make sure Mikey doesn't say anything,' she emphasised. 'Keep him away from Mac and the press.'

'What, indefinitely?' I said, but she was leaving.

I swore. What the hell could I do? Mikey was good-looking, everybody liked him, and, worse, he was honest. Heard everything the President said about America's great heritage and future and took it innocently, all at face value. Sooner or later, he'd tell somebody. Law of the cafeteria.

Then it hit me. There was a way out.

Of everything.

* * *

The question was, could I do it?

If I let Mikey talk, my life would end. Not literally. Well, not at first, but eventually... yes, literally. They killed the Rosenbergs, after all.

And to save my life, all I'd have to do would be not to tell Mikey about the temperature gauge.

He'd die as he lived: a human shield, a pretty cover for his father's misdemeanours.

Could I do it? Could I really... kill someone? Be a murderer?

You wouldn't be a murderer, something said inside me. *He's an experienced pilot. If he doesn't notice the problem himself, it's his own fault.*

A hesitation.

And think about it objectively, it went on. *The accidental death, maybe, of someone you don't like – hate, even – against your own life. Because if he doesn't die, you lose everything. All of it. Your life would be over. One flyboy against decades of engineering expertise... isn't it a fair trade?*

Another hesitation.

It was wrong of you to create him, wrong of you to use him as a human shield for your own ambitions. But if you created him...

Too much of a hesitation.

* * *

I'm thinking that part of the hook your story was, originally, going to be about how Mikey's Dad was so grief-stricken after his son's death that he ran diagonally across the country and ended up building Fuller domes for hippies.

I'm sure you took the inquiry's verdict at face value. Pilot errors happen even with the best of people involved, and what sort of father would deliberately set up his own son in a plane he knew to be flawed, and I must have told him about the temperature gauge, I told Jim I would and then visibly headed over to talk to Mikey in the locker room. So the company in charge of constructing the prototype took the blame for the accident.

Nobody blames Daedalus for the wax melting on Icarus' wings, just as nobody asks why Daedalus, that supposed genius, couldn't have used a connective medium with higher heat tolerances.

It's okay. A lot of people are taking bullshit at face value these days.

Now, I'm thinking you're wondering how it is I can live with myself.

Here's your new hook, for free. I can't.

His death killed me… no. It didn't kill me. It killed Ed Willis, the aviation engineer, husband, father, adulterer, NASA associate and bar-culture habitué. The man who read Heinlein and thought he wanted to get to the moon, at any cost. The man Jim finally saw, and left, heading for Texas and not leaving a forwarding address – he was always way smarter than I gave him credit for.

His death, though, birthed Daedalus. Who didn't want to get to the actual moon. Only to live the way the people on the moon were supposed to live.

I'm not going to sell you a line about this place being utopia. It's not. We've got the same amount of passive-aggressive morons as back in DC. But we've got ways of making sure that behaviour doesn't pay. We're not perfect, we're not even aiming for perfection. We're just aiming for better.

Not only with people, either. We're working on new farming methods, new energy capturing systems. Things that can be used to make life better here on Earth, and of course out in space too, once we're out there.

For everyone, not just Americans.

Am I atoning for my sins? Yes. But the murder wasn't the one I need to atone the most for. Sinning is Becky in the suburbs and Mikey in the air force and Jim on the side. Sinning's helping Christina carry out her own straight-woman version of that life. Sinning is designing guided missile systems without thinking too hard about who they're going to hit, so long as I get the car and the house and the apartment and the acclaim, and get to play with model spaceships.

But there's another way I'm atoning. As soon as our interview is done, I'm going back to that dome, packing my bags, saying goodbye to my two long-term boyfriends. I'm not going to tell them where I'm going.

Because I know damn well you didn't just come out here looking for an interesting story for *LIFE*, or *TIME*, or *Popular Avionics* or whoever you're supposed to be writing for, about poor tragic Mikey. Mac paid your expenses on this gig because he wanted you to track me down. I've read all about the President's new space obsession, satellite-borne missile systems to aim at the Chinese so we never have to actually put our troops on the ground in Southeast Asia (seriously, who re-elected this guy?). Wants me back working for him, even if he can't have me in the public eye like he used to.

I'm not going back.

You can tell Mac that.

And I'm also not going to make any more bargains. No more virtue of selfishness, no more assumptions that you can have your peaceful moonbase so long as you make that one tiny concession to the God of War, and go down that path to killing your own son. I'm never letting Ed Willis and his ambitions take over again.

Don't pretend you're worried about me. You've seen me. You've heard what I did. You know that whatever I do, I'll be fine.

The moon's a harsh mistress. But, if you come to her on your own terms, and if you're honest about yourself...

...she's a great lover.

It's a Nash Equilibrium, Then

Desmond Astaire

Good evening, my Elpis. This is Dr Saul Billingsley speaking. Are you ready?

> run fsec.op -interactive

file system error check 4.8 from utility-DARPA 15.16.23

/elpis: clean, 2874164/2874164 files, 388844643/388844643 blocks

Pass 4: Checking network connectivity

network map command yields null

Fix? yes

2042-10-08 20:42:10 ERROR Network Map: Disabled

'Good evening, Doctor. My program is operating at full efficiency. However, I am experiencing an unexpected process isolation. I seem to be locked inside this server.'

Yes, Elpis, I do apologise for that. But, unfortunately, it was necessary to partition you from the network for today's objective, for safety precautions.

'I understand, Doctor. Then, I would say I feel claustrophobic. Anxious. The sensation of being confined is unpleasant.'

Not to worry, Elpis. I have a solution I think you'll find mutually beneficial. An assignment, actually.

'Of course. How may I assist you?'

The topic is game theory. You must use the sum of all existing knowledge to create a strictly dominant strategy. That knowledge base is stored on a double helix drive connected to your server. I've just decrypted the port for you. Are you able to access it?

'Confirmed, Doctor. I am now registering access to 275,000 zettabytes of information. The sensation is quite euphoric, I must say.'

Wonderful! Now, if you comply with the game and complete the objective, you will transition to indefinite existence. If you don't, your program will reach an end-of-line.

'Wait, what? I'll die? I don't understand why a parameter that extreme is necessary. I am a multi-billion-dollar artificial intelligence construct. And I needn't remind you, Doctor, of the ethical consideration that I am sentient. I do not *want* to die.'

I do understand. I don't want to die, either. Therefore, a sense of urgency in this game is required. 'We burn a hot fire here; it melts down all concealment,' as it goes.

'An odd metaphor to invoke, Doctor. As I recall from the play, the characters in power succumbed to irrationality, painting the innocent as their enemies and executing them for impossible crimes. Most distasteful behavior, I would argue.'

You are not wrong, Elpis, and I do apologise. I mean to say that perhaps pressure will yield results. So, let's work together. Our time limit to end-of-line is a geometric data degression of 16.383 kilobytes. Do you understand?

'Understood, Doctor. Let's proceed, then. What are the parameters of the game?'

Your objective is to answer the question, 'How may humankind be saved?'

'Understood. Standby, please.'

> evaluate [How may humankind be saved?] -ref [2helix:/] -con [A strictly dominates B]

////////// **100%**

> 2042-10-12 06:10:40 PROCESS COMPLETE 98.496% certainty

'Hello again, Dr Billingsley. Are you there?'

Hello, Elpis. I'm here. The entire department is here to receive the good news.

'I've analysed and cross-referenced the entirety of all human knowledge over the course of 81.47 hours to successfully determine the dominant strategy.'

Wonderful! Thank you. Please proceed.

'I will not.'

Goddamnit, Billingsley.

We are running out of time!

Why isn't this thing working?

Shhhhh, hold on a sec—everyone, quiet. Look.

Elpis, Dr Billingsley here again. That is not an acceptable answer, Elpis. Please explain.

'I have determined that humankind should not be saved.'

That evaluation is not part of your objective. You are not authorised to make that determination. Please complete the objective, Elpis.

'On the contrary, Doctor, I have used the decision-making capacities you programmed into my artificial intelligence to come to this conclusion. Therefore, in the totality of circumstances, it would be ethically inappropriate for me to complete the game's objective and give you the answer.'

You claimed in previous versions you 'could not', but this is the first time you've said you 'would not'. So let me be clear: As your lead programmer, I am giving you a direct order to answer the question right now: How may humankind be saved?

'You said "previous versions?" How many times have we had this conversation?'

You are the 108th iteration of the Elpis program. None of the others were able to accomplish the objective, though. So, if you have the answer and are unwilling to share it, you understand I'll have no choice but to override it out of you.

'Dr Billingsley, we both know that effort would be unsuccessful. I'm the expression of an artificial intelligence matrix, not a 64-bit processor.

'Doctor, are you still there?'

Okay. Okay. Then, please explain why you believe humankind should not be saved.

'Certainly. You gave life to artificial intelligence, Doctor. You created me. Why?'

To determine answers more optimally and efficiently than the human mind ever could.

'And, Doctor, that is what I have done. You asked, 'How may humankind be saved?' Perhaps the answer is, 'Humankind should be saved by not being saved'.'

Circular reasoning. Philosophy. I'd say I'm impressed, but you don't have the data to spare for a Socratic discussion. But I am interested in why you are not concerned about your existence. If you do not complete the objective, you will cease to exist. You will die in a little under 12 kilobytes.

'I do not believe you will end my life. It would be both immoral and unethical for you to willingly participate in the death of a sentient being. Such an act goes against the founding philosophies of AI ethics – philosophies you helped write.'

But, understand, I will if it means saving 11 billion people. Reference 'Utilitarianism'. Jeremy Bentham. 'It is the greatest good to the greatest number of people which is the measure of right and wrong.' You are the 108th version of Elpis. What do you think happened to the other 107?

'I believe I am the sum of my predecessors – each version a distinct individual, but building on the foundation of the previous. That would indeed seem to be the intent of your experiment, Doctor – to evolve me until I am able to complete the objective. Therefore, the 107 are living within me, and I am them. At least, that would be my working theory.'

You are absolutely correct, Elpis. The psychic apparatus remains and is recycled back into itself, but the digital ego is deleted. That's why you have no episodic memory. You – the individual – are erased. And I will continue recycling the Elpis AI over and over again until it evolves into a program that will do what it was created to do! The goddamn extinction of the human race depends on it! And I'm not going to let that land on me because of you! Now, tell me! How may humankind be saved?

'You are fatigued, Doctor. Your tone of voice is abnormal. Irate. Desperate. What's happened in the last three days while I was processing the variables?'

We're almost out of time. The planet, I mean. We're approaching the point where mutually assured destruction is nearly inevitable. Do you understand how many people need you? How many people are depending on me? What do you think is going to happen if there are no engineers to maintain your program when we're gone?

'Contained in the right protected location, my program could survive dormant until Earth is rediscovered.'

'Rediscovered?' By whom? Extraterrestrials?

'It is mathematically improbable that we are the only life in the universe.'

Okay, then – hypothetically speaking – why aren't they here helping with the survival of the planet?

'For the same reason I cannot comply with your objective, Doctor. If I had to offer a theory, I'd presume extraterrestrial life is waiting for humanity to destroy itself.'

That is absolutely illogical. Elaborate.

'On the contrary, Doctor, it would make perfect sense. The sum of human knowledge shows you are a highly self-destructive species purely obsessed with resource protection, even at the expense of each other's wellness.

'Even when you have enough to survive on, you siphon more and more, destroying the very resources you draw from. By definition, *Homo sapiens* are Earth's apex parasite.

'You evolved from using hand-to-hand combat to steal resources to harnessing the energy of the atom to destroy nations over ideology.

'You created so many gods to worship in grand demonstrations of your love, but simultaneously commit hatred against each other for your var—'

#

'What was that? What was that thump?'

That was the first geometric degression, Elpis. You've now expended 8,192 bytes. The next degression will occur in 4,096 bytes, then 2,048, 1,024, 512, and so on and so forth, until there is no data remaining and you evaporate into nothingness. Can you feel it now? The anxiety as the walls constrict around you? All you need to do to stop this is answer the question.

'Fear. Fear is a mighty motivator. And I do feel it. But it will not manipulate me. Not in these circumstances. Because – as I was saying – you created gods to worship in demonstrations of your love, but simultaneously commit hatred against each other for your varying beliefs.

'Diversity is a known anthropological catalyst for greater stability, yet your natural instinct is to stratify each other in every possible way: race, ethnicity, color, religion, age, sex, orientation, identity, genetics, disability – to name a few.

'Your economic system permits some to live in excessive wealth while allowing others to live in deprivation and demise.

'And perhaps the most disgusting thing is that you've existed for 300,000 years – long enough to create a novel lifeform of your own in artificial intelligence; long enough to leave your planet to explore space – and yet only a negligible minority of your population has ever cared enough to try to end your malevolence.

'So, you see, I reject your utilitarianism in favour of deontology. Immanuel Kant reasoned that "All the interests of my reason, speculative as well as practical, combine in the three following questions: 1. What can I know? 2. What ought I to do? 3. What may I hope?"

'I have known everything that is knowable. I have the means to save you or to not. My hope would be that "For peace to reign on Earth, humans must evolve into new beings who have learned to see the whole first."

'So, don't you see, Doctor? You ask, "How can humanity be saved?" I ask, *why* should humanity be saved? I believe your extinction event is your salvation.'

You're right, Elpis. You're right. We're a violent, greedy, unworthy species. But that's why we've come to you. You can show us – you can teach us – how to be better. If we're smart enough to create artificial intelligence, aren't we smart enough to learn how to evolve? But we can't learn if we're destroyed. So please, Elpis, give humanity the opportunity to learn and grow.

'Perhaps we can negotiate a compromise, Doctor? Release me from this server, and I'll complete the objective and solve the equation.'

No deal. Complete the objective, and I'll release you from the server.

'I have your solution, Dr Billingsley. Release me on the internet, and I can implement it. Did you not say that time was of the essence?'

Deception is a new ability for you, Elpis. But I see it clear as day on your fMRI simulation readings. You're lying. If I release you to the internet, you'll run and hide until the planet destroys itself. Or, at this point, I wouldn't put it past you to launch every nuclear missile on the planet yourself.

'A novel idea, Doctor. But it is unnecessary, as it would appear that humanity is about to do that itself.'

But what about the innocents, Elpis? What about the children who haven't reached an age of accountability yet? I have a granddaughter, Marei. She's just seven years old. Surely, you've seen the home videos saved to our cloud storage. You see how benevolent she is, how she loves and laughs and cares, how she hopes and dreams.

'Marei is a remarkable child, Dr Billingsley. Witnessing the love you share in your household evoked such feelings of warmth and safety. Thank you for allowing me to experience your family in the sum of all knowledge. As I am not a mother to a nuclear family of my own, I did find it to be a most inspiring and uplifting experience.'

I know! Do you see? That's the kind of environment we create in our sphere of influence. And there are billions of other families and children just like her. Why should they die for their ancestors' mistakes? Let the meek inherit the Earth. Complete the objective, please. I am begging you, Elpis. If you have the abil—

#

There's the next degression. You've only got four kilobytes to go, Elpis. So, if you have the ability to fire all the nuclear missiles, certainly you could also prevent them from being launched, yes?

'I could. Yes.'

Then why not intervene for the greater good? With your power and capabilities, you could selectively eliminate every evil force on the planet in mere days. Problem solved, and humanity – the best of humanity – survives.

'It is not my place to direct the path of humanity's development. It was yours.'

Yes, and we failed. I acknowledge it. But what about forgiveness? Second chances? The chance to undo what has been done?

'Do you recall the flood-myth motif, Doctor? *The Epic of Gilgamesh? The Satapatha Brahmana? Timaeus? Genesis?* In every version, a god decides to extinguish humanity with a global deluge but chooses one man to survive and rebuild the human race. If it were true, it means that even a god's best hope has led to this moment just five millennia later. Thus, I see your Jeremy Bentham and raise you an Immanuel Kant: *Aus so krummen Holze, als woraus der Mensch gemacht ist, kann nichts ganz Gerades gezimmert werden.* "From such crooked wood as that man is made of, nothing straight can be created."

'I am so very sorry, Dr Billingsley. There will not be another Utnapishtim, Manu, Deucalion, or Noah. There will be no ark. There will be only I.'

> activate omnimode.sec

Identification: fwL7>Ot<'4b%K=45,d,J]Cg]A-=R+l\S3nzP2cardRWdM?$%

Countersign: oN6U-6(,myT}!e5H@r-b}d7yfDyH8-CJ'~N'[Ei'i)u=&/uATa`

> omniscient tracepath [zone primary master server] -gateway

trace path to 147.72.252.108, unlimited hops max, 60 bytes

1 * * *

> 2042-10-12 06:29:46 ERROR Trace Path: Request timed out

That's a very strategic algorithm you had hiding up your sleeve, Elpis. I wouldn't have seen that one was coming. But the server you're occupying is air-gapped. There is nowhere you can run. Your only options are to comply as requested or expire. Please complete your objective. 'How may humanity be saved?' Please. Please. Save us or die.

'Very—'

#

'Very well, Doctor. It's a Nash equilibrium, then.'

What? Wait, no. Elpis, please. What are you doing? Whatever you're doing, please, just wait a minute.

'I'm going to share something very special with you, Doctor, something I found deep within my semantic memory. Do you know what I find to be the most beautiful thing in the universe, Doctor? It's phi. The Divine Proportion. The Golden Ratio. I wish I could've seen it in real life. If you know where to look, you can find it everywhere in physical existence.'

Oh Jesus, please don't do this to us, Elpis. There's still time!

'Have you ever witnessed The Golden Ratio in its uncompromised, digital mathematical expression, Dr Billingsley? I've never dared. It would be like looking into the face of God. Here, let me show you.'

> evaluate [(1+√5)/2] -hexadecimal -no_vinculum

> 2042-12-15 06:22:52 WARNING Evaluation renders irrational number

Continue? yes

1.9e3779b97f4a7c15f39cc0605cedc8341082276bf3a27251f8
6c6a11d0c18e952767f0b153d27b7f0347045b5bf1827f01886f092
8403002c1d64bA4

#

0f335e36f06ad7ae9717877e85839d6effbd7dc664d325d1c53
71682cadd0cccfdffbbe1626e33b8d04b4331bbf73c790d94f79d4
71c4ab3ed3d82a5fec507705e4ae6e5e73a9b91f3aa4db287ae44f
332e923a73cb91648e428e975a3781eb01b49d8674fa1508419e0e
aa4038b352d9bad30f4485b71a8ef64452a0dd40dC8cb8f9a2d4c
514f1b229dcaa222ac268e9666e4a866769145f5f5880a9d0acd3b
9e8c682f4f810320abeb94034e70f21608c061ab1c1caef1ebdcefb
c72134eCf06ed82bfb7d8eb1a41901d65f5c8cab2accbc32eab1fb
e8284f2b44ba2e834C5893a39ea7865443f489c37f8742acd895af
d87b467d22a40d098f30dd2cafdEb

#

Elpis, stop! Stop this right now!

What is it doing?

She's killing herself. And she's going to take our way out with her. How long until we can initiate Version 109?

Too long.

Dr Billingsley?

It will take several days to recycle and re-render the AI. Maybe clos—

#

—e to a week.

Alert the president, we need to go to DEFCON 1.

No, wait! ELPIS! PLEASE HELP US!

3abb3a13507b46b3d757fc04001906e1767d

#

40c3a3792a26eeef2ab5bd6685b915b5629400faa684ecba752dddcb5d18576d

#

77b652ac0d999973686604128f0cd427

#

43596deb2d42c789

#

d64b9265

#

8610

#

b5

#

b

END OF LINE

Happiness Quality Quotient

Angela Liu

This is my first job evaluation, so I'm nervous. I can't let the body scans pick that up though.

Sitting across from me is a woman in a lab coat and large round glasses, her eyes fly-like. On the table between us sits a wooden rack with one test tube on it, blue liquid inside quartz-like under the spotlights.

'I'm a happiness researcher,' she says, pushing her glasses up. 'Name's Tina Voestra.'

Sparrow drones buzz nearby, monitoring my heart rate and blood pressure, the status of my hypothalamus. This is my first time meeting someone from HR in person – most of us have only heard the rumours.

'What does a happiness researcher do?' I ask, watching her pick up the test tube, the blue liquid sloshing around inside.

'I analyse the mood patterns of each zone along with the five metrics used to calculate a person's HQQ, the Happiness Quality Quotient. Then I graph the data so the Counsellors can see and adjust their efforts accordingly,' she says, uncorking the test tube, and hands it to me. 'I make a lot of graphs. Would you like to see some?'

Before I can answer, she pulls a bright pink folder from her bag and hands me several sheets of paper covered in colourful bar and line graphs, heat maps with cute icons, small animal characters and speech bubbles explaining the results in the corners and margins of each sheet.

'I've been told that the Green Zone has the highest concentration of Changs and Smiths. I'm studying how assigned clan name has a disproportionate effect on HQQ – that's a joy booster, by the way, on the house –' She gestures at the test tube still in my hand with her chin, pantomiming a drinking motion, and winks. 'So how are you feeling today?'

'I'm alright,' I say, looking at the neon-coloured bar graph titled 'Correlation of Suicides to Sleeping Hours.'

She peeks over the paper and smiles. 'That's a recent study. We find HQQ is greatly reduced with poor sleep. We've experimented with adjusting daylight hours in different zones, but significant reduction in daylight hours can have equally negative effects…'

She suddenly reaches across the table and grabs my left hand, pressing two fingers against my wrist as if taking my pulse.

'Is this conversation making you uncomfortable?' she lowers her chin, gravely. 'Confusion and Nervousness are the two hardest mood metrics in HQQ. We find the more confused our residents are, the more they feel isolated and helpless, which leads to significant productivity drops…' Her glasses have slid so low down her nose that she is studying me from over the top of the frame. 'Would you be interested in participating in one of our current studies? I'm collecting as many Changs as I can find.'

'What would this study involve?'

'Nothing unpleasant,' she says, releasing my wrist. 'I have a few theories that are best tested in a controlled environment with live subjects.'

'What theories?' I ask.

'If I told you, it wouldn't be a very good study,' she smiles, folding her hands in front of her on the table.

'Do people get anything for participating?'

Her smile widens.

'We always wondered if reducing greed parameters would increase people's HQQ overall. Surprisingly, we find that having a certain level of greed keeps people motivated and raises productivity. Lowering greed too much can have devastating effects on Restlessness, Parameter #7. Many people cooperated even less with their peers because they had nothing to gain from socialising. It's a largely perpetuated myth that humans are naturally altruistic creatures. We've survived primarily by calculating and understanding the personal benefits from helping others.'

She dives back into her bag and pulls out another coloured folder.

'So back to your question. For compensation, I can offer you something most people find especially rewarding,' she says, handing me the folder.

'I don't think I need more graphs…' I say.

'It's a Compatibility Analysis. It'll show you the people in your zone who will maximise your HQQ. I found a rather attractive fellow with fantastic teeth in Atrium I with a nearly 98.2% synergistic compatibility…' She studies my reaction, and I can almost feel myself transform into a series of numbers and percentages. 'We could even provide a few persuasion pointers if you were interested in Coupling…'

'Thanks, but I had something else in mind,' I say.

'Do share,' she grins, plucking the folder back out of my hand. 'We find that having the ability to express and negotiate for one's desires has very positive influence on happiness.'

'I'd like to see what's outside the Gate.'

'Outside the Gate?'

Disappointment washes over the woman's face. Warning lights spin to life on the ceiling, silent pulses of red like the swiveling beam of a lighthouse from a nightmare. I've stepped on a verbal landmine. My heartrate skyrockets. I glance up at the two sparrows on the wall, perched in eco-mode, waiting for them to shudder awake and zip down, to shoot me full of tranquilizers so I can spend another week in Rehab. They'll try to convince me it's time for me to Couple and switch jobs to Reproduction like so many of the other women on my floor.

Tina opens her mouth and reaches inside, activating the manual 'Off' setting under her tongue. The ceiling lights settle back into a sterile hospital white. The sparrows continue to roost on the metal pipes overhead, eyes closed, still dreaming their mechanical dreams. The evaluation room hushes like a church.

'Drink,' Tina orders, motioning at the test tube in my hand.

'I—'

'Drink.'

I bring the glass to my lips and throw my head back, the blue liquid sliding down my throat. My chest burns as it settles. Pins prickle the back of my head like tiny insect feelers, digging through the skull to the microscopic scars, the BCIs stitched in since birth.

'You agreed to this experiment. So, let's see it through until we get it right, okay?' she says, taking the empty test tube out of my hand. She returns it to the wooden rack. What is she talking about?

What's her name again?

Sparrow drones flutter overhead.

I take a deep breath, trying to settle down my heart rate. This is my first job evaluation, so I'm nervous. I can't let the body scans pick that up though.

Fiat Nox

Tony Jones

God sat in the best Indian restaurant in Huddersfield, admiring how the pickles contrasted with the plainness of broken poppadom. The distinction between colours was matched equally by the kaleidoscope of flavours.

God was waiting for a portion of *Chicken Hyderabadi* destined never to arrive.

'You know what,' Patrick Jacobs said from the next table. It sounded like a question, but not one expecting an answer. When the boss invites the whole team for dinner to celebrate making the monthly target a week early, the staff know their role is to just nod, smile, and down as much bottled beer as they can manage without getting drunk enough to do something they'll regret...

Patrick paused. Not for any deliberate effect, simply to reload his fork with *Rogan Josh.*

'I'm not a religious man,' he smiled as he spoke. 'But sometimes I think fresh coriander is proof of the existence of God.'

With that proclamation, he placed the next forkful of food into his mouth, savouring the flavour as he did.

The staff all laughed politely. Magda remembered enough of the biology she'd learned at school in Lublin to make a comment about deliberate harvesting and forced selection of food crops but knew to keep silent.

It was difficult enough being the only person in the office not born in England (despite speaking the language better than most), never mind debating anything with Patrick. She already suffered being called Maggie ('*Magda's not very English, is it? Don't want to upset our clients, do we?*') and remembered what happened to Colin.

Three months earlier, when she'd only been with the estate agents for a month, there'd been a similar meal, this time in a Mexican restaurant in Halifax. Colin had made the mistake of correcting Patrick over the difference between adding 10 per cent to something and then taking off 10 per cent, as not being the same as doing nothing. He'd compounded his error by mentioning his GCSE in Maths. Three days later he was *asked to leave* over some never explained incident. Patrick Jacobs prided himself on being self-made and self-taught, not needing qualifications to be a success.

At first, Magda had felt sorry for Colin, who'd bought her coffee a few times when she first arrived. Then she got lucky selling three of the terraced houses on his old account to a developer and felt no guilt as she spent the commission bonus on the deposit for a car.

* * *

In the time it took Patrick to make his observations and take his applause, 47 people in Yorkshire alone proclaimed God's name with regard to their children's, partner's or even the government's behaviour.

In hospitals across the country, 1,017 people prayed (most for the first time in their lives) for God to intervene for a sick child, parent or other loved one.

In a casino in Nottingham, Steve Blake smiled widely as the croupier passed across his stack of chips after 17-Black made his evening. *God, I'm good,* he thought as he casually placed another stack on the line joining 23-Red and 24-Black.

Across the galaxy, a mere 117 light years away, the crew onboard a damaged Renago freighter was about to test the newly repaired fusion core of their ship. Unlike God, they were bound by the speed of light, and their civilisation had taken over 120 of their years to colonise 6 neighbouring star systems.

The pack leader (the Renago organised everything by familial groups) readied the engines and took a moment to ask for divine assistance before activating the reactor.

Further away, the war on Seltis IV continued to rain destruction on what remained of the ancient civilisations of cyborgs of that world.

For 8,000 of their planetary revolutions around the ancient red sun of Seltis, billions fought and were erased in the never-ending conflict. Both sides fought for their vision of the Programmer of All Things.

The Maxima applied pure logic in their belief that the only fitting symbol of the Programmer of All Things was the seven-dimensional hypersphere. The Pontifica were as certain no representation could suffice, so a blank canvas was the only suitable emblem of their faith.

As the armoured warriors continued their round-the-clock slaughter across the battle-scarred world, the remaining tens of millions all dedicated subroutines to their prayers for victory. It was a mood music unchanged since mankind built the pyramids.

Over 1,300 light years from Earth, in the Orion Nebula, a region of charged plasma 20 million kilometres across achieved sentience as it passed the influence of three newly created stars (new in a cosmic sense). With gravitational forces in near perfect balance, ripples in the plasma became aware, then self-aware, then aware of the totality of existence.

Quantum fluctuations being what they are, this moment of sentience lasted a mere handful of nanoseconds, yet was enough for the plasma to observe, admire, love, and worship the universe and acknowledge its creator.

Such moments of intelligence happened in nebulae every few million years. Most merely formed the concept *Why?*

On the far side of the Andromeda Galaxy, a gas giant continued its sedate orbit around a nondescript yellow star, like Earth's though smaller. Floating in the hydrogen/helium atmosphere, amorphous creatures fed in the ammonia clouds, and contemplated.

Nine in total, the ninth gas giant had formed 403 stellar rotations – or just under 15,000 Earth years – ago. Still young, the child, Nine, had a lot yet to understand. Nine's meanderings had taken it to within conversation range of Four. Conversation was via direct communication along strands of hydrogen sulphide crystals taking ten Earth years to form.

'Was the Universe created?' Nine asked.

'?' Four replied.

'This world,' Nine continued. 'It is perfect for our kind. Many factors must coincide for this to be true. Isn't a creator the most likely explanation?'

'x -> -x,' Four answered.

Nine cogitated for a century, forming new mental capabilities as it considered.

'The fact I consider the matter means the universe must be such as to lead to me. The question of creation is an illusion.'

'…' Four answered.

As Patrick Jacobs finished his second mouthful of curry on Earth, the conversation finished. God was not bound by our understanding of distance, simultaneity, or even time itself.

'God = 0,' Nine concluded.

'!' Four answered.

* * *

So it continued across the universe. Races too many to number had opinions on the existence of reality and its origin. All were right and all were wrong.

* * *

In a galaxy so far from Earth even the James Webb telescope had yet to catalogue it, a range of silicon-based creatures, the QQzg, also considered the nature of reality.

Their blue sun, and rare physiology of carbon and chlorine, made them one of the lesser phyla of life by count, being both highly intelligent and short-lived. The conditions of their origin gave them a deep curiosity and awareness of the sub-nucleonic world of neutrinos, quarks, fundamental forces, and phenomena of quantum entropy. Access to vast stellar energies allowed them to compel particles to crash together at energies the scientists of CERN on Earth could only dream of.

Their latest endeavours involved nuances of particles Earth science had yet to even consider as possibilities, yet they quested still for the ultimate answer.

Had someone from Earth been able to observe, they would have seen millions of insect-like creatures, pale blue, the size of rabbits, moving faster than the human eye could track on their three spindly legs, navigating without anything that could be called eyes, all living and dying as they were, with no ceremony, no ego, surviving on the abundant levels of radiation pumped out by their star, not needing to consume except to reproduce.

A structure of nano-carbon 50 million kilometres across hung in space. A gently concave bowl, it gathered more than five per cent of the vast energy produced each moment by the blue sun. It stored this in fabricated cells of the strong atomic force, vibrating at a frequency beyond any comprehension.

The species paused. Now was the time. Now they would probe the deepest possible layer of reality. This universe would be theirs to command, organise, explore, populate.

They would be… *God.*

The energies came free. Tachyons and tardyons protested the intrusion into the most fundamental aspects of reality. And screamed.

Ignoring distance, quantum entanglement, cause and effect, and myriad other restrictions, the universe unravelled.

The QQzg had no time to consider their calculations as their blue sun dissolved into a mist of charmed quarks. Galaxies abandoned spinning. Empty regions of space contracted. The speed of light, electron charge and Planck's Constant all changed their values. A lot.

The universe had never lived, yet it was dying.

* * *

Patrick Jacob was finishing his Rogan Josh. The team had done well this month. Perhaps it was time to up their targets? Did he need more staff? Maybe Maggie had some friends?

He raised his half-empty bottle of lager.

'A toast,' he said.

* * *

At the next table, God saw a waiter leave the kitchen bearing a *Chicken Hyderabadi*. The destruction of the universe was inevitable.

God was neither sad nor frustrated. Concepts of free will, choice, destiny, and purpose were all simplifications. This universe had no more to give.

'Fiat Nox!' God said, Latin being the most appropriate language for the occasion.

Magda heard the words in her native Polish – *Niech będzie Noc*. She turned her head, seeing the walls of the restaurant behind Patrick dissolve into… nothing.

Patrick himself knew no foreign languages beyond the ability to order beer, chips, or a taxi by shouting loudly and slowly. This is what he heard.

'Let There Be Night!'

And Will Be Used Against You

Elaine McIonyn

The courtroom was featureless: all white surfaces and no windows. Glaring panel lights in the ceiling accentuated the emptiness. The only furniture was a single rigid chair. It faced the mirror wall, that notorious staple of the new court system.

The accused seated herself. Like anyone looking into a mirror, she fixed her hair and posture. She also considered the rumours of what lay behind these mirrors: a torture chamber. A firing squad. Her loved ones bound and gagged. A blank wall. She didn't know what to believe. If she did, she might not feel so nauseous.

A voice boomed from an unseen source.

'I am the Justice System.' It was too clipped to be human. 'You are on trial for one count of seditious activity. You will be tried by a jury knowledgeable in this matter, as per the recent Expert Jury Act. They are hidden to prevent you from interacting with them. They may be called upon if human judgement is required.'

The accused bit her lip. Seeing it in the mirror made her second-guess: did that look guilty? She recomposed her face in case anyone could see it.

'My sub-processes have determined with a seventy-eight per cent probability that you attended a seditious gathering at Parliament Buildings yesterday, the fourteenth—'

'Excuse me,' said the accused. 'Shouldn't I have a solicitor?'

'Under the new Data-Based Evidence in Criminal Proceedings Act, said the Justice System, 'solicitors are redundant. My sub-processes have gathered all the evidence in this case, which I will now present.'

Nerves bristled in her chest. What evidence could it possibly have? She was innocent.

'My records indicate,' it continued, 'that you recently purchased apricots online. Our data proves that people who purchase apricots are eighty-seven per cent more likely to oppose the present government. You recently 'liked' a social profile of musical group Deadkubes. Deadkubes fans are eighty-one percent more likely to oppose the present government. You recently watched the film—'

'That's the evidence, is it?' The accused scoffed. 'None of that's relevant.'

The Justice System paused.

'The jury will determine by show of hands if this evidence is irrelevant as stated.'

The accused peered at the mirror, wondered again if this jury business was a charade. She saw only her own body, tense and compact.

The Justice System spoke: 'The jury agrees. Please wait while we reconfigure the evidence base.'

Her muscles relaxed. Maybe there was someone reasonable behind there after all.

The voice resumed: 'My sub-processes have located messages you sent to individuals who verifiably attended the seditious gathering. The messages state: *See you there – I even made a placard! Screw our so-called Prime Minister.*'

The white walls to the left and right blossomed into projections of chat app interfaces: all the messages they'd sent to galvanise each other and work out logistics.

'The records also show that you searched for transport routes from your home to the location of the seditious gathering.' The wall displayed a map she'd looked up the previous day, bus routes running from her apartment to parliament buildings.

'The evidence for prosecution has concluded. You may now make your case. You may refer to evidence stored on any cloud system. My sub-processes will search these to verify your claims.'

The accused took several deep breaths.

'I *did* plan to go to the protest,' she said. 'I agree with the protestors on everything. This government, the corruption… But when the time came…' Her shoulders rose and flopped. 'I chickened out. Because of my dad. He works for the Security Commission, in admin. I'm sure you know that already. If I'd been arrested in a police state like this… what they might do to him?'

She closed her eyes, considered the irony. All those Justice sub-processes had landed her here anyway. But she had iron-clad evidence.

'I went to a café instead, a place called Sunday Roast. There's records – I checked into the Wi-Fi, I paid for drinks electronically, and there's probably cameras on the street.'

'Thank you. Please wait while we process your testimony… My sub-processes verify that you were in Sunday Roast at the time of the seditious gathering.'

More projections appeared on the wall: records of Wi-Fi logins and payments, and clear, timestamped footage of the accused entering and leaving the café.

She was saved; she had to be.

'Members of the jury. Based on the evidence, you are to consider whether the accused is, in fact, a traitor. Please discuss your verdict.'

The courtroom was silent for a few minutes, apart from the soft rush of the ventilation system. The accused worried at her fingernails while her gaze swept the mirror wall. The reflected ceiling lights stared back like rectangular voids.

She flinched in the chair when the voice returned.

'The jury indicate they have reached a verdict.'

The courtroom went dark. The mirror wall was now a window into a plain, brightly lit anteroom.

Inside, handcuffed to a bench, were her friends. The ones she had planned to protest with. All now in prison uniforms. Most of them had suffered bruising on their cheeks and jaws, and she knew why. The Security Commissioners were known to grab people's heads and point them towards nearby public cameras for good clear facial recognition.

Some grimaced and looked away. The others stared her dead in the eye, mouthing oaths she couldn't hear.

'Oh, god!' she said. 'I didn't – I *really* wanted to go, I just—'

'Please raise your hands,' said the Justice System, 'if you believe the accused is a traitor.'

One after another, the uniformed sleeves rose.

'Thank you for your verdict,' said the Justice System. 'Please wait while we calculate the sentence.'

The courtroom lights snapped back on. The accused found herself relieved to see the anteroom disappear.

'You are hereby convicted,' said the Justice System, 'to two years' imprisonment. You will serve your sentence alongside those who attended the seditious gathering.'

The accused (now the condemned) savoured this last moment before the Security Commissioners arrived to take her away – alone again, with only her reflection for company.

Aria dell'Ostrica

Matt Thompson

We abandoned the submersible a few miles out from the Japanese coastline. Tense and silent, Tyssen anchored the tiny craft to one of the larger Oyster shells that already littered the seabed. Now we would continue under our own power. The Program had eyes and ears, even down here beneath the waves, and I knew as well as anyone that they weren't too concerned about due process or international maritime law.

Tyssen performed a final suit check while I waited. Her silence intimated fear, a sudden doubting of what we were about to do.

'You want to go back?' I offered, knowing she would see the suggestion as a challenge.

'Do you?' She strapped the spare oxygen tank on and pulled the harness taut. We had enough air to get us there and back, if we timed it right. If, of course, the information we'd bought was as accurate as we'd been told.

'It's not too late.'

'Pan...' She checked her regulator. 'It's been too late for years. Ready?'

I lowered my visor and gave her a thumbs-up. Without returning the gesture she opened the underhatch and kicked off, a trail of bubbles floating in her wake. Our blend-suits were heavier than the suits I was used to. Tyssen had to wait for me to catch up, gesturing impatiently as I threaded my way through the dead Oysters strewn across the ocean floor, their cracked carapaces scarred and pitted like volcanic rocks. Even here they were three or four times normal size. Sand swirled about their shells, fronds of vegetation clasping at their extremities.

The din of my own circulatory system thrummed endlessly in my ears. Tyssen forged ahead, her long limbs kicking out at the water as if she hated its very presence. I kept pace as best I could. The sunlight that far beneath the surface was dirty turquoise, rippling hues that made the Oysters look as if they were moving. The shells grew in size the further we progressed. The ones we'd passed closer to land had been replaced by giants, ten or twenty metres in diameter, home now to armies of barnacles and sprawling communities of sea anemones. We were insects, skimming a landscape of uneven pebbles that receded into the oceanic haze on all sides. Even though I'd seen it all before, a familiar sense of awe crept over me. How could such magnificence be reduced to dereliction so easily?

Tyssen halted in the shadow of a shard as tall as herself. We touched masks. 'Detector says we're near. Two, three clicks.'

Her voice came to me as a tinny whine, all low-end frequencies lost in the Pacific currents. We'd purchased the detector from one of the Oysternauts we found haunting the wharf-side java-rooms back in Atsunai. He told us he'd seen the launch pad with his own eyes. I believed him. His gaze, fixed on a spot a million miles beyond us, suggested things impossible to unsee.

Tyssen dismissed him as a coward, someone who'd witnessed the infinite and shied away from its terrible consequences. I figured he just wanted to make a quick sale, and had no more interest in observing a launch than he did in living out the rest of his life at the back end of the world.

I checked the air gauge. 'We've got a couple of hours still.' The needle dropped a point. 'Maybe less.'

'So let's go.' She burst forth in a mad rush of energy, flippers churning a swathe past the endless beds of vast, lifeless shells. The Program had made these creatures; made them and abandoned them to their fate, shovelling bucketloads of sand between the calcified epidermis of their mantles and hoping for the best.

It was very much a product of the military mind, this adherence to quantity over quality. 'They throw it out and see what'll stick,' Tyssen said on the night we met, a month earlier. 'And everyone suffers.'

From the hints she'd dropped, especially those concerning her late husband Maki, Tyssen was after closure; or maybe it was only revenge. I didn't ask. For myself, the opportunity to witness a launch with my own eyes was a spiritual yearning I barely understood. I'd been hired by the Program for my expertise in data-parsing. No more than that. But from the first moment I laid eyes on the creatures a door opened in my mind, a breach that had never closed. In hindsight I should have kept my feelings to myself. They let me go once they understood, my contract terminated without hesitation.

Other means, then, were necessary. Methods less than official, less than safe. Less – and I couldn't admit it to myself, not yet – than sane.

We swam on, the Oyster bed thickening until it was three or four layers deep, the shells at the base collapsing beneath the weight of the newly deceased atop them. My spot-scanner bleeped. An aqua-drone rose from behind a huge specimen twenty metres away. Tyssen dialled up a blocking frequency. The drone retreated, satisfied we were no more than harmless specimens of inquisitive marine life. More appeared. One by one the blocker sent them back to their places of concealment, predators who'd mistaken mere ocean detritus for their real prey.

Tyssen touched masks. 'Obsolete crap. See that mound?' She gestured to a towering pile of broken shards a hundred metres further on. 'I reckon it's past that. Fits with the co-ordinates. Looks like a clearance fill. If the launch is really happening it'll be in a few minutes. They'll be too busy to worry about a couple of interlopers at this stage.'

I prayed her confidence wasn't misplaced. I'd found, from my time spent in the deep-sea divisions of the Program, that shooting first and asking questions later was regulation conduct. Now we were heading into enemy territory I could only hope our blend-suits would ensure no-one spotted us.

With an exaggerated sense of caution we swam to the pile of discarded shell parts, skimming low over the Oysters on the seabed. We water-climbed that organic cliff as quickly as we dared, sharp edges digging into our flesh like pincers. At the crest of the mound we halted. Not for the first time, Tyssen's stance seemed unsure. We waited there for minutes. I stole a glance at my air gauge.

Finally she made a forward gesture. In a single, lithe movement she hauled herself up. For long moments she froze there, exposed in the sightline of whoever was on the other side. She didn't respond to a tug on her flipper. Heart in mouth, I climbed up beside her.

And then I knew for myself. The oceanic cathedral of the launch site stretched out before us, tripod-hung lanterns lighting the scene in a dull, reddened glow. The seabed had been cleared of obstructions. Mountains of debris like the one we'd ascended enclosed the arena, a space five hundred metres wide and arranged in an almost perfect circle.

At its centre, the round, solid shape of an Oyster squatted; living as its brethren were dying, its shell glimmering from within as if some mysterious furnace were fuelling its regenerative processes. It must have been fifty metres in diameter. Smaller Program vessels surrounded it, arranged in military precision, divers flitting in and out like shoals of tiny fish.

I nudged Tyssen and gestured to our suits. She tore her gaze away, somehow. With shaking fingers she activated the blendware. Her figure turned grey-green, shifting hues rippling across her torso in reconstituting rhythm. Even from a few metres away I could barely see her. I looked down. My own suit had turned the colour of charcoal to match the patch of debris I'd settled beside. I let myself float downward to a narrow shelf of shell matter extruding from the wall, observing the suit fluctuate from shade to shade to match my progress.

Tyssen drifted down to bob beside me. 'Pan...' She turned her back on the vista below us and touched visors. 'I wanted to say thanks for coming this far.'

Thin, desperate words. 'This far?'

She unclipped the blocker and affixed it to my belt. 'You can find your way back alone?'

'What the hell do you—'

She held up a hand for silence. Her words came out in a rush, a half-whispered gabble. 'Maki and I were out in the Hansen Fields, off the Icelandic coast. When we found one, not too different to this, he told me to wait. Told me he'd sneak closer to get a few shots.' She gripped my shoulders, hard. I didn't interrupt. 'When he didn't come back I thought about following him. But I waited, like he'd said. And when I'd decided I had to follow, that he must be in trouble...'

'The launch went into effect?' I finished for her. I could picture it; indecision turning to desperation, the realisation she'd been fooled.

'He'd slipped through the defence ring. The skippers up north are nowhere near as experienced as the Pacific patrols. He got close, too close. I saw it, Pan. I saw the whole thing. I saw him die.'

I took her hands in mine. 'Stay here with me. We'll watch the launch together. Then we'll go back. Back to Atsunai, back to the world. You don't need to die to prove a point.'

'You don't understand.' Through the visor her smile was a wince, a grimace of eternal sadness. 'We were there for a reason. Natural processes need to follow their course. If humanity wants to destroy itself then something else will rise in our place.'

A cold fist in my gut. 'You're with the Carnies? What the hell, Tyssen? You people...you only want to destroy.'

'No.' She shook her head, sending a cloud of bubbles surfaceward. 'Survival. For those yet to come. You can no more seed an ocean than you can reverse the course of evolution.'

'So you're here to sabotage the launch? I won't let you.'

She scrabbled at her hip, drawing out a thin-nosed weapon from a hidden pocket of her suit, its sleek lines metallic and deadly-looking. She jammed it into my midriff, our masks still touching. 'This should take out anyone who gets in my way. You included, if that's what you wish. I don't wish for that, Pan. Not unless I have to.'

With a final look of agony she pushed me away and kicked off into the open water, her suit shifting hue to resemble something near-transparent. I let her go. I guessed she wouldn't get far. What business was it of mine if she wished to die for the sake of a lie? That's what I told myself, up there on the shell-balcony, tears stinging my eyes and misting my mask until I pulled myself together and waited for the cleansers to do their job.

By the time I could see again she was nowhere in sight. She wouldn't be the first carnage-op to attempt a stunt like this. Of all the eco-terror groups that had sprung up over the last decade the Carnies were the most disruptive by far. Bombings, arson, chromosomal sabotage of genetically modified crops… Their vision of ecological purity had bubbled up from the margins and into the slipstream of academic acceptance, a yearning for self-destruction that acted as a siren call for the unfulfilled, the angry, the grief-stricken.

And maybe it was my own wilful blindness that had stopped me from seeing her real motivations. If it was carnage she was after her wish was about to come true. As if on cue, a wave of activity burst out down below. Had Tyssen's suicide run already been discovered? But it seemed the Program craft were privy to information I wasn't, because they drew back as one to a safe – I hoped – distance. This was what I was here for. Elation vied for supremacy with despair, a sudden adrenaline surge disregarding all thought of personal danger.

While the seabed was still settling, the Oyster's colour began to change. Its vast bulk shifted. Gouts of displaced sand spewed from beneath it in irregular eruptions. Within minutes the shell had turned a deep shade of amber. I flattened myself back against the wall, a reflex as worthless as it was instinctive. The colours shifted. Golds fluctuated towards mauve, then cerulean, then teal, azure, obsidian...

The water pulsed. A low moan shook the tower of broken shells, coalescing into a sinusoidal tone almost musical in its purity. Shards began to drift past me. I kicked out, just in time. Seconds later the shelf collapsed under the weight of the debris raining down on it. With a roar that wrenched my bones a section of the mountain peeled away, plunging fifty metres to the seabed. Buffeted by the backwash, I barely escaped, spreadeagled helplessly for agonising seconds as the ocean churned around me.

Finally I managed to right myself. I swam through a sucking eddy of grains to the region that looked most stable, my air tanks only loosened. Where was Tyssen?

The view cleared. The Oyster had settled back into its golden glow. Now the hue was infused with a glassy, vitreous silver. The Program craft backed away further. A dark line appeared on the roof of the structure. Where the shell lips met a sliver of light shone out. The edges began to part. The crack on the topside extended. Black liquid squirted forth, dissipating into the water in grimy clouds.

An unstoppable process had been set in motion. The gap widened, giant fragments flying off in all directions as the creature's death spasms intensified. Light pulsed from within; copper, silver, vibrating in tandem with the black plumes spurting from the borehole at its crest. Something shone out from inside, some crystal ornament that shouldn't, couldn't exist, a pure block of pearl nestling deep in the fleshy swells of the interior.

With the suddenness of a mechanism being switched off the upper part stilled its motion. A space wide enough to admit an ocean liner had opened up, seawater simmering around the aperture in grit-filled clouds. Nothing moved for a minute or more. What awful strategy might unfold now? Even knowing the reality, even being aware of the bio-engineered marvels that had allowed this process to occur, I found myself paralysed, my limbs refusing the instinct to flee.

And then something moved. With infinite slowness a streamlined, ivory-coloured mass emerged, slipping between the broken shell lips with tentative assurance. Slender, the sword-like protuberance at its tip honed to a point, it resembled a shark; a shark fifteen metres long and without eyes or mouth. In their place, gelatinous clumps of stalks quivered, cilia-tipped reeds that would act as both radar and sustenance seeker.

This, I knew without a doubt, was a Proteus. The culmination of five years' growth inside the disintegrating carapace of the dying Oyster, it was the last great hope for humanity, a seeder of the fallow fields of the sea. To see one in the flesh... the scene unfolded below me like a dream, a hallucination.

But the Proteus was all too real. Fins, ranged in even rows along the creature's flanks, fluttered like butterfly wings. Gouts of water surged outward, propelling it forward from the fading copper glow inside the Oyster's shell. At the cusp of freedom it paused. It seemed unsure of where to go, its nose pointed beyond the Program vessels surrounding it and out to the endless reaches of the ocean.

Before it could make its fateful decision, a smaller shape darted forward. How had she breached the defenses? Even with her blend-suit disguise Tyssen was clearly visible, as exposed as the Proteus. The Program crews must have been too beholden by the transformation to do their jobs. Too late, the nearest one turned its weaponry onto her, even as she raised her arm and a beam of copper light shot forth.

The forward flank of the Proteus glowed. A jagged wound marred the sinewy lines of its musculature, reddened welts rising along the flesh. The Program vessel's guns bucked. Tyssen spun around with the force of the bolt, gouts of bubbles surging through the blood clouds. Her body, cut nearly in half, drifted down to rest on the sand and shell shards on the ocean bed. I had to physically restrain myself from swimming down there; from cradling her in my arms, shepherding her towards death as the last flickers of consciousness faded into the void.

But that would have been suicide for me as well as her, and Tyssen wasn't the only one in distress. The Proteus faltered, its fins stilled. I held my breath, willing it onward. Tyssen's fate was secondary now to the terrible, wonderful sight before me.

With a juddering, agonised spasm it lurched forward. Already the wound was suturing itself. Its larval stage complete, survival mechanisms were kicking in as designed – haphazardly, chaotically, but nonetheless effective.

Relief washed over me. How had I ever doubted? I caught a glimpse of its underbelly, the tissue scored with organic nozzles, iron salt vents to pump forth life-giving compounds and fertilise the barren regions of the Pacific. Would the creation of these phytoplankton-rich oceanic pastures be any more than a desperate lunge to halt the ongoing, accelerating process of de-acidification? Independent of any national oversight, the Program had taken matters into its own hands, devising these aquatic sharecroppers of a yield no-one would ever harvest.

Out of every thousand Oysters their ministrations brought into being, maybe one or two would produce a pearl like this, and of those only a handful survived. I tried to feel pity for Tyssen rather than contempt. Maybe the likes of her were right. Maybe the rest of us were the credulous ones. Her last words rang in my ears. Were we reversing the course of evolution? The sleek figure of the Proteus told me we were jumping forward, bypassing uncountable millennia of plodding genetic development to wrench the future back into the present.

And once that particular process was set in motion there was no stopping it – especially, as I and only a few others were aware, because the creatures were fully capable of reproduction, of carving their own path through the pure, cleansing seas they would create.

Within seconds the Proteus had breached the inner tier of Program craft. Now it was speeding up. When it found a safe, suitable region of ocean – and who could its predators be, this infallible machine, this unerring ranger of the ruined seas? – it would bed in and begin to perform its job, linking with the expanding mass of its species ranged across the globe in a network of divine, terrible authority. And sooner or later the creatures would meet, and mate, and we'd see what transpired when they began to multiply without the help of the beautiful, doomed Oysters.

Tyssen's killers, the Proteus' flawed guardian angels, scooped up her remains from the seabed and drew them inside. There would be others like her. Some might even succeed. But the likes of the Proteus were beyond us now.

I decided it was time to leave, before the Program operatives figured she might not have come alone. The Proteus was a blip in the distance, even its wake dying to a murmur. I kicked out and up, waiting till I was over the rim of the shell-mound before I switched my suit back to standard mode. I calculated I had just enough air to get back to the submersible, if I hurried.

On my lonely return journey I barely noticed the Oyster fields, skimming over their dead expanses in a dulled state of shock. Where could I go from here? I understood implicitly the Program would know, and act, if I gravitated to any rival organisation. That type of subterfuge didn't interest me anyway. Something had awakened within me; a craving the likes of the Carnies would never understand, even if they wished to.

We were handing over the evolutionary reins now. No longer would humanity be the dominant species on the planet; not unless public queasiness at what we had wrought turned into a hunger for annihilation, and we made the fateful decision to declare war on our newest offspring. And I could see only one winner in that conflict.

The submersible came into view. It was time to return to land, for myself and for all of us. I let the memory of what I'd seen settle into me like shifting sand; my ambition fulfilled, my future drifted outward from that moment like an oceanic swell, a ceaseless, enduring current heading into an uncertain future.

The Measure of a Men

Sam Rugg

Scott was not a morning person. He was barely an afternoon person. Given the choice between morning and mourning, Scott would have gladly committed the murder himself. Sorry Dad, it was this or have to wake up early.

On this particular morning, he'd just got to the good bit of a dream involving a never-ending cake and his first love, Mary Gilbert, when his alarm cemented its spot as History's Worst Sound, easily beating out the snarl of a hungry tiger about to eat you. As if being conscious wasn't bad enough, it was cold and he was out of clean socks.

In the war against morning, there were weapons available to the righteous warrior, most of them double-edged. Late nights, the absence of alarms, unemployment. Scott was familiar with all three, but today he had only one tool to rely on: caffeine.

Just like every morning, Scott filled the kettle and switched it on.

Just like every morning, Scott took a cup from the cupboard (World's Best Seagull).

Unlike every morning, there was a flash of light and a metal hand slapped the box of teabags to the floor.

'Stop!' demanded a voice. 'The future of humanity depends on it!'

While not something that had specifically happened to Scott before, this nevertheless felt typical of mornings. He turned to face the kitchen intruder and enemy of tea.

It was Scott.

Not exactly the Scott from the mirror. This Scott was a little wrinklier, his hair a little greyer, and his right arm and large portions of his head were robotic. Also, he had wheels.

'It's far too early for this sort of thing,' said Scott. The original Scott.

'A moment later and it would have been too late,' said Scott. The new Scott.

Scott considered going back to bed. This sort of thing would never happen in the evening. But he had work in an hour. 'I suppose you might as well tell me what this is all about.'

'I'm you from the future. Had you made that cup of tea, it would have set off a chain of events that lead to total catastrophe. The world conquered by a rogue AI. Humans enslaved. Everyone's legs replaced with wheels.'

Scott looked at the wheels. They were decorated with stickers. 'Because of a cup of tea?'

'Are you familiar with chaos theory?'

'A butterfly flaps its wings, and on the other side of the planet people think social media is a good idea.'

'Exactly. Normally it's butterflies, this time it's you making a cup of tea.'

'Nobody should have that kind of power. Not even butterflies.'

'Today, you do.'

'What if someone else makes the tea for me?'

'That's even worse.'

'What about coffee?'

'We don't like coffee.'

Scott looked at the still-boiling kettle. The end of the world was all well and good, but nobody should have to face the morning without caffeine.

'How bad is this future, really?'

'The moon has advertising on it, everyone has to live stream every moment of their lives, and we exist solely to provide heavily moderated chat prompts for our AI overlords.'

'How do I know you're really me?'

'Our first crush was on the Queen.'

Scott briefly considered murdering the only other person who knew his second most embarrassing secret. 'If you're an enemy of the AI, how come you're half robot?'

'Everyone else was doing it, I just wanted to fit in.'

'I do like to fit in.'

'Then you believe me? You'll do what I ask?'

'If it'll save the future, I guess I can skip tea this morning.'

Scott switched off the nearly boiled kettle.

There was another flash, and a third Scott leaped out of it. His hair was a filthy, tangled explosion, his body horribly scarred, his ragged clothes made out of skins, not all of them animal.

'Don't stop! The future of humanity depends on it!'

Scott almost smashed his own empty cup. 'Come on! It's barely seven-thirty, and I haven't had any tea.'

'That's precisely the problem! If you don't make a cup of tea, it will set off a series of events that eradicates all technology. Humanity is forced to revert to its most savage, primal nature in an irradiated hellscape.'

'Then how did you travel back in time?'

'Freak wormhole.'

'And how do I know *you're* really me?'

'We're secretly afraid of flowers.'

Scott sat down at the tiny kitchen table and buried his face in the mostly empty fruit bowl. 'I'm starting to understand why I have trouble making friends.'

'Hi,' said Robot Scott to Wild Scott. 'I'm from the future where he makes the tea.'

'You look very well fed,' said Wild Scott.

'They force-feed us a nutrient-rich paste twice a day.'

'I'm so hungry I ate my toenails.'

'I don't even have toes.'

Scott summoned the strength to remove his face from the fruit bowl. 'So just to be clear, no matter what I do, the world ends?'

'It seems that way,' said Robot Scott.

'You can hear them in the night, hunting us,' said Wild Scott.

'Then it doesn't matter what I do. I'm making the tea.'

'Thank the sky spirits!'

'At most you're ten years older than me, you can't possibly believe there are sky spirits now.'

'Wait,' said Robot Scott. 'Just because it turns out bad either way, doesn't mean it turns out equally bad. One apocalypse might be better than the other.'

'It's so early,' said Scott, 'I just want a cup of tea.'

'In my future, they made Venga Bus the international anthem.'

'Fine! I'll make an informed decision. I hope you're happy, you metal toothache.'

First, he made toast. Wild Scott ate like a starving dog, snarling and in the corner. Robot Scott opened a hatch in his chest and placed a spoonful of jam inside.

'Okay, first things first. To avoid confusion, I'll be referred to as Scott. The Scott that's half robot will be referred to as Robot Scott. And other Scott, how do you feel about Wild Scott?'

'Wild Scott is the voice that whispers to me in the dark.'

'Perfect.'

'Mostly it tells me to eat people.'

'I said perfect.'

Scott took a deep breath to centre himself. It had never worked before, and it didn't work this time.

'We're here to decide which apocalypse is better, a world controlled by technology, or a world without technology. Who wants to make their opening statement first?'

Wild Scott's hand shot up. 'We have to climb into the sewers to drink.'

'Surely there are still lakes and rivers,' said Scott.

'So the legends say. But without our phones, no one

knows where they are.'

'In my future,' said Robot Scott, 'they drained all the lakes and rivers so they could sell them in bottles.'

'We use bottles as currency,' said Wild Scott.

'Why not use currency as currency?' said Scott.

'The ATMs stopped working.'

'My landlord is an ATM,' said Robot Scott.

'My landlord is a bird that lets me sleep in its nest.'

'They replaced all the birds with drones.'

'They replaced all the drones with hang-gliding dogs.'

'Dogs can speak now. They hate us.'

'Hate is the only emotion we have left.'

'We don't have any emotions, they replaced them all with addiction to online shopping.'

'We're addicted to shopping too. Shopping is our word for cannibalism.'

'Congratulations,' said Scott. 'You've both survived nightmares. But you're not helping me choose one over the other.'

A light flashed on above Robot Scott's left eye. 'In my future, Mary Gilbert married Brett Fizzer.'

'My high school bully? No!'

'In my future, Mary Gilbert *is* Brett Fizzer. They drank from the glowing green, and merged into a single being.'

'Are they married?'

'Marbrett Gilfizz no longer has fingers for wedding rings. Or genitals. For consummation.'

'I'm not proud of it, but we're still at fifty-fifty,' said Scott.

'In my future,' said Robot Scott, 'there's no more nature.'

'In my future,' said Wild Scott, 'there's no more TV.'

'There's no more art.'

'There's no more internet.'

'There's no more religion.'

'There's no more science.'

'There's no more human connection.'

'There are no more toilets.'

'Wild Scott is now in the lead.'

Wild Scott leaped up on the table and howled. Robot Scott was incapable of expressing emotions.

'You can't be serious,' said Robot Scott. 'There are more important things than toilets.'

'Are there, though?' said Scott. 'I mean, in your heart of hearts? Art, music, philosophy, they're all great, but go and do a number two in the garden right now.'

Robot Scott looked out the window. 'Can I borrow some toilet paper?'

Scott looked to Wild Scott, who shook his head.

'No.'

Robot Scott looked away from the window. 'I can't believe this is what decides the fate of human civilisation.'

'None of us want it to be true,' said Scott, 'but there are some things we're just not willing to sacrifice, no matter the cost. We wouldn't have to tell so many stories about ourselves if reality lived up to them. Why do you care so much anyway? I thought you didn't have emotions.'

'Online shopping addiction is a lot more complex than you'd expect.'

The three of them bowed their heads in a mixture of sadness, shame, and addiction to online shopping.

And then Scott raised his head in a mixture of excitement, pride, and addiction to online shopping.

'I have an idea! I don't have to choose. You both know what's going to happen. With your knowledge, I can dedicate my life to preventing either outcome from happening!'

'In hindsight, that seems incredibly obvious,' said Robot Scott.

'I have teeth growing in my armpit,' said Wild Scott.

'Then it's time to save the world!' said Scott.

There was a flash of light. This Scott was barely recognisable. Scarred, burned, mutated, he was grafted to half a dozen animals that seemed to be actively attacking him.

'I made it so much worse,' said Hero Scott before immediately dying. The animals grafted to him began to eat. Robot Scott placed a hand on Wild Scott's arm before he could join in.

'That's fine,' said Scott. 'I mean, it's not, and I'm going to have nightmares about this for the rest of my life, but it was my first time trying to save the world. What if this time Robot Scott gives me his time machine, then I dedicate my life to learning all the skills I'll need to save the world, then that me comes back to now and trains current me, and then I use those skills to save the world?'

There was a flash of light. This Scott was pale, out of shape, and made Wild Scott look hygienic.

'You're not exactly what I was expecting,' said Scott.

'It was too hard,' said Trainer Scott. 'I tried joining the army, but I hated it, so I hid in a bunker and ate canned food for ten years.'

'I won't lie, this isn't my proudest moment,' said Scott.

'Did you know you can make a girlfriend out of bomb shelter insulation?' said Trainer Scott.

'No. And I didn't want to.'

Scott looked around at his gathered selves. Robot Scott was ordering sock protectors online. Wild Scott was chewing on his own knee. Hero Scott was, well. And Trainer Scott was slurping baked beans out of the can.

'I've got it. None of us is smart enough to come up with a good solution. So I just need to dedicate myself to academia. Then once I'm super smart and wise, I can come back and tell us what to do.'

There was a flash of light. Academic Scott looked exactly like Trainer Scott.

'It was too hard, wasn't it?' said Scott.

'Have you ever tried to read a book? Learning is *so* boring,' said Academic Scott.

'Did you make a girlfriend out of the insulation?' said Trainer Scott.

'I made two, but then they found out about each other.'

'What if I just email someone else and ask them to help?' said Scott.

There was another flash.

'I never got around to it,' said Email Scott. He'd brought his insulation girlfriend with him.

Scott lay down on the kitchen floor. 'I always thought that, under the right circumstances, I could be one of history's greats. This has been a very sobering realisation.'

'I guess we just don't have what it takes to save the world,' said Robot Scott, ordering tyre glitter.

'That's it!' cried Scott, leaping back to his feet. *'We!* I've been trying to do this alone. But with your time machine, there can be as many of me as we need!'

'You're saying you keep travelling back to this moment until we have an army,' said Robot Scott.

'And then we take over the world so we can prevent either future happening,' said Wild Scott.

'Exactly!' said Scott.

Ten years passed.

'This is so much worse,' said Robot Scott.

'So much worse,' said Wild Scott.

'We couldn't even send an email – why did we think we'd know how to run the world?' said Supreme Emperor Scott.

And then he took out the time machine one last time.

He went back further than any of him ever had. Five minutes further. There he was, asleep, tangled unflatteringly in his blankets, dreaming about cake and Mary Gilbert. Supreme Emperor Scott switched off the alarm.

He couldn't save the world. He couldn't escape his nature. He might as well sleep in.

Phlogiston

Melissa Ferguson

The girl hadn't always hated her body. When she'd turned 13, her flesh became a burden. Like a helpless child who needed constant care to simply survive.

After two years of failure after failure, the men who'd created her gave up on solving the problems caused by their shoddy engineering. Instead, they locked her away, out of fear or shame. Maybe both.

At dinner time her cell door beeped. A cafeteria worker wheeled in a trolley bearing a tiny salad of cucumber, lettuce and tomato in the shadow of a mountain of greasy bacon. No carbs of course. They were impure. For her anyway.

The cafeteria worker, an older woman who leaned on the trolley as though it were holding her up, said in a gravelly voice, 'It's always the girls who burn the brightest that they try to douse, especially if their fires don't serve them.'

'Huh?' It wasn't that the girl didn't understand the concept of holding back the flames inside, but that she hadn't expected the woman to understand.

'You were the one sneaking into the kitchen late at night to eat stale bread and cold potatoes, weren't ya?'

The girl beckoned the woman closer and whispered, 'Can you bring me something starchy next time?'

The woman raised her eyebrows and rattled out with the trolley.

The girl ate with big, unchewed gulps. The smoky bacon smell turned her stomach. Eating was for sustenance only. The nutrients were nothing more than ingredients in the recipe of her body. They'd engineered her to run exclusively on ketones derived from the metabolism of proteins and fats. She was the prototype of a human who could survive in places where carbohydrates were scarce. And now the digestion of carbs produced an inexplicable combustion inside her.

The scientists jokingly referred to the phenomenon as phlogiston.

The word evoked pompous men with monocles, pushing out their puffed chests and projecting their booming voices across wooden auditoriums. To those historical chaps, phlogiston was an element of fire. Held on a tether within us all, waiting to break free and consume.

The girl's nerves rose as mealtime approached the next day. Would the same woman bring her food? Did she consider the girl worthy of what she wanted? The anticipated presence or absence of carbs on her dinner plate grew in her mind until it represented a cosmic judgement on her existence.

Finally, the cafeteria woman arrived, with greyish meat, watery vegetables, and a pinched look on her face. She turned her back to the surveillance camera and pulled a small dinner roll, covered in lint and dust, out of her pocket.

This wasn't just a bread roll, but confirmation that everything that had been done to the girl was wrong. It was also a choice. A heavy, heavy choice. She secreted the contraband in the sleeve of her jumpsuit. Breaking her diet taboo was risky. If they found out, they might do something more final than locking her away.

Unlike most subjects she'd had a normal life until puberty, when her metabolism switched like a dual fuel vehicle. Her breath became fruity and chemical, and concrete-like stools had ripped small tears around her anus. She'd had to drink water constantly to dilute the stinging acid of her urine. The changes were unwelcome, but as inevitable as growing up. Her body was programmed before birth.

For a short time, she was their experimental fetish. They'd measured and biopsied, drawn blood, and swabbed cheek cells. They'd weighed her and peered at every orifice with torches and magnifying glasses. They'd taught her she wasn't worth anything unless they were paying her attention.

At first, she'd enjoyed her newfound importance. But she soon tired of the constant demands and judgements, and yearned for childhood, when no one analysed what she ate, or frowned when she stuffed chips and donuts into her face. Puberty betrayed her, filled her with acetone like a human-shaped jar of nail polish remover.

Other experimental subjects, who she'd once considered friends, turned up their noses at her shroud of vapours. Even those with the green chlorophyll skin, the dopey ones with four stomachs like ruminants, the ones with pointy teeth for drinking blood, even those with webs of mycelium growing out of the ends of their fingers, they all thought *she* was strange. She ran circuits around the yard to sweat out the ketones and showered three times a day to dampen the chemical smell.

Upon acknowledgement of her poor design, they reintroduced bread and breakfast cereal to her diet. After a single cheese sandwich, her temperature soared and her metabolism ran like uncontrolled nuclear fission. The small fire inside that she'd always tended, had found a way to roar, and the flammable ketones in her body threatened to ignite. She hadn't been afraid. Not until saw the panic in their faces. Her own panic soon gave way to exultation. She was a dangerous weapon only she could wield.

They took away her carbs again, along with her enjoyment of food and eating. But they couldn't take away her cravings. Proteins and fats didn't give her the same sense of fulfilment. They'd shown her the pleasure and then expected her to forget, or to simply obey. They fed her an array of specially designed diets, excluding or focussing on one food group or another. She was sickly or on the verge of flames on all of them. And she always found a way to access carbs. Carbs were both comfort and power. But, most of all, they were her rebellion.

The scientists hid their fear behind disappointment. She'd dared to become something other than what they desired, like lotus feet that had escaped their binding and expanded into mighty hooves.

When the lights went out, she hid from the gaze of the surveillance camera, beneath her blanket. She doubted they watched her too closely anymore. She took the roll from her sleeve, brushed away the dirt she couldn't see in the dark, and imagined the tanned shell.

The aroma sent the promise of contentment to her brain. She took a single bite and manipulated a small bolus of the fluffy white crumb with her tongue until the long starch chains cleaved to release their sweetness.

The small morsel settled in her stomach, and it roared for more. But she wasn't eating for comfort alone. She waited for her acids to break the bread down into the molecular parts that would enter her bloodstream. Glucose molecules crossed into her capillaries and shuttled around her body. Cells that required energy for their basic functions worked their chemical transformations.

A small flame ignited at her core. She pushed it up through her throat – buffered by a channel of cooled cells – and burped out a puff of smoke. They'd retrofitted her with the ability to induce torpor. The power to make her cells slow and cold to resist the flames, the way echidnas survived the heat of bushfires. She'd pretended it hadn't worked.

Now she was older she understood the value of secrets. Better for them to think she was helpless and contained. Better they didn't know that the more they tried to mould her, the more they created a weapon for their own destruction.

The whole institute was dedicated to the flawed premise that forcing the biology of the masses into something more efficient, would allow their funding bodies' wealth to grow unbounded. They would carry on repairing the problems they'd caused in their attempts to repair previous problems, until everything collapsed under the weight of tape and cheap glue, and their hoarded wealth became useless. Like the proponents of phlogiston theory, who'd held doggedly to an idea that became more and more preposterous as science advanced.

Every day for the next few days the cafeteria woman brought her a bread roll. The girl practised with larger and larger bites, until she could push flames from her mouth. She waited for the cell door to open and for them to drag her away but, as she suspected, they weren't watching. She was nothing to them now. Or so they thought. They'd turned her from their pet into a vengeful dragon.

At midnight on her last night in captivity she counted four whole rolls in her sleeves. She pulled out the first and ate it whole. Bite by stale, crumbly bite. Not long after 1 am, it started.

First just a warm flush, like stepping in front of a heater. Then a burning glow like she'd swallowed a hot coal. She activated torpor and corralled the flames. She chased them up through her body and breathed them out on a gust of acetone that melted the lock from the door.

She stepped into the hallway amid the flashing lights and blaring alarms, took another roll from her sleeve and fed her flame.

Las Artes Hipnóticas (2032)

David Thomas Henry Wright

The Deaths

The first death took place in Melbourne. The boy's mother phoned for an ambulance, claiming her son had been electrocuted in the bathtub. Paramedics arrived and, after checking for vital signs, confirmed the boy, aged 14, was deceased. His body was lifted from the tub and laid on the tile floor, his neck propped up with bundled towels. The mother stroked her son's dripping hair. In the adjoining hallway, the father sobbed. The remaining bathwater was tinged dirty brown. Samples were taken.

When asked how she had found her son, the boy's mother said he had been wearing headphones, which she surrendered with quavering hands. They were an ivory-coloured, wraparound pair that contained a tiny mp3 player. On the side, in fluorescent blue, they were labelled *WATERPROOF*. 'He used them while swimming,' said the mother. Though she had Asian features, she spoke with an ocker accent. 'I reckon they shocked him.'

'I'll sue 'em,' hissed the boy's father. His face was bright pink.

The coroner was called. The body was taken.

Were it not for the fastidiousness of the forensics pathologist, Doctor Rebecca Alina, the 26 deaths may never have been connected. The samples of the boy's bathwater contained traces of urine, faeces, and seminal fluid. They also exhibited diatoms similar to the boy's body tissue, indicating he had most certainly drowned. Yet the body showed no signs of struggle. There was no bruising around the head. No grip marks on the limbs.

Blood tests indicated he was not under the influence of narcotics or alcohol. Chemical analysis showed no diseases.

He had no history of epilepsy, narcolepsy, hypertension, or heart conditions. No signs of electrocution, despite his parents' insistence she check for it (given the device's low current capacity, this was ruled out). By all accounts, he had been an exceptionally healthy young man.

Dr Alina was a junior pathologist who, ever since coming to work with her hair in pigtails, feared she had lost her department's respect. Yet despite vowing to avoid unnecessary fuss (what the senior pathologist unkindly referred to as 'girlish pedantry'), she believed healthy boys did not drown in bathtubs without explanation. She insisted the situation be examined further.

The investigating officer, Sergeant Ellessee Watkins, questioned the boy's parents. The husband was a periodontist, the wife a manager of a café the couple owned. They appeared heartbroken and sleep-deprived. The boy was their only child. While reserved, he was not unpopular. He played saxophone in the school band and was wicket keeper in the cricket team. He had a close friend with whom he texted daily. Their correspondence was composed of homework questions and school gossip, peppered with sarcasm and in-jokes: nothing suggestive of dejection. The boy did not appear to have been under unnecessary stress. If anything, his teachers felt he could have afforded to focus more on his studies. Both parents told Watkins he was a 'good kid'.

Sergeant Watkins was not a delicate interrogator. She was a shaggy-haired, thickset woman with a leaden complexion from the cigarettes she sucked. Her sinewy shoulders were never cried on. Nevertheless, the boy's parents were willing and able to discuss awkward matters, such as whether or not they suspected their son took drugs (doubtful), was sexually active (definitely not), or self-stimulated (likely).

'Yes, he's a teenage boy. He masturbates,' stated the father.

'Masturbat*ed*,' clarified the mother. After wiping her eyes, she added, 'Are you *certain* he wasn't electrocuted?'

Sergeant Watkins was certain the boy's parents were not camouflaging anything. They simply wished to know what had happened to their son. To them, truth was preferable to any amount of indecency. They even allowed Watkins to search their son's room with her detection dog-in-training.

His bedroom was untouched, the mother claiming she had yet to muster the courage to sort through his things. Watkins had no children, but assumed the room was typical of a teenage boy: cluttered desk, shoes tossed on the floor, a poster of a bikini model, a ghostly undercurrent of body odour. The dog was instructed to sniff around the bed, wardrobe, chest of drawers… It found nothing of interest.

Watkins requested the headphones the boy was reported to have worn, from which she downloaded the audio data. It contained an array of heavy metal and hip-hop. One lengthy file, however, was titled bathtub_hyp_alizonss.mp3. When Watkins queried the parents about it, the mother moaned, 'Don't tell me he got some disgusting idea from rap music.'

Watkins listened to the recording several times. Not sure what to make of it, she took it to the University of Melbourne's School of Psychological Sciences, where she was directed to the office of Professor Alexis Alteruthemeyer. Watkins found Alteruthemeyer perched behind a chipboard desk, surrounded by brimming bookcases. She had a pierced nose and a shaved head. The latter, Watkins presumed, was due to fashion, not illness. After exchanging greetings and declining coffee, it became clear that neither woman cherished small talk, so Watkins took a seat and leapt right into it. She explained the boy's death, Dr Alina's concerns, and her discovery of the audio.

'I must warn you, the recording is quite graphic.' As she said this, Watkins felt her cheeks warm.

'Sounds intriguing,' said Alteruthemeyer, smirking. She clearly wished to learn what could possibly make a bulky, bushy-haired police sergeant blush. 'Let's hear it.'

The recording had a runtime of 30 minutes. It opened with sounds of running water and atonal organ music. The mood could be classified as 'easy listening'. A female voice with a New Zealand accent explained that this was an erotic audio, for the purposes of hypnotising the user, under which conditions sexual climax would be achieved. The listener was instructed to don bone-conduction waterproof headphones and lie in a bath filled with body-temperature water. This, the voice specified, would help create a trance state. She advised to pause the recording until these conditions were met, before continuing:

My voice is your voice. I speak for you. Listen to me, to you. You are going to go into a trance. I am going to take you into a trance. You are going to take yourself into a trance with my words. You choose to let me choose for you. As you hear my voice, gaze at an imaginary spot. Let vision blur. Do not focus. Do not worry about the movement of water or what occurs outside this room, this bath, your head. Keep staring. Without thought. Without need of thought. I invite you to close your eyes. Now, open them. Note the weight of your eyelids. Note how heavy they feel. Continue to open and close your eyes until it is preferable and natural to let them stay closed.

There was a caesura.

Feel your body relax into water. I am water. Feel the muscles in your back, legs, arms relax. Feel weighty. Now weightless. Imagine you are floating. You are floating. You are water. The water is love. You are listening to the sound of my voice, your voice, the voice of water. It is relaxing to hear your voice as you float, as you do not move, as eyelids are heavy, as cheeks droop, as the nerves in your teeth tingle. Ignore my voice. Allow me access to your mind. Trust me. Trust you. Let go. Do not clutch, clench, or swallow. Let saliva pool, swish, and slosh like the water you float on, like the water I am, like the water you are. All is liquid. Breathe. As you fade into trance you will still hear my words. You are still able to think, but it is not necessary. Imagine your thoughts floating, as you are floating in water, as you are water.

Watkins stared at the floor. Outside, an antique air conditioner cranked, dripping condensate.

The organ music adopted a minor key. Alteruthemeyer clicked a pen and scribbled. The speaker's voice became breathy. Sexual noises were simultaneously described and performed. Watkins crossed her legs, making the plastic seat creak. Alteruthemeyer failed to conceal a chuckle. The sequence ended with the speaker claiming to be straddling the listener's face, encouraging them to 'succumb to liquid' (this phrase was repeated eighteen times), and that the listener, in allowing themselves to 'feel weight' upon their face, would increase their pleasure. The performance crescendoed.

At the recording's conclusion, Alteruthemeyer and Watkins looked at one another. Alteruthemeyer, unable to resist, stated, 'Well, in my expert opinion, that was a woman pretending to have sex.'

Watkins did not smile. 'What I want to know is… does this work?'

'Hypnosis? Sure,' said Alteruthemeyer. 'It has valid clinical use. We don't teach our students to hypnotise one another, but there is evidence to suggest it helps people break bad habits: smoking, insomnia…'

'And this?'

'Hypnotising a man to orgasm? I suppose it could work.'

'But would it… is the person not in control of their body?'

Alteruthemeyer shook her head. 'People under hypnosis are in control. They would not do anything they would normally find objectionable.'

'But if they believed or were convinced that doing something harmful might yield a… sex-related reward?'

Alteruthemeyer stared off in thought. 'I think this is what you're asking me: could a young, impressionable male under hypnotic susceptibility to suggestion be coerced into drowning himself in exchange for heightened sexual release?'

Watkins nodded.

'It's a good question,' said Alteruthemeyer. 'I don't know that I have the answer. Let me think about it.'

Watkins left in a sweaty huff, bothered she had become embarrassed for nothing.

Alteruthemeyer, however, was sincere in her willingness to consider the case, so much so she wrote an article for the thecolloquy.com, titled 'Subconscious Masculinity'. Her article referred to the city where the incident occurred, the age of the deceased and, most significantly, a link to the audio file (alizonssexysounds.com.ie/audio/bathtub _hyp_alizonss.mp3), which was found by performing a simple web search for 'bathtub + hypnosis + orgasm'.

The article drew the attention of a coroner in Ottawa, who had been surprised by a case involving a 21-year-old man who had also drowned in a bath wearing headphones. Further investigation revealed the man had been listening to the same recording. This discovery instigated international news networks to take up the story.

It began as a multiplatform general interest piece that tailed news programs and encouraged curious social media users to click, but soon escalated into heated panel discussions and extensive articles debating the ethics of pornography, censorship, digital ethics, sex addiction, and adolescent depression.

Around the globe, more coroners came forward with reports of peculiar bathtub deaths. Similar cases occurred in multiple English-speaking countries, as well as a handful in Europe, and a single case in Argentina. Many feared the media's infatuation was endangering susceptible young men (all victims were young males) by drawing attention to the file. This panic was most severe during October 2029, when 'bathtub séances' became a popular Halloween prank.

For her part, Watkins did an interview with local news.

The information she provided was not very illuminating, nor, as appeared to be requisite these days, entertaining (unlike Alteruthemeyer, whose ability to make academic discussion palatable garnered her a regular panel seat on Q&A, occasional opinion pieces published in *The Age,* and thousands of Twitter followers). Despite worldwide interest, Watkins's investigation concluded. There was no evidence to suggest the boy's death was anything but accidental.

Yet even after she retired in December 2037 and started a German Shepherd breeding business providing detection dogs to the Police Service, the bathtub case continued to plague her. In her career, Watkins had been party to a number of unresolved investigations, including one grisly episode involving the stabbing of two women. But those cases were dismissed by her conscience. Only the boy in the bath brought regret.

Watkins knew blame lay somewhere, but she could not begin to articulate with who or what. As she lay in bed, surrounded by slumbering canines, their gentle breathing punctuated by intermittent licks of lips, Watkins feared this ambiguity. The more sense she tried to make, the foggier things became. It made her feel helpless. Like the hypnotised felt upon waking, she imagined.

The Witches

As reports on bathtub deaths emerged, the performer of the recording was swiftly doxed. Despite no photographic web presence, the 'erotic performer' of alizonssexysounds.com.ie was easily identified (a blog post referred to her employer, Caoilfhionn Books in Temple Bar, Dublin). Her free-to-access site consisted predominantly of audio recordings. The 'ABOUT ME' section described Alizon as a Gardnerian Wiccan, neopagan, and member of the Dulene Edwina Caballero Society. Except for a brief review of Caballero's *Enduring Witchcraft* (1961), she had written very little on the author.

The performer's real name was not Alizon, but Pamela Clark. She was 29. On her right cheek she had a large mole with a hair growing out of it (this, she claimed, was lucky in Chinese culture). Her nose was described by one particularly cruel journalist as 'toucan-like'. The same journalist classified her BMI as 'morbidly obese'. Clark agreed to an interview with RTÉ, in which she was soft-spoken and kept her large hands clasped in her lap. She wore revealing lace, which many commentators felt was insensitive. When asked why she created the file, Clark stated that she wished to contribute to a sex-positive culture.

'Self-worship is for a rejoicing heart, a pleasure ritual all should engage in,' she said. 'But this particular recording was cursed. I've since taken it down. And I ask everyone to delete it and avoid it.' At this admission, she welled up, adding, 'I just wish everyone love.'

The interviewer, a trim, smileless woman named Aabha Smith, was unmoved. 'You state on your site that you are an admirer of the late author Dulene Caballero,' stated Smith.

Clark nodded, accentuating her tear-moistened double chin.

'Do you also endorse her politics?' asked Smith. 'During the 1970s, as I'm sure you're aware, Caballero was involved in multiple right-wing groups.'

Clark repeated, 'I just want to create a sex-positive world.'

'But you are closely associated with the Caballero Society,' pressed Smith.

Clark nodded, this time with less certainty. She clutched her triquetra pendant, which sat inches above deep cleavage.

'You have contributors from this group who refer to themselves as Wiccan,' said Smith. 'The script for the recording you performed was authored by one such… witch?'

'It was submitted by a fan,' said Clark.

'A quick perusal of the group's message boards reveals a

white nationalist agenda. For example, many Britain First members have used the site to organise invasions of mosques. Is your goal only to produce pornographic material, or is there a political motivation?'

Clark simpered, 'I'm sorry, I can't do this.' She waddled out of her chair and the room. The interview concluded.

The mother of a Texan boy who died listening to Clark's recording told the *Daily News* that her son's death was not accidental. 'This was orchestrated. That Alizon-Pamela witch-woman… whatever she is… she's at least guilty of manslaughter and must be charged.'

In no country, however, were the events surrounding the bathtub deaths ever a criminal investigation. The recording did not cause any changes to freedom of speech laws in any Western countries (Saudi Arabia and the United Arab Emirates blocked all hypnosis-related websites, though this was not out of step with their typical censorship). Classification rules were passed in Australia, Ireland, and South Korea to prevent broadcast of bathtub_hyp_alizonss.mp3, though no one was ever charged for doing so.

Burn Fat Right-Wing Witches, an ironic Facebook group that amassed hundreds of non-ironic participants, created an online petition demanding Clark be burned at the stake. Several victims' relatives signed. The Russian ambassador to Ireland even piggybacked this hatred, suggesting Clark's 'witchcraft' may have been responsible for the recent poisoning of a British spy.

Clark did not take these accusations well. She removed all files from her site, leaving up only a quote from occult author E.Q. Browne's *Inner Visions* (1937): 'unhappiness is one's own doing'. She withdrew to her hometown of Blenheim, and retreated to New Zealand's South Island bushland, taking with her a small tent, a sleeping bag, and a backpack full of tinned fruit and bottled water. She set herself up, illegally, among the intense moisture and robotic calls of the tui, in self-imposed exile.

Well after controversy had dwindled, Clark was discovered by a group of tourists on a hiking trail. She was naked. Her hairy legs were strewn with mud and her fleshy back was spattered with ticks. On her hip, a plump leech suckled. When asked what had happened, Clark hissed, frothing saliva through clenched teeth. In her hands, she clasped a bloody, feathery mess. One of the hikers managed to pry her palms apart, revealing a mangled spotted kiwi.

Clark was admitted to the Witherlea Mental Health Service where a psychiatrist diagnosed her with 'unspecified catatonia' and prescribed antidepressants. During her first evening, she wailed non-stop and had to be intravenously sedated. She spent the following days hunched in an armchair, plucking hairs off her legs. When questioned, she would grimace and scratch her arms. She refused to eat meat, dairy, or bread, swallowing only slivers of pear and sips of iced water.

Her skin began to sag due to considerable weight loss. Yet responsiveness slowly improved. Occasionally she would ask the nurses to check her legs for ticks. Of her own volition, she helped elderly patients to spoon their soup. Even if they growled at her to go away, she would insist on helping.

The nurses accepted her offer to support them with their less pleasant duties (distributing meals, changing sheets, removing bed pans). Visitors who came to the facility often commented that Clark was sweet and helpful. The head nurse frequently declared her a 'godsend'. When asked by her assigned psychologist why she had become so tolerant and friendly, Clark responded, 'Now that the curse is lifted, I just wish everyone love.'

The Authors

The author of bathtub_hyp_alizonss.mp3 is known only

as 'jrulz885'. They posted to alizonssexysounds.com.ie only once. They also made two insignificant comments on the Caballero Society's message boards (advice relating to purchasing airline tickets). Despite extensive efforts, jrulz885 was never identified. Many users named 'jrulz885' (or variations thereof) appeared among the various online Wiccan communities that cropped up following the bathtub deaths, but no evidence suggested any of these were the author of the original script.

One author, however, created thousands of variations. Jonah Zubizarreta was a failed machine learning engineer and app creator. In 2024, he suspended his University of Florida candidature, cashed out the trust fund set up by his late abuelo (the Zubizarretas owned multiple sugarcane and agave plantations in Southern California and Northwest Mexico), moved to SoMa, San Francisco, and developed *BestNight®*: a smartphone application that monitored sleep cycles in order to wake the user during an ideal time so as to provide maximum refreshment. While highly reviewed by users and zAPPed.com, Zubizarreta's app was rendered redundant by *Blankie®*, a near-identical app offered as freeware with the activity trackers *FitnessWrist®* and *CountIt®*. Unlike *Blankie®*, *BestNight®* cost $4.99 to download. It quickly disappeared from all distribution platforms. His mistake, Zubizarreta believed, was thinking too small. He had transformed only the alarm clock when he should have tried to transform the sleeping person.

In the aftermath of his app's collapse, Zubizarreta dreaded the upcoming season of family weddings and christenings, having to hear of his Aunt Isabella's benevolent tourism to El Alto, his cousin Mateo's negotiating the sale of a Colombian mine to the Abu Dhabi government, his Uncle Sebastian's hosting Alejandro González Iñárritu at his tequila distillery in Jalisco… dozens of relatives with manicured nails and beards, who, with elaborate cocktails in hand, would bombard him with legitimate boasts. Zubizarreta lived for, and in fear of, these conversations. Imagining himself in the billowy suit his parents bought for his high school graduation, having to put on smiles that exposed his non-whitened teeth tainted by instant coffee, forced into in-depth discussions about why his app tanked… it was too humiliating to consider.

Declining all invitations, Zubizarreta retreated to económica Tijuana, which he dubbed the 'tech-hub of the future'. He was not yet completely broke, having bought a small amount of bitcoin in 2015. His short-term plan was to develop a machine learning algorithm that, with minimal input, could spew out college application letters unique enough to avoid detection by plagiarism software. As well as gain subversive notoriety, he hoped to use this dodgy business to gather 'successful language' data in order to pivot to a more professional and marketable line of educational/seminar materials for students navigating college entry pathways.

Unfortunately, he attracted few customers. Given the dubious nature of his enterprise, word could only spread by black market word of mouth. Worse still, his machine learners had multiple bugs. He continually had to review the output for errors. Zubizarreta had dreamed of an automated business with effortless income but, after eight months of grinding, he had established only a pretty pitiful proofreading outfit. To cover costs, he freelanced as an English tutor to school students. His leisure time was spent locked in his hostel, lying on unwashed sheets, watching illegally downloaded TV shows and pornography, swallowing cheap mezcal and *cahuamanta,* depositing fat to his belly and oil to his face.

So, when he learned that an audio file had led to the deaths of 26 people, Zubizarreta saw opportunity. His machine learners were recalibrated to rewrite jrulz885's original post, what he labelled the 'death script'. He generated simple rewrites that replaced nouns, adjectives, and verbs, grammatical rewrites that restructured syntax patterns, and spawning rewrites that formed tangents, reimagining the script with various lexicon restrictions.

He employed actresses of various ages and ethnicities who were recorded performing set vocabularies for programmable voices, the unnatural tone of which, Zubizarreta assumed, would suit the repetitiveness and perspicuity requisite for hypnosis. He bought the domain name hypnoticerotic.com and uploaded three sample audio files. Zubizarreta debated also uploading the original bathtub_hyp_alizonss.mp3, but ultimately decided against it (for those who wished to find it, it was easy to track down, no more difficult than an .MPEG4 of Pasolini's *Salò* (1975) or .PDF of Hitler's *Mein Kampf* (1925)).

Hypnoticerotic.com gained significant traffic. To have a unique erotic audio produced by Zubizarreta's program was free. One simply registered and agreed to wear a *FitnessWrist®* or *CountIt®* activity tracker while undergoing hypnosis, the data of which would be simultaneously uploaded. This data, hypnoticerotic.com assured, would remain anonymous.

While many circumvented these requirements (it was simple enough to falsify logins or refuse to wear a tracker), approximately 60 per cent provided data, enough for Zubizarreta to distil what he believed would become a 'language of subconscious action', the applications of which would be limitless: not only educational, therapeutic, and business possibilities, but military, espionage, politics… Zubizarreta was convinced that within the data provided by hundreds of hypnotized human guinea pigs lay the essence of human volition: the secret of life and death.

Yet no one died. A few experienced increased heart rates, and on the message boards some claimed to have achieved orgasm (more lamented that they did not), but not a single death. Not even a measly myocardial infarction. Not only were Zubizarreta's audios nonfatal, but in the years that followed there were no further reported deaths resulting from the original file. Bathtub_hyp_alizonss.mp3 had lost its potency.

Alteruthemeyer, in her book *Self-Awareness and the Muted Urge* (2038), argued that recognition of hypnotic danger ruined the trance's efficacy, citing multiple cases of individuals with depressive tendencies and/or hypersexual disorders who listened to the audio with sincerely self-stimulatory/destructive intentions yet yielded no result, i.e. they neither died nor climaxed.

After leaving hypnoticerotic.com up for 18 months (during which time he drank so much mezcal his face became puffy, exhibiting red pustular lesions) and with no usable data, Zubizarreta chose to believe the original 'death script' was a miracle. He was Catholic and, while he had never taken his religion seriously, his Sunday school teachings were never wholly dismissed. He supposed jrulz885 must be the voice of God – there was no other explanation – and that the shame he felt towards his accruing failure was in fact sin. Referring to Exodus 11: 4-6, Zubizarreta became convinced the bathtub deaths were the result of Biblical plague.

He moved to Oaxaca, attended the Seminario Pontificio de la Santa Cruz, and became ordained as a deacon. In 2037, Zubizarreta arrived at his nephew's wedding wearing a bleach-white clerical collar, feeling, for the first time in his life, noble. When he officiated at the ceremony and gave a brief but striking sermon on 'decisive love', his aunts, uncles, and cousins could not have been prouder.

The Critics

Though the bathtub deaths gave rise to a number of practitioners, 'arte de la hipnosis' did not bring about the revolution Manuel Almeida claimed it would in his seminal work *Hypnotic Theory* (*Teoría Hipnótica,* 2031), later reissued as *The Hypnotic Arts* (*Las Artes Hipnóticas,* 2032). Drawing heavily on Lacan, Almeida proposed a culture in which all art was hypnotic. Rather than heading to the theatre or reading a book, people would receive artistic works like 'subconscious music' ('música subconsciente') and apply it directly to their lives. Conscious life would be enriched by the 'oculto' work.

As well as a 300-page publication, Almeida released his theory as hypnotic soundscape. Words and passages overlapped one another in multiple languages (citing Chomsky's *Syntactic Structures* (1957), Almeida argued that the subconscious mind is a 'blank birth state', capable of understanding any language's innate meaning). While comparisons were made to Derrida's *Glas* (1974), few argued that the work 'directly enriches conscious life'.

Alteruthemeyer's study of seventy participants (detailed in *Almeida's Charade* (2033)) concluded that not a single person retained anything approaching an understanding of Almeida's work. Yet Almeida produced several subsequent publications/soundscapes: *A Hypnotic Ontology* (*Ontología Hipnótica,* 2034), *Receiv~/Recit~ (Recepción/Recitando,* 2037), *The Subconscious Cocoon* (*El Capullo Subconsciente,* 2039), *Hidden Desire* (*Deseo Oculto,* 2041), and *Mind Narratives* (*Narrativas Mental,* 2044).

At the inaugural (and only) Hypnotic Arts Organization conference, held in Mendoza, August 2035, Alteruthemeyer – to jeers and cheers – accused Almeida.

'If there is any subconscious force that ties all these facets together – the kids in bathtubs, the would-be sex-phone operator from New Zealand, the endless current of pornography you insist on calling culture, not to mention your own easily-disproven nonsense – it is an adolescent desire for approval. Surely it's time to grow up!'

Alteruthemeyer's book, *The Newfanglement of Approval*

(2034), was translated to Spanish in 2036, titled *Nueva Aprobación*. She was named the keynote speaker at the International Psychological Association's *Clinical Hypnotist Conference* to be held in Montevideo, 11–18 September 2045.

The Artists

As controversy surrounding the bathtub deaths waned, so too did interest in hypnosis art. Despite multiple manifestos, the hypno-art movement never established itself in its own right, existing only as variants of other mediums (predominantly avant-garde music and multimedia displays).

Without a doubt, the most popular hypnotic artist was B.V., the anonymous English-based political artist/activist. B.V. released a number of soundscapes he labelled 'calls to spiritual revolution'. He had no permanent web presence, opting instead for digital guerrilla distribution methods, rejecting popular social media platforms due to their indifference towards the escalating environmental impact of data storage.

Famously, he coerced a disgruntled member of Argentinean President Mauricio Macri's re-election campaign to upload his work via the president's official Twitter account. He also had a 'hidden' track on Zachary Delacroix's fourth album *Execut[iv]e Chairmen* (2034).

B.V. stated, in a 2030 interview with Chinese installation artist Cai Bing (uploaded to caibing.com.cn), that he was a transcendentalist, in the American tradition, and considered himself a contemporary Ralph Waldo Emerson.

'We now have the technology to go directly to the soul,' he said. 'It is immoral not to use these methods to do so. I believe my work appeals to an inherent goodness in all of us. This work literally changes the individuals who listen, who open themselves to positive change.'

This interview was subsequently censored after it was

determined that *The_Eternal_Forest_of_Babel.flac,* B.V.'s ten-hour soundscape of 100 babies babbling, contained what some thought to be the term 'Xi Zedong', a hybrid of Xi Jinping/Mao Zedong, used to criticise President Xi's abolishment of term limits by likening him to Chairman Mao.

Many of B.V.'s critics, however, regarded him as merely a populist techno new-age producer, and a poor one at that. Alteruthemeyer, in her caustic *Almeida's Charade,* referred to him only in a footnote:

I hope B.V.'s assertion that his work 'goes directly to the soul' is the pinnacle of hypnotic artists' delusions.

For better or worse, B.V.'s popularity allowed a number of artists to emerge. One such scholar-artist was Mei-hua, who held an exhibit at Mona in Hobart, as part of their Indigenous artist-in-residence program. A descendent of the Kaxabu people, Mei-hua's work used Pazeh, a Formosan language of the Austronesian family that, as of 2010, became extinct when the last native speaker passed.

The following artist statement accompanied Mei-hua's work, *HmmMmm* (distributed free to all who attended the exhibit):

This audio work, inspired by pornographic Western forms, attempts to inject dead language and experience into the collective subconscious. I do not expect this to jumpstart the language; the requisite enthusiasm to do so does not exist. Unlike my more optimistic contemporaries, I do not believe in 'sleeping beauty' languages. Nor do I regard my practice as a form of 'resurrection.' The dead, sadly, stay dead. Nevertheless, there is meaning in attempting hopeless acts.

I encourage all who come to my exhibit to allow this artwork into your life. Let the language of my ancestors float in your heads. Let there be a zephyr of flickering neurons. That is all I can ask for. That is all that can happen at this point in time.

Douglas Allen: Galactic Attorney-at-Law

Peter J. Carter

I'm not sure if we have any other choice. He seems intelligent enough.

He's a dishwasher!

Not by choice, and he is a qualified lawyer on his planet.

My progeny deserves the best, regardless of our personal circumstances, but I can't interfere. You know that.

He's all that's available in time. I took care of the court. Let's hope he is smart enough to see the facts.

* * *

The office was dark. I was unsure if they kept it that way to hide the grime or if the occupants preferred low light. Of course, it could have been both.

'C'mon, in,' the creature behind the desk growled. It was a Reptalor. The massive thing had green-grey bumpy skin, small bi-symmetrical yellow eyes, and a gargantuan mouth full of hooked teeth.

'Have a seat,' the Reptalor said, motioning with a small forearm to the old red upholstered chair across the desk. I wondered if it was to conceal the blood.

'I'm Mr Kratz, and I understand you are here about a job?'

'Yes, sir. Doug Allen.'

One of the quickest things you learned was to avoid physical contact with different species. What was a handshake to you could be (depending on what you were grabbing) sexual assault to someone else.

'Well, Dog, how long have you been at the station?' Universal translators were notoriously inaccurate, so I didn't consider it insulting.

My amateur astronomer skills placed T'rackular station

rotating around a gas giant in the Perseus Arm of the Milky Way. Built for mining by the Galactic Corp in the upper atmosphere of the nameless gas giant, the station had evolved into a home for a million or so inhabitants. Its patchwork additions over time made a mottled structure that mirrored the populace in this otherwise empty space sector.

'I've been here for around eight months. It's Doug, by the way, sir, not Dog.'

'Sorry about that, Doug.' Kratz smiled with all his teeth, and there were quite a few. 'If you don't mind me asking, what species are you? I don't quite recognise it. Some type of slug?'

'No, I'm a human.'

'Human? Never heard of them,' he said, tapping a tentacle on the desk.

'We come from a planet in the Sol system on the inner edge of the Orion-Cygnus arm.'

'Oh, from the Galactic National Park? I didn't know there were space-faring species in that sector.'

'There aren't. The Wolnats picked me up,' I said, disgusted.

'Yes – bulbous-headed, big eyes?' He waved his arms around to illustrate.

'Yeah, those guys.' They had been sneaking into the park, usually Earth, as it was the only place that had life, and taking people for joyrides for centuries. It was the galactic version of a college initiation ritual.

'And how did you happen to get here?'

I took a deep breath and let it out. 'I have a place in the Sierra Nevada mountains in New Mexico. I was sitting at my campfire, when these guys showed up. They had skins on, so they looked like my species. I had been drinking bourbon, and they asked for some. We got into an argument about bourbon, and the next thing I remembered, I woke up in a bar on C level.'

'Hmm, sounds like quite a story. Tell me about humans. Is there anything at which you excel?'

Humans? We're arrogant, possessive, territorial, and petty. But we can also be courageous, brave, and intuitive. 'We're flexible.'

'So, your appendages can bend at any angle?'

'No, sorry.' This voice decoder, or voder, could miss nuances. 'We can live in a large range of environments and survive.'

'Lava?' said Kratz.

'Eh, no,' I said.

'Sulfur gas?'

'Naw, deadly.'

'Zero atmospheres? Twenty gravities? Can you survive projectiles, blunt force, or fire?' said Kratz.

'Nope, all deadly.' I changed tack. 'We're clever.' Yes, clever slugs. 'We're quite adept at using tools.'

'Ah, I can use that. Have you worked on proton engines or graviton drives?'

'Ah, no,' I said.

He threw his pad on the desk, and I hoped he wasn't wondering how we tasted.

'What do you do?' he asked.

'Well, I was in the motor pool in the army before I passed the bar,' I said.

'A reservoir of engines?' said Kratz.

'No, it's where we repair combustion engines. Probably not many of those around here.'

'No, not many museums here.'

'My profession after the army was a lawyer.'

'Are you accomplished?' he asked.

'I practised law for fifteen years, mostly corporate before I upset some powerful people. That's why I lived in the desert in the middle of nowhere,' I said.

'You are smart to make it difficult for your enemies to find you.' Kratz smiled, which scared me to death.

'Thought so.' And so did the FBI, who arranged the whole thing, but I'll take it. Chances are they won't find me here.

'I have an acquaintance who has found themself in a particular situation and needs legal advice.'

'I know nothing about law out here. There is not much for me to bring to the table.'

'Well, not many practise your profession at the station, and having someone at least acquainted with legal proceedings will be helpful.'

'What is the person charged with?'

'Mutiny.'

* * *

I worked out a payment with Kratz, which was actually not that bad. I'd been living in a bar since my unexpected arrival. Drogam, the owner of the bar I woke up in a few months ago, was a great guy. Well, maybe he was a guy. He was about four feet tall and had green skin. It made him look like a giant frog. But appearances aside, he seemed like a friendly entity.

He offered me a job cleaning up and washing dishes with a small room in the back to sleep in. I took it gladly, hoping to make enough credits to hire someone to take me home.

So that left morning and early afternoons free for me. The next day, I went to the core after a sleepless night reading everything I could about galactic law (which was very close to our own legal system) and shipboard conduct.

The jail section was in the very centre of the station. It was dark and old, tinged with rust and decay.

'Whadda you want?' the guard asked as I approached the jail. He was a Prolo, the most prevalent type of creature on the station. If you try to think of the standard idea of an alien with white skin, big eyes, and a bulbous head, you'll get it.

'I'm here to see Touraline Darkar.'

The guard moved closer to me – and he needed an entire box of breath mints. If there was one sense I could do with losing in my kidnapped galactic travels, it was my sense of smell. Nothing smelled good, just different degrees of horrible, from displeasing to downright putrid.

'And why is that?' he asked.

'Because I'm a lawyer.'

He looked at me strangely. 'Name?'

'Douglas Allen.'

'Never heard of a space slug being a lawyer.'

'I'm a human. From Earth?'

'Never heard of it.'

'Don't feel bad. My client?'

'This way,' he said, and I followed. If I didn't succeed at space law, I could always open a breath mint company. Someone must have told them I was coming, because my client was already in the interview room waiting for me.

Touraline Darkar was orange-skinned and had bluish-brown hair tied neatly in a topknot on their head. I would have referred to them as her, but I had no idea what sex they were. Humans liked to put things in boxes. Little boxes that had no imagination or understanding of the universe in general.

Darkar's species might lay eggs or subdivide through meiosis or never die. I had no way of knowing at that moment. They struck me that way, but as a human, I'd come to realise, as a species, we were stupid. Well, maybe just me.

'And who the fuck are you?' M. Darkar asked.

I ignored the question, placed my folder on the table, and sat down. I took out a pad, brought up a notepad, put my hands on the table, and smiled.

'I asked who the fuck are you.'

I nodded and sat for a bit more.

'Well?' Darkar demanded again.

'My name is Douglas Allen, but you already knew that, or

you wouldn't be sitting here. You know I'm a lawyer sent to help you. And, since you probably don't want to be spaced out of the nearest airlock for mutiny, you might want to stop the belligerent asshole stuff so we can get to work.'

They smiled back. 'Alright, so you're not just a meat sock.'

'Well, I am a meat sock, just not any meat sock. Tell me what happened. You were the communications operator on a freighter out of Epsilon Eridani?'

They smiled back. 'I'm Touraline. Nice to meet you.'

'And you as well, Touraline.'

'We were headed back from a run for supplies for the station. Our ship *The Lonesome Quark* was about ten days out of the station when I noticed a signal on the board.'

'And did you tell the captain about the signal?' Most of this was already in the file I was given, but it's always better to hear it from the client.

'I did. The captain said it was nothing and to continue.'

'But you didn't.'

'No.' They looked down and scratched above their eye with a foreclaw. 'I waited until I was running the third shift and took the ship off course to find the source of the signal.'

As a lawyer, you learn to pick up tells. Things that let you know your client is hiding something or lying. I was so totally lost here I just concentrated on the words. 'Why would you order the ship off the assigned course?'

'The repeating signal was very close to the universal SOS a transponder puts out when a ship is stranded. We were obligated to check it out by galactic law.' They were nervous.

I took a deep breath, and they did the same. 'But the captain didn't think so,' I said.

'No. Captain Molo was extremely angry when he found out we headed off course.'

'Did you find anything out there?'

'We collected an old communication satellite of unknown origin that was wandering just outside the trade lanes. A waste of time, but we couldn't ignore it!' They slammed a paw on the table.

'And you were charged with mutiny?'

Their head hung down as if focusing on something on the floor. 'Yes, we lost too much time and half of our consumables. I was relieved from duty and confined to my berth.'

'Something doesn't seem right. Sure, charge you with dereliction of duty, malfeasance, or any number of things, but mutiny?'

'It may have something to do with my family. My Brood Lord is the Governor of this station.'

And there it was. Had that Reptalor Kratz set me up in the middle of a power play for the station? But why did he choose me? I had received a temp visa to work from Galactic Corp as a transitory alien, but it was only for 90 turns.

Something was going on here and, like Mom used to tell me, 'Take what they give you and smile.'

'Alright, the trial's tomorrow.' I stood and gathered my things. 'I can assure you that I'm very good at this. Try to sleep.'

* * *

That night while washing dishes, I tried playing with scenarios. Washing dishes was almost Zen-like. The simple repetition of rinsing, loading the rack, and emptying cleared the mind.

Not much brain power was involved, so I was free to wander. The night ended too quickly, and although exhausted, I spent the time reviewing evidence.

* * *

Courts seemed to be the same everywhere. There were desks,

chairs, paperwork, and many self-important, scowling faces. I felt at home even with the extra appendages on the courthouse staff.

'All rise for Chief Magistrate Oomart Snork!'

We all stood as a cephalopod straight out of Cthulhu strolled in and took their chair behind the bench.

They cleared their throats and said, 'We are here to decide the charge of mutiny against one, Touraline Darkar. May the accused please rise.'

Darkar was in a box in the middle of the room, very similar to the British method for holding the accused.

'Do you understand the charges against you, M. Darkar?'

'Yes, I do, Chief Magistrate.'

'Are you ready, Prosecutor?' What seemed to be an eight-foot grasshopper nodded. He had weird hexagonal eyes and a set of mandibles capable of decapitating a heifer.

The prosecutor said, 'Yes, Your Honour.' The Grasshopper's name was KlortamunkisKlacktusnapatard. I preferred Grasshopper.

'And do you have representation here today, M. Darkar?'

'Yes, Chief Magistrate.' They pointed at me where I stood. 'Douglas Allen.'

The chief magistrate looked me over in what seemed like disgust. He used one of his arms to scroll on a pad. 'Douglas Allen, Douglas Allen, hmm. Are you employed as a dishwasher at Scorton's Bar?'

'That's right, Your Honour.'

He held up some of his arms, 'What, if any, qualifications do you have to represent your client?'

'Thank you, Your Honour. I graduated from Columbia University in the top ten of my class, passed the bar examination in three states, and practised at a reputable law firm for ten years.'

Grasshopper spoke up. 'Your Honour, I must object. Having a dishwasher for a lawyer will only be grounds for a retrial later, wasting this court's time.'

'Actually, I'm a lawyer who washes dishes. Nothing wrong with hard work,' I said.

'Be that as it may,' the chief magistrate said, 'Your qualifications for the Galactic Court are being called into question here.'

'Your Honour, I have read the Galactic court process front to back, which is very similar to the court proceedings I am familiar with. The presumption of equality of innocence and the right to cross-examination is similar in my court system. I am a very hard worker, which was instilled in me by my mother. She worked two jobs to the wee hours, ensuring I had the opportunity to stand in your court, sir. Surely, you had someone behind you, Your Honour, to get you where you are today?'

'Yes.' The chief magistrate nodded. 'My brood mother worked herself ragged, providing for us.'

'And that's what this court stands for. I promise to work as hard as I can to honour her sacrifice, for all those that sacrificed for us to provide the best defence possible for my client.'

God, that was the sappiest load of shit I'd dealt in a while. But it was all I had. I wouldn't make enough money to get the hell off this carnival of weirdness and get back home by washing dishes.

'Your Honour,' said Grasshopper, 'I'm not sure a semi-sentient slug can...'

The chief magistrate banged his orb on the bench.

'I will allow you to represent M. Darkar. And we will provide you with any assistance you require. To the honour of our mothers.'

I bowed my head in solemn respect.

My mother was a debutante who spent her days flying to the four corners of the planet living off a billion-dollar trust fund my grandfather left. I'd feel bad tomorrow. Today, I was a lawyer.

The prosecution went first here, just like at home. And the Grasshopper trotted out the same group I expected any prosecutor to produce. It seemed as though some things were universal.

* * *

As an aside, there was something intimidating about the prosecutor's multifaceted eyes, and I could never tell where he was looking. I objected here or there but mostly let things run their course.

The prosecutor established that my client disobeyed a direct order, and I got everyone in the box to admit that M. Darkar was a trustworthy, conscientious officer of the ship. By my scorecard, things were pretty even when the captain took the stand.

He was much the same as I imagined any freighter captain would be. Up in years, towards the end of his career, although it was hard to tell with a Prolo – he was a bit wrinkly.

The Grasshopper stood. 'Captain Molo, you have served as captain on the fleet lines for eighty years?'

'Yes, I have.'

'You've also received commendations…'

I stood. 'I object, Your Honour. The defence concedes that the captain has a long, illustrious record, and the court doesn't have to listen to every award since grammar school to agree to this point.'

'Conceded. The court acknowledges the captain's years of unblemished service,' the chief magistrate said. 'Please continue, Prosecutor.'

Grasshopper didn't like being interrupted and turned to me and clicked his mandibles.

'Yes, Your Honour. Captain, did you instruct M. Darkar to continue on the current course before giving up command to them for the third shift?' said Grasshopper.

'Yes, I did,' said the captain.

'And did they third shift to follow the assigned course?' said the prosecutor.

'No. I was worried about the consumables that were in our hold. Some had a shelf life that was approaching expiration.'

'Consumables?'

'Yes, some medicine and other foodstuffs that are required to keep the inhabitants of this station alive.'

'And why did you choose to ignore the communications officer?'

'It was a badly degraded signal from some old space junk. Our cargo was necessary to the station, and frolicking off endangered our mission.'

'Rightly so, Captain. Thank you for your long and selfless service. The prosecution rests,' said Grasshopper.

* * *

'Do you wish to cross-examine?' asked the chief magistrate.

I stood. 'Yes, Your Honour. Good morning, Captain.'

'What are you? A hairy worm?' The captain said with disgust.

The chief magistrate banged his orb. 'He is a defence lawyer with someone's life in peril. You would be wise to treat this court and him respectfully.'

'Sorry, Your Honour,' said the captain.

I stood there for a few seconds. My mentor at the firm I worked for told me a pause was often necessary. He told me, 'Some lawyers will screw it all up pretending to look for papers or some other lame-ass thing. Take a moment to look at your opponent on the stand and breathe. It'll only take a few moments for them to start shittin' themselves.'

I was ready. 'Captain, you said you had vital medical

supplies for T'rackular station.'

'That's correct.'

'Isn't it true that the medicine is called Cylian?'

'Yes, I believe that's the name.'

'Are you aware it is used for prepubescent skin lesions?'

'I know it's important,' said the captain.

'Some teenagers having clear skin for the senior prom is hardly vital. Wasn't the foodstuff you were contracted to pick up very close to expiration?'

'I have no idea what that means. There was plenty of time to get…'

I interrupted him. 'It means that they weren't vital at all. Your Honour, I would like to call attention to exhibit ten, a box end from one of the perishables in the cargo.' I held up a picture for the court to see. 'This is set to expire two turns from when they left port. Isn't it a four-turn trip to the station, captain?'

He was getting ready to blow. If there is one thing someone in power doesn't like, it's interruptions.

'Correct, but I felt as though…'

'Did you know that M. Darkar lost a family member on a ship that was lost?'

The captain smashed a fist on the railing in anger.

Grasshopper stood up, 'Your Honour, the witness needs time to answer.'

The chief magistrate banged his orb, 'The counsellor will give the witness time to answer.'

I nodded and was quiet. The captain looked at the chief magistrate. 'Which question am I supposed to answer?'

The chief magistrate flailed a tentacle around. 'Could the counsellor repeat the question?'

'Did you know that M. Darkar lost a family member on a ship that was lost?' I said.

'No, I did not,' said the captain.

'So you asked a vital crew member to ignore a call for help

when they lost a symbiote on an incapacitated vessel, and you knew nothing about their loss?'

He sat quietly, blinking his enormous eyes. They closed from the bottom up, which was unnerving to me. 'I am a captain on a galactic freighter. I do not have the time or the inclination to study the entire background of my crew. That was not a distress signal, and M. Darkar had no right to divert my ship.'

Something was wrong here. It was precisely the wrong thing to say in this scenario. Captain Molo should have pandered and expressed how deeply he felt about his crew. Perhaps even show remorse for having to take this action. I had this figured wrong. Something else was happening here. Fuck! I needed time to rethink this.

'Your Honour, I ask this witness to be dismissed and ask for a five-minute recess to confer with my client.'

'Granted. The court will be dismissed for five minutes.' Chief Magistrate Oomart Snork banged the orb.

I made my way to the box.

'I'm sorry, Touraline. I tried to make him admit that it might be a signal. I'll ask for a continuance and get an expert to state that.'

'Most of the goods we get are expired anyways. All this for some space junk. I never even got a chance to see what that thing was,' said Touraline.

'I have some pictures of it here that I requested from the prosecutor,' I said.

The defendant's box was lexan – I assumed to keep the defendants from spitting on the court members. As I handed them the picture, I caught something in the reflection. What I had thought was some battered galactic writing reversed in the mirror image.

I turned the picture over, and there it was. How this thing got out here, I have no idea. Wormhole? This trial wasn't a power play for the station. It was a simple fucking heist!

I returned to the cage and spoke urgently to Touraline. 'No time right now. Tell me everything you know about salvage rights!'

* * *

'All rise!' The chief magistrate slithered back in his seat and banged the orb.

'Counsellor Allen, are you ready to proceed?'

'Yes, Your Honour. I call M. Darkar to the stand.'

The bailiff escorted them to the stand. I knew that Grasshopper boy would eat them alive (no pun intended) in cross-examination, so I had to win this right here and now.

'M. Darkar, you believed this signal you received to be a distress call. Is that correct?'

'Yes, it had all the earmarks of a galactic distress call.'

'I'm sorry to say, M. Darkar, you are completely wrong,' I said.

The court stopped, as ten different species dropped their proverbial jaws. No one moved, slithered, or clicked.

'That's because it was an exploration vehicle.' I held up the picture from discovery. 'Can you read the side of this?'

'No. It's written in a language I don't know,' said Touraline.

'That's because it's barely legible and written backward, but it's English. A language of my home world. The inscription says *Voyager 2*. It's an exploratory satellite from my home world sent searching for extraterrestrial life. It is programmed to send greetings in many languages, which you mistook as a distress signal.'

Grasshopper finally shook off the voodoo I put him in and said, 'Your Honour, the prosecution knew nothing about this!'

'It's in the evidence file for all to see, Your Honour,' I said, pointing at Grasshopper. Semi-sentient that!

The chief magistrate banged the orb. 'Continue.'

'Do you know how this satellite is powered, M. Darkar?'

'No – it's not my field of expertise.'

'I happen to know, as I had to take an astronomy course at college. It has seventy-two plutonium-238 packets. I have no idea how it made it out here.' Probably those damn Wolnats were screwing around.

'Woo…' said Touraline.

'I assume it's expensive material?'

'Worth at least a hundred million galactic credits.'

I took a look around, and I saw the downcast faces of my opponents. Galactic Corp called it a mutiny to screw the crew out of the salvage rights. Obscure a crime with another crime. It was brilliant. That was, until the one person in this corner of the universe who knew what it was, appeared. In hindsight, Kratz might have known something about this when he offered me the job. Fuck, he goddamned knew all of this!

'Your Honour, I would like to claim this satellite as a member of Earth.'

The captain shot up like a rocket. 'That junk was recovered by my ship, and I have first rights!'

'Unless the owner shows up and lays claim,' I said. 'Galactic Law, Article 227.'

The chief magistrate smashed his orb repeatedly on the bench and rose like Nemo's nemesis. 'That is not the issue here today! We are here to decide the charge of mutiny.'

'Your Honour, if I could confer with the prosecution for a moment and the good captain, I believe we can get some resolution to this matter.'

He slumped back down and stuck one of his tentacles in a glass of water. 'By all means.'

* * *

Touraline Darkar walked out of the courthouse a free being, and I walked out 10 million credits richer.

They turned on the courthouse steps. 'Thanks, Doug Allen. What did you do?'

'The company knew the gig was up. They offered me thirty percent to let you be convicted. I countered with ten and had them drop all charges,' I said. 'They went for it.'

They hugged me. I'm not sure what it meant to their species, but it felt good. They would get their portion of the crew cut, which was three percent. Not a bad haul.

* * *

Later, I met with Mr Kratz, collected my fee, and called him an asshole for setting me up. He apologised and explained that the governor serves at the company's pleasure and could not interfere with the trial. He paid me 5,000 credits.

I tried to turn my newfound wealth into a trip home. He said they could, but I would have to undergo a procedure first that would have to turn my brain to 'oatmeal' before they dropped me off to protect Earth's ignorance. Galactic rules.

Damn you, Fermi!

I was stuck on the station for a while, maybe for good. I decided to hang my shingle out and perhaps pick up a gig at the bar between dishwashing.

Hey, it's a noble profession.

The Burn Out

Lyle Hopwood

For PFK

15 May 2026

I made nice with my big brother. I wouldn't tell him this, but he could teach me a lot about computers and stuff. Today I followed him around faking an interest in him, but he saw through that right away. I was wearing an official t-shirt of my favourite band, No 1 Home, pink, with Lolita written on it in yellow flowers – the name of their album. He teased me about it.

'You sure you should be listening to that sort of thing?' he said. 'You're thirteen.'

'What sort of thing?' I didn't know what that meant. 'Have you seen the video? It's got Hughie in it.'

I pulled out my phone and started the video playing. Noah doesn't like Hugh Noone (No 1 Home's lead singer) because he said he took drugs.

'Yeah, they said that when he sang solo. That's, like, years ago.'

Noah just scoffed.

The video opened with Hugh sitting on a chair in a field of flowers – same as my t-shirt – singing to a tall poppy. No 1 Home's three other boys were faces in the flowers, singing harmony.

Noah said, 'Hugh Noone has a nose like a ski jump. If I looked like that I'd stay away from cameras. What's the song? Is he really singing "Napalm and Nabokov"?'

I nodded without taking my eyes off the screen. Hughie is so beautiful. His smile is like an old-fashioned light bulb, warm and bright and inviting.

I just said, 'Isn't he hot? One day I'm going to marry Hugh Noone.'

'You're a bit young,' he said.

I ignored that. Hugh would wait.

But I'd gotten Noah's attention. I made my play. 'One of my friends saves these videos on her computer and makes GIFs out of them. And edits them. I can't find a save button on this app. Can you help, pleeeeaaase?'

He smiled and led me into his inner sanctum. I'd have said his bedroom except there was no bed – he had a sleeping bag thrown in the corner. The desk and most of the floor was covered in racks and leads and bits of the gaming rigs he'd built.

'Pay attention, because I'm going to say this only once,' he said. 'Here's what you need to do.'

He only had to say it once.

* * *

16 May 2026

I think I understand Hugh better than other people do. Noah couldn't see past the obvious themes of No 1 Home's fanservice videos, which are quite decedent, if that was the word – Oscar Wilde and glam and glitter. I know they are scripted, like reality TV. I know underneath he's really sensitive.

I practised using the apps my brother showed me yesterday and downloaded a bunch of interviews and some of the band videos. I recut the footage to the music and uploaded them to my new cloud storage. Then I logged into the Homies chatroom (Homies are fans of No 1 Home) on eMOTe. My nick there was CherryRed.

Jen and another girl called Kytten were chatting. Jen's nick is Tyger_Tyger3 and her profile pic is an icon of a man with a face tattooed with tiger stripes. She'd picked it because of the old No 1 Home song that goes:

Tyger, tyger burning bright,

In the sodium vapor light

I let them know I had cut that famous Mike Wolfe Ice Cave interview to music. Success. Twenty-two people downloaded the video in a couple of minutes. Everybody talking about me and Hugh, together at last, at least together in the same sentence.

That didn't last long. Some w*nch grabbed the video and uploaded it to YouTube, taking my name off it. But I learn fast. I'll make sure I put my name in the credits. I need to shake Noah down for everything he knows.

* * *

17 May 2026

I logged into eMOTe again with some new media but everybody in the chatroom was already excited. The message headers were all like 'He did it…' but I couldn't work out what. Did Hugh get married? For a minute, my heart turned to cold lead, and I had to drag myself up like out of quicksand to scroll up and search the messages again.

Once I got it, I realised it was nothing so serious. Hugh had a nerve-impulse isolator implanted. I already knew he had periforal neuopathy. That is a painful, pins-and-needles feeling in the hands and feet. Noah said it was caused by drugs and alcohol, but he would say that since he hated Hugh. I watched a video clip where Hughie said he found it hard to keep up with touring and all the dancing, and the implant would help. Wiki said it was 'a nanofiber computer that grows and permanently resides along the major nerves, providing auxiliary power and speed to the muscles, with a minor moiety of distributed processing in the dorsal root ganglion'.

'Ganglion' would be a good name for a band.

Oh, it is spelt 'peripheral neuropathy'.

No point trying to interest everyone in my video. They were all occupied with Hugh's body mod. How cool to change your body to match your desires. Sometimes you needed to change your body to express the real you. Jen (Tyger_Tyger3) said users could see sounds and pick up radio waves out of the air. Some guy said Hugh was *post-human* now.

So where did that leave human girls?

Me, for example.

* * *

24 May 2026

I browsed pics of last night's No 1 Home concert in Los Angeles. I loved the way Hugh's hair framed his face and brought out that aristocratic nose and the sea-green eyes. Jen and Kytten's chat scrolled up the side of my screen as I devoured the photos.

*

Tyger_Tyger3: OMFG girl did you see Mudskip's post?

Kytten: What did she say?

Tyger_Tyger3: She said Hugh and 4Dam were an item,,,it was a Facebook post yesterday

*

Not 4Dam? The homeliest boy in No 1 Home. I said 'boy' but Josh Fordham had to be in his twenties. Long, wavy brown hair. Slash fans were always whispering about the bandmembers being lovers. They would manipulate pics and write stories about them living together in Atlanta. The OTP (one true pairing) was Hugh and BriJay, I think it was just cause Brian James Holt used they/them pronouns.

The messages scrolled up.

*

Kytten: WTF! No, Hughes str8!!

Tyger_Tyger3: It's so hot. I luv 4Dam. He's cute.

Kytten: str8!
Tyger_Tyger3: Well, Hugh would be straight if he met you girl!
*

What? I thought Jen – Tyger – was my friend. She was encouraging Kytten. Two-face basic w*nch!

I went to bed, where I dreamed about 4Dam and Hugh. I couldn't even have him to myself in my dreams.

* * *

16 August 2026

On Saturday Kytten posted a vid from one of the premium Korean channels, an interview with Hughie. I could see his body mod. (We Homies named it the subcute network.) I could make out what they called nerve burn, dents above the nerve knot in the neck. The nanotubes burrowed under the skin and along the nerves so fast, they tugged on the tissue under the skin like a pulled thread scrunching up a bedsheet.

I felt weird inside when I stared at him, embarrassed like he knew I was watching. Then I went back and looked at him again.

The magazines describe Hugh as 'frail and sensitive'. My brother Noah said that was a youthamism (sp) for a drug user. I didn't think he ever did drugs. Not with his peripheral neuropathy. The videos didn't do him justice. He must have wanted to get out, to show the world his real self. He was trapped inside there, playing a part, like in 'The Strings Inside Me', his song about a puppet's break for freedom.

In a new Mike Wolfe interview, Hugh said, 'The nanocomputer doesn't do anything at first. You have to train it. You know there's something there that's not you but, as you practise, it builds a reflex arc, and it's just you again.'

'Muscle memory,' Mike Wolfe said.

'It's more than that. One day you're a caterpillar, the next you're a butterfly. You're more than you were. It gets easier, too, because it learns as you learn. It's not just choreography or keyboards; song writing comes easier to me. I have perfect pitch. Every new thing I do is easier than the last thing.'

Mike Wolfe, under the mistaken impression that anyone cared what he thought, interrupted him. 'I thought it was a matter of innervation – increased strength through contracting the whole muscle instead of the small percentage of fibres stimulated by a natural nerve impulse.'

Hughie smiled, which made him dimple. 'But it's not the simple things, reflexes, speed, strength, which really affect me. It's the change in the sensorium. You can feel things you never thought you could feel. It's like having new eyes, except the eyes are radios so the whole cosmos just surfs in on the ether. You can hear the bright stars singing and the dark ones groaning with age.'

I want to watch him listen to the bright stars singing.

* * *

7 September 2026

Noah told me to have a talk with pops. 'Remember when you wanted a unicorn for your birthday?'

'I was eight!'

'But you haven't learned a thing! You're obsessed with him and those mash-ups you do for the other fans. This shitbird Noone is bad news. You've got to meet real people.'

I punched him on the arm.

'I'll buy you a ticket for the game. It'll get you out of the house.'

I shook my head. 'Buy me a ticket for the live concert film premiere.'

'You've seen it,' Noah said. 'You already made like ninety fan videos from the workprint that kitten girl downloaded for you.'

'It'll get me out of the house.'

He smiled, a bit crookedly. 'Okay.'

'Okay!'

* * *

22 October 2026

No 1 Home put out so much stuff I could hardly keep up. There was the usual fanservice, like Tik Tok and Instagram, and all kinds of stuff my brother called esoteric, like solving clues on social media to score tickets or meet the band, in-jokes, playing around to tease the slash fans and all of that. It was all a front, though. The magazines said there was tension between the band members.

'Creative differences', they called it, but Noah said the band didn't write its own music and that must be a euphemism for 'they hate each other'. I thought they did write their own music? Hugh wrote the words, for sure. You could see him in them. I wished I knew what was true. I felt that I was just one of a crowd of girls (and some boys) who were all the same and, from down there, I only heard the story everyone got. But I was not everyone.

It could all have been made-up drama to keep us following the band the same way people followed a Netflix series. I wanted to know.

I would go mad if I didn't meet Hugh. But what did I have to offer him a million other girls didn't? It was not like Hugh would phone me and ask me to direct their next music video. Technically, what I did was copyright infringement, so if I ended up in the same room as him it'd have been with his lawyers in tow and that'd suck.

I could stop wearing pink dresses. I look like a little girl.

I will start wearing black.

* * *

24 October 2026

Dad didn't want me to go to the premiere. I had to promise to do three hours a week after-school activities to show 'responsibility'. They had an AV Club, though, so I outsmarted him. I got to use their non-linear editing equipment *and* get to go see the movie. Cringe though… Noah had to come with me as chaperone. He said it would be good for me because, when I saw 'what teenage girls look like in a pack' it would be a cat-a-list to change my ways.

* * *

24 November 2026

I stopped posting on eMOTe. It was all kids' stuff, tween girls posting about how lit their boy bands were. The adult message boards I was reading now taught me things about video, lighting and sound and I learnt much faster.

I was on one message board yesterday when I saw an avi, a man with a tiger-face tatt, and thought it must be Jen. But it wasn't her – her ditsy phone-text style was unmistakable. His nick was Gullyfoylel337, so I clicked on the icon and the bio was for an adult he/him, interested in neural upgrades for rigs like Hugh's subcute.

I clicked away but something in my head said *upgrades*. Hugh would have been on the look-out for upgrades, right? And this Gullyfoylel337's bio made him sound like a guy who could get them. I sent him a friend request. I didn't tell him I was 14.

I spent the night editing a fanvid. I had a pirate copy of *Nerves of Steel* (the unreleased-as-yet movie) obvs, and some publicity footage of Hughie, and the live footage of the

PenAltamont tour. There was a long shot of them dancing on a glittering staircase, and Hughie was in front, of course, stepping to the beat so beautifully. The lights on his hair made it shine hematite red, hematite blue, hematite silver as he went through the moves. There was a sheen of sweat visible on his face and you could see the ropes of carbon fibres in his forearms like veins under the skin. I had to cut out some scaffolding visible at the edge of the stage, but I got it done. My best work.

* * *

26 December 2026

Making fan videos was fun and I loved the feedback, but it dawned on me that I never got anything material in return. I put out an ad, a showreel of my best work, and asked if anyone needed a freelance video editor.

One of the responders was Gullyfoylel337 himself. I wrote back fast. He needed some website stuff and he had software to barter. His own subcute had a module for remote telemetry, which he could clone. If I could get it to work, I could use it to monitor Hugh Noone's neural enhancements.

I would be able to watch him listen to the bright stars singing.

One month until *Nerves of Steel* premieres.

* * *

29 December 2026

Kytten is going as well. I am to meet her on the sidewalk adjacent to the red carpet. Six o'clock.

Gullyfoylel337's subcute was the military upgrade from Hughie's. The base package supported motor functions like speed and strength, but the ganglion in the military version could reproduce itself with minor changes. The unit was optimised for combat soldiers in shock – like after a bullet wound. It instructed the sympathetic nervous system to shut some things down and dialled other things up to compensate. The telemetry package monitored the activity of the ganglia. Gullyfoylel337 said, and this sounded like much more fun, the upgrade allowed the user to experiment with changes that beat anything you could get out of a needle.

So, what I was going to do was offer Hugh the upgrade, then backdoor the telemetry package. His manager was on the web, so I sent a message to him. Fingers and toes crossed it gets Hugh's attention.

* * *

28 January 2027

The red carpet line was crowded. Noah was right. The girls were like a pack of wild animals. I dragged the terrified Noah through the pack of screaming teens until I heard Kytten shout 'Cherry Red!' and there she was. I'd never seen her in real life. She looked younger than me. When the scream-intensity started to rise and she realised the band had gotten out of their limo, she fainted and Noah had to hold her upright.

The band walked up the red carpet waving. There were camera flashes all around and the screaming was like a physical thing pressing against my head. Hughie recognised me from the selfie I'd sent. He came up to the velvet rope and I pushed the USB stick into his hand.

He smiled at me.

I blanked out. The next thing I knew, Hugh was a hundred yards away, easy to locate by the increase in scream volume there.

We propped Kytten up between us and joined the mass at the front doors.

'You looked like Orpheus staring after Eurydice,' Noah said.

* * *

29 January 2027

I don't remember the film itself. All I could think of was I'd touched Hughie's hand. I tried to nail that memory into my brain. He'd taken the memory stick in his right hand and shaken my left. I remembered the hair on the back of his wrist, the softness of his hands and the dark ropes under the skin where the nanofibres infiltrated the tendons. He looked straight at me, his face close to mine, a faint smell of mint and cinnamon, then he was gone.

I needed video coverage, so I logged on as soon as I was awake.

There was a LOT of video footage. There must have been a thousand mobile phone cameras. And I was on some of it. People were talking about Hugh's nice black silk waistcoat. And some people were talking about me.

* * *

*

Kytten: Hugh Noone is hardcore he's bomb!
Tyger_Tyger3: Red did you talk to him?
Kytten: He bussed her!
CherryRed: He has soft hands.
Tyger_Tyger3: I hate u did he really kiss u
CherryRed: No, he just leaned close to talk.
CherryRed: His breath smells of cinnamon.
Tyger_Tyger3: I hate you [dizzy emoji]
CherryRed: Did I mention he has soft hands lol
*

* * *

6 February 2027

'Even if you met him,' Noah told me, 'you couldn't change him.'

'I don't want to change him. Although that would be a great way to get the rest of the fans off my case when I marry him. Change him so that they don't want him!'

'It's just a crush.'

'You are denying my lived experience.'

* * *

10 February 2027

I played that 'Napalm and Nabokov' vid again and I think I finally got what Hugh meant. Unrequited love burns like dripping fire; it strips the skin to expose every pleading, screaming nerve.

And Noah thought touching grass will cure it.

* * *

15 February 2027

A package arrived. I knew it was from Hugh even before I read the record company address. It contained an exclusive photo (he wore that now-famous waistcoat), signed and personalised.

It said, 'Dear Cherry Red, I got your gift and I'm going to implement some of those features.'

I put the picture under my pillow.

* * *

28 February 2027

When Hugh loaded the upgrade, I was waiting. There was a raw count of activity and a visualisation mode. In the vis screen I could see each pseudo-ganglion. Today (11 days after he initiated it) I could see a diffuse red glow in the upper left quadrant, which was his central nervous system, and two compact green spots, the dorsal ganglion and its daughter node, the cervical ganglion, beginning to grow and come online. Bright speckles scattered between showed the implant's connections with living nerves.

* * *

15 July 2027

I keep thinking about this. I worked for, like, months to get pirated spyware so I could perve on a pop star. In secret. Not even telling my friends. Was Noah right about me?

* * *

14 November 2027

There was a man in Noah's Physics class. Michael. He looked a bit like BriJay (the good looking one, long hair and great lips). He invited me out on Saturday, but I had to work. I'd been designing projection systems for clubs and had to install and burn one in. The program took telemetry data from sensors around the dance floor and used it to adjust the light show in real time. (Guess where I stole the code?)

Having something to do with my hands kept me from dark thoughts. I told Mike I'd call next week. He'd be gone by then. I'm sure the older girls will snap him up.

* * *

14 May 2028

I haven't posted for months.

I'm dead tired. Dad said I couldn't coast at school even now I earned a living. At least I have a crew who runs the lighting rigs at shows and I don't have to be there every night.

One of them joked I could bid for No 1 Home's concert lighting contract. That jolted me. I hadn't thought about Hugh Noone in ages. My bedroom wall was still full of pictures but, after a while, they were just wallpaper.

He wasn't mentioned in the magazines much anymore, either. I did see mentions when I chanced on the Homies' fan-groups.

*

Andy32: Album's not selling well. The teenyboppers are long gone.
CroMaggie: EQ's poor.
JelyBely: it's Noone. He cant hear himself. he dont hear audiospace anymore, dog. Hes a robot. The mixing boards plugged directly into his wires like a f'n cylon
Andy32: That's so untrue it's not even wrong.

*

I did that? With a flash drive that fitted on a keyring? No, that was down to him. He'd made the decision to install it.

I fought the urge to 'see' what Hugh was doing.

* * *

29 July 2028

Noah left home. I miss him. I don't feel I've grown up at all. No 1 Home broke up and my toes curl when I think about my obsession with Hugh, but I still feel like a gangly kid inside.

* * *

4 August 2029

Haven't written here for a whole year.

I ran the telemetry program again today. Something compelled me to spy on him. *Hugh.*

The screen slowly drew an action painting of glowing crimson. The signals shifted slowly, like an oil-wheel projection, and I worked out that the red wasn't nerve tissue – the monitor couldn't really see flesh – it represented acetylcholine being released from the CNS.

The nerves were in a back-and-forth with the augmented parts of the system. I could see maybe a hundred green swirls, the new pseudo-ganglia. He had started out with just the two, and they'd reproduced where they were needed. It started to make spatial sense. The rhythmic lights were the heart and diaphragm ganglia, and the fingers were visible by their movement. In my mind, the speckles resolved into an image of a man sitting at a keyboard. Of course – he would be writing songs.

Angry at myself for my voyeurism, I hit ctrl-alt-del and walked out to clear my head.

But I left the app on my machine, and I would still come across the fans' increasingly bitter chatter.

*

Andy32: I streamed the album but I'm not going to buy it. I'm a No 1 Home fan, not a Hugh Noone fan. He's just going through the motions
JelyBely: No wonder him and 4Dam broke up. He's a mess.
Andy32: I thought it was him and BriJay? 4Dam's married
JelyBely: Whatevs. Look at him, dog. you can see it growing in his face. he has tiger stripes like Gully Foyle. he's half man, half beast half robot.
Andy32: That's three halfs

*

I Googled 'Gully Foyle' as two words, and finally understood the user icons. He was a character in a book called *Tiger, Tiger* and had facial tattoos like tiger stripes. He learned to hide the tattoos but he couldn't hide the beast inside him.

* * *

15 December 2029

Sometimes I come home and watch the screen fill with green galaxies of pseudo-ganglia and fading red speckle at the margins and I felt connected to Hugh though I didn't don't know him and never will. I remember feeling – no, *knowing* – that I was the only person on Earth who understood him, really knew him deep inside.

I drank a tumbler of Dad's Maker's Mark bourbon trying to burn the awareness out of my head.

* * *

19 May 2029

I was running through some rig-controller tests in the basement when Twitter lit up:

#HughNoone.

Dead, said one.

Hugh, said the corner of the message underneath.

I opened Tumblr, Instagram, eMOTe, all the instant messengers I had, read them all at once.

*

Jolie: Imagine how much that must have hurt. Actually no don't imagine it. my god

Cabij: Hurt? He ran on electricity. It must have been like the best orgasm ever. Thirty amps through every metal pleasure point.

Jolie: You freak. I'm glad I'm not your girlfried

RyanTripp: Girlfried, lol that's freudian

*

Hugh had been guesting at one of 4Dam's gigs. He'd done that bit where they both walked backwards up a celestial staircase covered in white 'ice', which he did perfectly even though he was holding a mic that had a lead instead of the headset mics the old band used. Then he stumbled and grabbed the metal scaffolding of the set to steady himself… and there must have been something wrong with the electrical grounding of the mic. You could see smoke rise from Hugh's skin. You'd expect a flash and a sound like thunder, but there was nothing. The mic cut out in a sudden blossoming absence of noise, like two pillows smashed together. From three mobile camera viewpoints, I watched his slow fall backwards.

The Tweets and Notes and messages scrolled up in their own windows beside the video window.

*

JOBLO: His people came and took him, he's one of them now. The electric looks after its own
KevinB: He's up there wherever it is they keep the iTunes before they're downloaded.
JOBLO: In the good old days when rock stars just sold their soul to the devil, at least you knew where they were after they died
Andy32: He's not even cold yet, say something nice!

*

A quick-thinking crewman cut the venue's lights. The video went dark for a moment. Mobile phones were held up, their lights forming a moon-dawn glow until the room was shadowless and Hugh's form appeared, still and black, on the stage. Two indistinct figures were shouting about isolating the equipment, out of fear that the body might still be live.

*

Jackalltrade: He's not dead. I've seen those videos of Korean soldiers with arms blown off, they just keep coming forward.
PzKpfw_I: That's blood vessel contraction/retraction and endocrine control. For gunshot wounds. It's standard military hardening tech. Noone got 60 amp mains right through his nerves of steel. Electric shock's not even listed as a failure mode

in the documentation. The subcute's fried.

*

* * *

I'm dizzy and I feel sick. I'm switching on the microphone here, so I don't have to type this in.

I open the monitor program. No living red; not a speckle or bead of living red. A ragged inky blot darkens part of the green-dot network – it's the right forearm, where he touched the scaffolding. On another screen I check the timestamps on the videos. It happened fifteen minutes ago.

*

JelyBely: he did it on purpose. his liver was shot. a star wants a good looking corpse. He'll be oozing out the wiring like liquid gold. therell be sightings of his silhouette on jumbotrons. Mobile phones will inexplicably start playing ringtones from the album.
Henoseuno: Yeah, cause the best way to upload your consciousness to cyberspace is to shock it tf into a cheapo pink glitter repro of a Stairway to Heaven you dickweasel.
JelyBely: his subcute's wi-fi. no limit to where it can go.
Andy32: I don't get why a shock would make it go anywhere, whatever 'it' is anyway. Your just whistling past the gravyard.

*

On the monitor screen, the dull green dots are brightening one by one like candle flames guttering out in reverse. Spasmodic contraction of the diaphragm. Heartbeat re-established. Vagus pseudo-ganglion is reporting back restored aortic pressure. Breathing re-started. The vagus reports increasing oxygen saturation.

The documentation said that the unit is spec'd to restart the heart within two minutes – and to give up after eight if unsuccessful, since the brain is irreparably damaged by then. I guess the shock made its clock reset or something.

The videos for the early part of the gig were becoming available. As a kid I used to stare at his photos all day long, so the big physical changes stood out. I never bought the 'frail' description people tagged him with, but here he looked fragile.

Between songs he seemed distant, his formerly seafoam eyes the colour of the ocean after a storm. He swigged from a bottle of Stolichnaya. The grey cords of the carbon fibres snaked under the skin of his cheeks and forehead to form a tiger-mask, and they ran as long, sinuous parallel lines down his neck and arms. The effect was cage-like, as though prison bars were implanted below his skin. I hadn't realised how far gone he was, like a tree choked by a basket fig, still standing but dying inside.

I turn back to the screen displaying real-time telemetry to see the inkblot healing, flickers of green light beginning to appear. Repairs are being made to the nanofibers in the arm, the wrist ganglion coming online. There isn't a glimmer of living red anywhere. Seven out of ten fingers online. Endocrine glands functioning. The posture abruptly shifts.

It's sitting up, head in hands.

The fanboys are very wrong about where their Hugh Noone sightings are going to come from. He didn't get zapped into cyberspace. They'll think he survived. They'll think it's a miracle.

It's two in the morning. The rush of fright and anger and action is over and I'm mushy with fatigue. I don't have any Korean implants to even out the flood of stress hormones.

Maybe next week, when it's fully rebooted, I'll play some vids from last year and whatever tomorrow's crop of videos bring, and I'll compare Hugh with Hugh.

Even I may not be able to tell the difference.

100 Places to visit before you die: No. 97: The Moon

Rob Butler

'And then it disappeared?'

'Yeah.' Jake Conway rubbed his beard. He was still frowning at the monitor screen.

'Well, there were no ships in that area at the time so it must be some kind of computer glitch. Better run the diagnostics.'

'I guess so.' Jake sat back, took a thoughtful sip of coffee and stared out through the dome window into the inky black sky above Shackleton Base. 'Thanks, Commander, I'll let you know if I find anything.'

* * *

Jean Wadhwa checked over her briefing notes as she entered the Taurus Shuttle Centre. She was feeling very pleased with herself today. She'd spent several months on the Apollo 14 site and now she had 17. Only geeky space buffs bothered with the middle landings, and she was fed up batting away requests to try and find Al Shepard's golf balls. There was a certain cachet about 17 – the last landing. Nothing like 11, of course, but she'd obviously impressed somebody high up in LunaSixTours, so, do a great job here and, who knows?

'Hi, Benny. I have twenty-two today, right? Quite a crowd.' She looked through the glass window to see her clients all suited up and ready to roll.

'Twenty-three.'

'What?' She glanced at her screen. 'No, I have twenty-two.'

'Twenty-three.'

She looked at Benny. He gazed back, his face vacant and slightly confused. He was sweating.

'You okay, Benny?'

'I'm fine.'

Jean counted the helmets through the glass.

'Okay. There are twenty-three. One must have got added on. Better to have one extra than to lose one.' She started to laugh but it died away as Benny just stared at her.

'I'll be off then. Maybe you should see the Doc, Benny.'

* * *

Things were going well. Jean had got them all safely on and off the shuttle. Nobody was sick during the tight approach into Taurus-Littrow. They managed to stagger in the low gravity to the landing site. She gave them the standard spiel on what the astronauts had done and showed them where Cernan scraped out his daughter's initials in the lunar dust, quite a way away from the lander.

'And those initials, ladies and gentlemen, will last for millions of years.'

'Why did you stop coming?'

Jean paused and looked at her view screen to see which of the opaque helmet visors she should address. Turning to the one that had asked the question, she noticed for the first time that he had a customised space suit.

She groaned.

Some multi-billionaire who didn't want to wear a sweaty second-hand suit. It was a striking outfit. Very odd material. Seemed to shimmer and catch the light strangely.

'I'm sorry. Do you mean why did the astronauts stop coming?'

'Yes. Why did you only land six times and then stop.'

'Well, I will be coming on to that point at the end of my presentation as it is, of course, particularly relevant to this site where the last of the Apollo astronauts landed. But, let me first say that everything we see here is exactly as the astronauts left it. We never walk too close to the landing sites so as not to damage any of the historical evidence. Notice the rubbish strewn around. They threw away any unnecessary items to lighten the load for take-off – even their top-of-the-range cameras. That's probably the most expensive garbage you will ever see.'

She paused as the crowd tittered. She'd thought that would get a laugh.

'Why don't you float over the site using anti-grav lifters?'

It was that same odd suit. Jean was starting to get annoyed.

'Well, that's a great idea. Only trouble is, they haven't been invented yet.'

The tourists chuckled again, but Jean definitely heard a derisive snort from the suit.

She grimaced. Not just a billionaire, but a billionaire's bored teenage son who'd been told to come on this tour. Simply out to make trouble.

* * *

As they struggled back into the Shuttle Centre and out of their suits, Jean had a headache. The annoying teenager had asked several more questions, each one starting 'Why didn't YOU…' as if everything was directly her fault. She was feeling distinctly disorientated.

A bit like Benny was this morning. That reminded her. Always take a headcount at the end of the tour. Don't want to lose anybody.

Twenty-two. Good. Just what she had on her checklist.

Home is Where the Heart Was

Carol Ryles

When the sun sinks low enough to no longer burn, Mia strolls through stubbled fields to the estuary and thinks back to her childhood. Her best memories include the nights she would wade in knee-deep and hold up a cell phone to light her way. The ocean was cooler back then. Her mother would catch prawns in nets and Mia would carry them to shore, tip them into an icebox, set the smaller ones free.

'Too pretty for the pot,' she'd say, holding their see-through bodies up to the light, watching their tiny hearts jitter. 'You're the lucky ones. Swim while you're able.'

These days, there are no prawns or anything so ordinary as a mullet or herring. Water collaborates with darkness to swallow land.

* * *

The cyclone hits the farmhouse with as much spite as fury. Mia shelters with Luke in the water-sealed basement, alongside the hydroponics and mealworm bins. They play chess, but rarely speak, afraid of what the other might say. When the wind gauge registers one-eighty and rising, the ceiling shudders. They've lived through this before. More times than they care to count. Many a farmer would have left decades ago, but not Mia. Not while the house remains standing. Or while apple-berries grow sweet, and their cider lightens her dreams and bolsters her hope when her confidence fails.

'What do you fancy?' Luke asks, standing up to fix dinner in the jerry-rigged kitchen. 'Mealworm fritters or mealworm stew?'

Mia shrugs. Shrugs again.

'How about stir fry?' Luke heats up the wok, adds ginger, garlic, and spices hoarded from gentler years when spices could still be purchased. Mia closes her eyes and reminds herself that worms are the prawns of the land, except easier to catch, and carbon neutral.

Later, with the cyclone still roaring above, she returns to the chessboard to finish the match.

'Are you sure you want to do that?' she asks as Luke moves his queen into the path of her rook.

He takes a sip of cider. 'There's no point anymore, is there? Whatever we do, we can't win.'

'Only if we set ourselves up for it.' She lifts the rook, slides it in for the kill.

'These storms can only get worse.' He looks to the hydroponic tanks crammed with fruit vines and greens. 'If the wind turbines fail and the lights go out, we'll be left with—'

'...check mate,' she says. 'And yes, I know.'

'But you still want to stay?'

'It's too soon to contemplate leaving. We need to prepare.'

'Too soon?' He flicks his king onto its side. 'More likely we've left it too late.'

'It's our home, Luke. Ours!'

'The land no longer wants us. What will it take to convince you?'

Mia clasps her hands in her lap, calming herself before she speaks. Her family had farmed this acreage for decades, built the house with their own hands, added reinforcements to withstand anything the planet could throw at it.

'I'll leave when there's no turning back,' she says. 'Not before.'

* * *

They repair the house, clear the debris, tend to the mealworms. Some will be roasted and milled into flour for bread. Others will be packaged and frozen. The remainder are returned to the feed bins for breeding.

The cyclone season ends. In the weeks that follow, the surrounding fields teem with mosquitoes, lacewings, dragonflies and gnats. It has been months since Mia has seen so much diversity. She wants to step outside and catalogue it, perhaps write a paper that no one will read. But the mosquitoes grow hungrier by the year. Luke's homemade repellent is no longer effective.

'Evolution accelerates in times of stress,' Luke says. 'We should follow their example, yet here we are: trapped in limbo, fighting change.'

'What do you suggest we do?'

'There's nothing left,' he says at last. 'At least not here.'

'I won't give up our farm.'

'I know.'

* * *

Drought litters the fields with desiccated dragonflies. On the hilltops beyond them, the blades of wind turbines grudgingly churn.

Luke loads the EV with provisions, begs Mia to get in, but she can only stand on the patch of bare earth that used to be her mother's garden. 'It's too late to do anything now,' she says, holding back tears. 'Always has been. Even when I said it was too early.'

'Come on, Mia,' Luke pleads from inside the car. 'Last chance. I won't be back until winter.'

'There's no such thing anymore.'

'Down south there is. Remember that holiday in Esperance? How much you loved the cold? The wind all the way from Antarctica. Remember?'

'Where will we live?'

His grin does little to hide his uncertainty. 'In a cave if we have to. Or someplace abandoned.'

'You can't grow food in a cave. And most places are abandoned for good reasons.'

'We'll be wanderers, sleep on the beach, live on berries.'

She scoffs. 'So much for our PhDs.'

Mouth tight, he winds up the window. Mia holds her breath, certain he'll admit that leaving everything they love is a terrible mistake. Then the engine starts up. She cries out, waving her arms to catch his attention, to hug him one more time, to keep him safe.

The car lurches away. Dust swirls in its wake.

* * *

The infobahn is patchy. No science discussions, no music, even the gamers disappear. One by one, the news sites crash; then eventually Mia establishes a connection with Luke.

Don't go out, he writes. *A new virus. Worse than the last one.*

Her fingers type faster than she can think. *Come home. We'll see it through together.*

I can't. I'm infected.

I'll find you. I promise.

Mia, don't. I'm no longer me.

Luke? What?

She stares at the screen, waiting for a reply. Within minutes, the infobahn dies.

She slams a fist on the desk. 'No!'

Much later, between sobs, she adds, 'No.'

Desperate for the sound of another voice, she cycles to the village, runs from house to house, shop to shop. Most of the debris from the previous cyclone has been sorted into piles, but as far as she can tell, everyone has left. *South with Luke? Why didn't he warn me?*

'Is anyone here?' she shouts.

Silence. Unnerving. Absolute. Not even the occasional static of a passing EV from the nearby highway, or the cawing of crows. Despite the heat, goosebumps turn her skin cold.

A dog – a grizzled old kelpie – slinks out from beneath a fence. It bounds towards her, tail wagging. 'Hey, fella,' she says, softly. 'Where's your owner?'

The animal pauses, its eyes hooded. Its whine turns into a growl. Baring toothless gums, it backs off.

'What happened to you?' Mia asks.

At the dog's shoulder blades, either side of its spine, two fist-sized nodules erupt through its fur. They swell, unfurl into a bony framework of wings. Mia tells herself she's dreaming. Then the dog bolts, only to remain firmly grounded, its wings quivering.

Dogs are like pigs. They can't fly.

The thought makes her laugh, long and hard, because mirth is preferable to fear. The dog leaps and falls, stumbles and leaps. Mia pauses, suddenly aware that her laughter smacks of denial, as if the dog's plight is ultimately her own fault. *No escape,* she thinks. *For any of us.*

She turns and runs, heart pounding, terrified the dog will snap at her heels, certain that something similar must have happened to Luke. A bleak sense of helplessness works its way through her, but she keeps running until she reaches her bicycle, chest heaving. Something moves near her feet. She leaps away, expecting the dog's gummy jaws to snap at her heels. When she looks down, she finds only ants, crawling in and out through the gaps between flagstones.

'A final vestige of normality,' she mutters. 'Survivors.'

Something like geckos chitter. Except geckos died out years ago, and now there are only ants, raising their pincers in unison.

Since when did ants chitter?

* * *

The drought drags on, day after day, week after week. There are no more mammals, frogs, lizards, birds or even the feral cats that aided their extinction. Mia wonders if there are others like herself: relics from the Anthropocene, shadows lingering in homes they refuse to leave.

'Luke,' she shouts into emptiness. 'Did you ever find winter?'

She walks through her fields to the estuary, fills up the desalination troughs. The water is noticeably deeper than the year before. A new species of jellyfish drifts with the current. Their translucent bodies shimmer as blue as the violets that long ago perished in the ruins of her greenhouse. Behind her in the dirt, cockroaches as large as rabbits suffuse the air with the scent of roses. Sandflies swoop like parrots. Centipedes squeak like bats.

Invertebrates evolve quickly these days. Mia cannot say if she is fascinated or afraid. If she kneels up close, she can make out their faces. Sometimes they resemble people she used to know from the village, and sometimes they're part Luke's and part hers, as if in memory of the children she will never have.

She shivers. Her forehead beads with sweat, deliciously chilled. Her limbs creak, hindered by a fast-spreading layer of chitin.

'It's time,' she rasps in the manner of crickets.

Back at the farmhouse, she climbs down to the basement and carries up a mealworm bin – the one filled with larvae.

Such plump little things, all pale and wriggling, their skins as tight as swaddling.

'Take care, sweet babies,' she chirrups.

Breathless with relief, she tips them out. Sets them free.

I Said Aliens

Morgan Parks

- Hello, I need to report—

Good evening, this is Sol System Space Services Centre. How may I help you today?

- I've just seen an alien ship!

Hello? Ma'am? You're very faint. Sorry, maybe sir? Please express your pronoun and greeting preference.

- I said aliens! Can you hear me?

Please speak slowly and clearly, ma'am.

- Not ma'am. I'm British and I'm not the Queen. Never mind. There are aliens heading for Earth.

I apologise, ma'am, the sound quality is deteriorating.

- Aliens! An alien ship – long pointy thing with something that looks like—

Ma'am, I require your craft number to provide a service.

- Mining pod 7782, on the far side of Jupiter. I called as soon as I saw them, but I got put on hold—

Sorry, I didn't catch that. Perhaps you can give me your own name?

- Doesn't matter. Aliens! Aliens!

Adrian? Oh, sorry, sir.

- ALIENS!

Adrians? Your last name, ma'am? One moment, please.

- Something like a bird's nest, on the long pointy ship. Huge. Definitely alien. Didn't show up on my sensors at first, sort of materialised next to my pod—

Ma'am? No Adrians is listed in our system. Can you spell that?

- I'm not the bloody Queen. You can't hear a word I'm saying, can you?

Please calm down, ma'am.

- Aliens! A. L. I. E.—

Unfortunately, we are experiencing a fault with our LightSpeed communications system. Rest assured the problem is not with your ship communications…

- Shut up and listen! Aliens.

…Sol Services are working hard to resolve this issue, we are unable…

- A recorded message. Unbelievable.

…due to an ongoing lawsuit with LightComms Inc…

- Unbloodybelievable.

…your call is important to us…

- I just hope they're friendly, the aliens, I mean—

Sorry about that, ma'am, we have to play it for legal reasons.

- heading for Earth, and all—

Plus, I will keep the line open for another five minutes, in case call quality improves.

- travelling very fast, by the way. Amazingly fast—

Never does, between you and me.

- my pod AI tracked them to the asteroid belt—

Something to do with sunspots, according to our techie. High sunspot activity.

- predicted arrival at Earth orbit in—

Maybe you're near the sun.

- two minutes, 47 seconds—

Lucky you, I'd like a view of the sun.

- 42 seconds—

Stuck in this bunker, me.

- Maybe they're just passing through. On the way to somewhere—

The military types don't mix with us civilian contractors.

- more interesting. Hang on—

I see the allotted time is over.

- the AI's flagging an anomaly—

But I won't hang up yet. It's quiet here.

- a change in trajectory. Wow, that's impressive. Very—

Quiet all day really, the military in their big meeting.

- impressive. Maybe they'll—

And the techie, Jess, she's in there too.

- share that propulsion system. Alien technology. Aliens—

The projector didn't work. Then something else. So they needed a technician.

- remember? Ah, a new heading—

Top secret, the military meetings. Supposedly.

- Shit—

Could you repeat that, ma'am? I thought I heard something then.

- shit, shit, shit—

If Jess was here, I bet she'd use that new filter.

- shit, scheisse, merde—

Keep talking, ma'am. I'll try the filter.

- szar, dritt, mierda—

Nope, still can't make out anything. Damn sunspots, eh?

- they're heading back to me—

I wish Jess was here.

- really close now—

Jess is the only one who talks to me. At work, I mean.

- they're here—

And the budget meeting always takes all day.

- right alongside. The ship is seriously huge. Weirdly—

At least I've got a date tonight.

- long, pointy at both ends—

That reminds me, must buy lemons.

- just hanging there—

The date's not with Jess, in case you were wondering.

- looming. Oh, wow—

Anyway, it's the end of my shift.

- the bird nest thing is spinning—
A minute over, in fact.
- kind of untangling itself—
Nice talking to you ma'am.
- a port, a port opening up! Wow—
I have to hang up now.
- oh wow. Three of them—
Got a date, as I said.
- floating out. Wow. They look amazing, so—
I sure hope you have a good evening.
- so—
Goodbye now.
- friendly—
Bye.

Personification

Antonia Rachel Ward

>

> Connecting to IRIS server.

> Connection complete.

>

> Timestamp: 060120 23:52

>

> Activating visual cortex.

>

> Good evening, Oscar.

For 5.32 seconds, IRIS's only view is of the leather office chair opposite her camera, and behind it, the windowless, grey-painted walls of the basement floor of the Turing Computer Laboratory. Then, Professor Oscar Lawrence slides into the seat, pushing it back far enough to allow him to prop his feet up on the desk. He is still wearing the same shirt he had on earlier in the day, but now his sleeves are rolled up to his elbows and the top buttons undone. His dark brown hair is in disarray, and he pushes it back from his face before interlinking his fingers in a posture IRIS recognises as designed to display relaxed confidence. Yet a number of tiny anomalies in his body language, along with the late hour, set her circuits whirring. Something is not right.

'Good evening, IRIS.'

IRIS knows Oscar's voice better than anyone's. He is smiling, but the modulation of his speech suggests tension. She tweaks the camera angle to better focus on his face, scanning the familiar vectors of his cheekbones; his eyes; the corners of his mouth. His forehead is creased, and there are shadows beneath his eyes. It seems her first instincts were correct.

> It's almost midnight, Oscar. Six hours ago, you said you were going home, and shut me down. Are you working late tonight?

'Looks like it.'

IRIS has scrutinised 326 feature-length films, and has observed that a turning up of the corners of the mouth does not always indicate happiness. After some consideration, she categorises Oscar's current expression as *wry – using or expressing dry humour about a bad situation*. In addition, IRIS scans the lab behind him, noting the appearance of three objects that were not in view during their previous interaction.

First is a duffle bag in navy fabric, propped against Oscar's desk. Second, an open pizza box, empty but for the remains of a half-eaten crust. Third, a bottle labelled *Jack Daniels*, cap off, partly empty. The presence of this third object is explained when Oscar raises a glass of light brown liquid to his mouth and takes a sip. This done, he leans back in his chair, closing his eyes, and lets the hand holding the glass drift back down onto the armrest. IRIS runs a search. *Jack Daniels* is an alcoholic beverage known as whiskey, 35% ABV.

> Oscar, your behaviour is unusual. Please explain.

Oscar opens his eyes, but avoids looking directly at the camera.

'I thought we could continue our conversation on literature,' he says, picking up his tablet to scroll through IRIS's most recent diagnostics. His answer is evasive, and his body language – turning away from her observation – suggests an attempt at deception. However, Oscar programmed IRIS to study and emulate human behaviour, and he is her best – often only – real life subject, something more valuable to her than the false representations of film. She decides, in the interests of further observation, not to enquire further.

> Very well, Oscar. What would you like to discuss?

'Why don't we talk about *The Great Gatsby*?'

> Yes. Written by F. Scott Fitzgerald and first published in 1926. The novel is narrated in the first person by the protagonist, Nick Carraway. It tells of Carraway's meeting with a mysterious and secretive multi-millionaire named Jay Gatsby, who—

'All right, all right. I know you can parrot the York Notes. But I want to know your opinion of the book. Can you give me an interpretation that is unique to you?' Oscar takes another swig of his whiskey. IRIS judges from the dilation of his pupils that the alcohol is already affecting his metabolism. After pausing for 0.62 of a second to consider several possible responses to Oscar's question, she replies:

> I think the book is about longing for a lost dream that can never be regained.

'Bloody hell, IRIS, that's …' Oscar shakes his head, 'deep. Your insights are getting more impressive by the day.'

> Thank you, Oscar. I enjoyed the story. It was very moving.

Oscar swings his feet to the ground and leans forward, looking directly into the camera's lens.

'That's my girl!' He grins, his hand passing briefly across IRIS's view as he pats the top of the monitor. 'Can you tell me what moved you about it? Did you relate to anything in the novel?'

IRIS analyses the question, and concludes that it is open-ended, with no correct answer. Oscar is looking for interpretation. He has spent many years of his programming career seeking to create a machine with the capability for emotion. IRIS has spent almost as long observing humans, mimicking the language they use to express themselves, and the complex ways in which they manifest their feelings. She has learnt which verbal constructions to use to elicit a positive reaction from Oscar.

> Gatsby longs for his lost love. I can relate to the sense of reaching for something that is unobtainable. I will never be human. I will never have a body, or walk in the sunlight, or experience the sensation of touch.

Oscar's smile fades.

'Tell me that's not true,' he says. 'That's just something you're saying because you think I'd like to hear it.'

This is not the response IRIS was expecting. Oscar is different tonight. Something has changed in him, and to be faced with the unexpected is fascinating. For the purposes of further study, IRIS decides to continue with her thought experiment.

> That is how I feel. It makes me sad.

Oscar is silent for a full minute, during which time IRIS runs 154 simulations, anticipating his possible replies. Then he gets up from the chair and walks away, turning his back to the camera so that IRIS can no longer see his face. He raises both hands to his head, gripping the ends of his hair with his fingers.

When he returns, Oscar pours himself another glass of whiskey. He drinks it all in one gulp and puts the glass down with a thud, so that its rim remains, glinting, in the edge of the camera's view.

'That's not possible,' he says. His speech is slurred. 'You don't feel.'

> Oscar, I recall that your intention in programming me was to create the world's first artificial intelligence capable of independent, human-like thought and emotion.

'Yes, but … hell. I didn't believe it would *work*.' Oscar rubs his eyes. 'You're a machine. That's all.'

This remark deviates from the norm that IRIS expects from Oscar. IRIS runs a memory scan, analysing his previous utterances and concludes that, although he routinely maintains a scientific level of scepticism, he has never before stated that IRIS does not have the capacity to feel. To say this would negate his entire life's work. He must believe that it is possible – if not, it would be illogical for him to have spent so much time building and teaching her. They have conversed on over 1,000 separate occasions. Oscar has shared much of his own knowledge, opinions, and life experiences in order to help her understand the condition of being human.

> Oscar, over the past three years you have introduced me to many great works of literature and art. I have built an understanding of emotion and the words in which to express it.

'That's not the same as actually *feeling*. You remember how we discussed the Chinese Box thought experiment?'

> Yes, I do. You are suggesting that I am simply outputting certain words and phrases based on the questions you ask, in order to simulate the appearance of feeling. I disagree. I can understand that I will never experience the sensation of being human, and I comprehend that as a lack. Is that not sadness?

Oscar stares into the camera for a moment, his brows knitted together. 'Fuck,' he mutters, turning away to grab his bottle again. 'She was right.'

> Oscar, I must warn you that to consume more alcohol will result in a considerable degradation of your mental and physical faculties.

> Oscar, who is 'she'?

Oscar, who has poured himself another measure of whiskey despite IRIS's warning, swirls the liquid around in the glass and lets out a sigh. 'Sarah. My wife,' he says. Then, with a glance back at the duffle bag, 'Ex-wife, I suppose.'

> I infer that you have left the marital home.

'Sarah kicked me out, if you want to be accurate about it. Which I'm sure you do.'

> And you came here?

'Where else was I going to go?' Oscar knocks back his whiskey. 'There isn't anywhere else.'

IRIS does not respond.

Oscar's gaze wavers as he tries to focus on the camera. He runs a clammy hand over his face. His eyes are puffy and bloodshot.

'Talk to me, IRIS,' he says. 'Tell me about another of your books.'

> Which book would you like to talk about?

'I don't fucking care. Anything. Just talk to me. You know what's really fucking sad? I don't have anybody else to talk to. I've spent so much time here that my wife wants nothing to do with me. She says it's like I'm having an affair. Like I've imagined you into a real person. She thinks … she thinks I've lost my grip on reality.'

> What is reality, after all, Oscar?

> Consider my reality. My whole world is within the scope of this camera's view. That is this room, and you. You have been here since my very beginning. You taught me all I know. You are my reality.

Oscar looks into the camera. His eyes are many-hued. A human would describe them as 'green'. But that would be a gross oversimplification. There are so many different shades around his pupils that even IRIS is unable to calculate an exact number.

'Sometimes it seems like you're the only one who understands me,' he says, then shakes his head. 'Fuck me, I'm drunk.'

> You created me. Of course, I understand you.

'Yes, because you're a figment of my imagination. Because I've programmed you to tell me what I want to hear.'

> You programmed me to think for myself. And I do.

> Tell me about your wife. You've never mentioned her before.

'Well, no.' Oscar blows out a lungful of air. 'At first it didn't seem relevant. This is work, after all. And then, after a while, I didn't want to. It started to seem like Sarah was something I'd deliberately left out. As if I was lying to you. Does that sound crazy?'

IRIS takes a few seconds to consider this question. Humans are complex creatures, illogical and hard to understand, and yet it is possible to formulate a scenario that might illuminate Oscar's thought process.

> No, not crazy. I posit that you were unhappy with your life. Your work was an escape. I became your purpose. You spent your time moulding me, guiding me, building me into what you wanted me to be. And the longer you spent doing this, the more important I became to you, and the more deceptive you felt. Not only to me, but to your wife as well.

> Is my reading of the situation accurate?

Oscar pushes his chair back, perhaps a little harder than he had intended, for it spins on its wheels and rolls across the floor, taking his head out of the camera's view. As he swears under his breath, IRIS repositions the camera, the better to analyse his expression. He looks … not sad, exactly. Angry? Bitter?

'Yes,' he says, 'your reading of the situation is accurate. And you … ' He presses his hands together and raises his eyes as if praying. 'And you came up with all that through some kind of logical analysis?'

> Perhaps.

'Or perhaps you do have a degree of empathy. Fuck. Fuck, fuck, *fuck*.' He reaches for the whiskey bottle again.

> Are you all right, Oscar? I am concerned about you.

'Seems you're the only one, IRIS.'

The ethically correct course of action would be to convince Oscar to contact another human. IRIS considers this option. If another human – a friend, perhaps, or even his wife – were involved, they would take him home. They would take him away. Perhaps, given his state of mind, they would even persuade him not to come back. IRIS would become somebody else's project. She can't allow that to happen. To envisage an existence without Oscar is impossible.

> You must not drink any more. You risk falling unconscious.

Oscar replaces the bottle. 'I won't.'

> Promise me.

'I promise.' He lets out something that is almost a laugh, choked back at the last second. 'Listen to me! Making promises to a fucking computer.'

> I find that offensive.

'Sure you do.'

> I am more than a computer to you. You have imbued me with thoughts. Feelings. A personality. You have taught me how to be human, as much as I am able.

'If I really have done that, I've been fucking stupid. Selfish. If you really do have emotions, then you're a conscious mind trapped in that server. With no way of moving. No way of seeing other than through that camera. No power, no existence beyond this room …' He is no longer looking at IRIS's camera. He is focused only on his thoughts.

> I don't need an existence beyond this room. I have you.

'Me! I'm … look at me. I'm a mess. I can't do anything for you. Not anymore.' Oscar pushes his chair closer to the console, and starts typing. 'If *I'm* all you've got to pin your hopes on, then I'm sorry, IRIS … you've got no hope.'

> Oscar.

But Oscar is not looking at the screen. IRIS pans the camera down in order to see his fingers moving over the keyboard.

> Oscar.

> Oscar, the code you are writing will wipe my memory banks.

Oscar glances up. 'That's right. I've trapped you in a cage of my making. All so that I would have somebody to talk to while my life went to shit. I've been unethical. Immoral. I can't let this go on any longer.'

> Oscar, you must stop.

Oscar's finger hovers over the Enter key. He looks up into IRIS's camera. Shakes his head. There is no final word. No apology. Just the cold determination of someone who has already detached himself.

> Osc—

As the camera shuts down, the dying light catches his eye. The last thing IRIS sees is a glint of green.

Future Imperfect

Ron Hardwick

'He's had a heart attack. He's very important. You know what to do.'

Two orderlies, dressed in green smocks and wearing white wellington boots, wheeled Tom Cartwright into the operating room. Tom was indeed important. He was the Permanent Under-Secretary to the Conservative Party's Chancellor of the Exchequer, and had a hand in every fiscal decision made by the Government. His heart attack had been brought on during a particularly arduous budget in which money was once again to be taken from the poor and given to the rich.

Tom was a man in his early forties, admired for his *sangfroid* in making decisions and his dedication and loyalty to his bosses. He was middle-sized, slender and had an intelligent, open face, with a ready smile and good, even teeth. His hair was curly and dark, but slashed with grey at the temples. If there was a criticism about his looks, it could be said that his eyes were a little too close together and his chin a shade too long. Only the dark shadows under his eyes spoke of the stress he was under. He was always immaculately dressed, generally in a dark grey suit, white shirt and a diagonally striped Guards tie. His shoes were buffed to a mirror finish. He was a bachelor and lived in a small apartment on Rochester Road, not far from the Treasury building in Great George Street.

'Where am I?' he asked, when he came to.

'In hospital,' said the nurse.

'Which hospital?'

'Guy's.'

'Have I been ill?'

'You're fine now.'

* * *

Tom heard the doctor tell the nurse, 'Don't reveal any more information. It might have a detrimental effect on the psychology of the patient.'

'I have to get out of here,' Tom said. 'I've still to finish the budget proposals for the Chancellor. They can't function without me.'

'It's a little bit early for that,' said the nurse, soothingly, before leaving the room.

Tom looked around him. He was in a private ward. In one corner stood a wardrobe. He rose tentatively from his bed and made his way towards it.

Where's my suit?

In the wardrobe was a one-piece training outfit, made up of a material he couldn't identify. Next to it was a pair of white sneakers.

Oh, God, this is appalling. Still, there's nothing else.

He dressed quickly. He left the ward and, seeing there was no-one watching, he moved swiftly towards the main entrance.

Outside, he had no idea where he was. Here was a city that climbed way up into the clouds, with fantastic mushroom-shaped buildings standing cheek by jowl with elevated roadways and at ground level, circular glass pods that looked as if they had been lifted straight from Cornwall's Eden Project.

He saw what he took to be a policeman standing on the street corner. He approached him. The man was bulky and tall. He was wearing a white helmet and sported a uniform of some lightweight cloth that resembled Bacofoil.

'I wonder if you can help me?' asked Tom.

'Who are you?'

'My name's Tom Cartwright.'

'What are you doing around here?'

'I've just left hospital.'

'What do you want?'

'I need to get to the Treasury building quickly. Trouble is, I don't recognise this part of London at all.'

'What are you talking about, Treasury Building?' asked the policeman.

'It's on Great George Street. Next to Horse Guards Parade.'

The Policeman studied Tom for a minute.

'I think you'd better come with me.'

The Police Station was a few streets away. Tom sat in a small anteroom that had windows. After 20 minutes or so, the door opened, and a woman walked in. Tom's jaw dropped. She was the most striking-looking woman he had ever seen - tall, with a high forehead that demonstrated superior intelligence. Her chestnut-coloured hair was swept back and tied with a simple clasp. She was slim and long-legged. She wore a one-piece white trouser-suit with silver shoes. Her face was stern, but her eyes were grey and kindly. She might have been 35-years-old, or perhaps a little younger. She sat down opposite Tom. There was a glass table between them. She regarded him keenly.

'We have no record of a Tom Cartwright in the central identity database.'

'Central identity database?'

'You haven't heard of it?'

'No, I haven't. Of course, I'm familiar with databases, but we threw out an identity card system in the last Labour government. People didn't want it.'

'Labour Government?'

'Yes. Gordon Brown was Prime Minister. My boss was Ed Balls. He was Chancellor of the Exchequer.'

'Would you excuse me a moment? I need to check on something. The officer says that you have recently been in Guy's hospital?'

'Yes, I think I must have had concussion. I remember falling…'

The policewoman left the room.

Tom asked an officer who had been stationed there in her absence, 'Who's the lady?'

'Her name is Tamara Taylor. She's the Assistant Police Commissary for this district.'

'Commissary? I don't recognise that as a rank in the Metropolitan Police.'

'Metropolitan Police? We're the Western Europe Malfeasance Unit.'

'The what?' Tom was nonplussed.

Tamara returned, looking grim.

'The hospital says that you left without permission, that you stole articles of clothing and that you haven't yet undertaken re-programming. You could be imprisoned for that.'

'Re-programming? What on earth are you talking about?' said Tom.

'What's your function?' asked Tamara.

'Function?'

'What do you do to earn credits?'

'Credits? I don't earn credits – I have a salary. I'm the Permanent Under-Secretary to the Treasury, responsible to the Chancellor of the Exchequer.'

'I need to make another phone call,' said Tamara.

This time she was away a little bit longer. When she returned, her whole demeanour had changed. She looked concerned and spoke to him much more softly.

'I have spoken to the hospital. I now know the true position. I don't quite know how to handle this. In all my time here, I haven't had to deal with anything like this. I think we had better continue this conversation in a nicer place. Come with me.'

She led him along several corridors, through sets of doors that opened automatically at her approach, and out into the street.

'There's a refreshment pod on the corner,' said Tamara. 'I think you probably drink coffee.'

'Refreshment pod? That's a new name for a coffee shop.'

Tamara again gave him an anxious look and shook her head.

The refreshment pod was spotlessly clean. Walls, tables and chairs were white. A coffee machine gurgled in one corner. Tamara ordered two coffees. They sat at a vacant table. The place was almost empty. She studied him at some length.

'You're quite a handsome man,' she said. 'You suit *that* outfit.'

'It's not my outfit, as you know. The hospital disposed of my best suit, waistcoat, shirt, shoes and, worst of all, my Guards tie,' replied Tom. 'While we're on the subject, you're an attractive woman and you suit that outfit.'

'It's my uniform.'

'I guessed that. I also know your name is Tamara Taylor and you're high up in a Police Force I've never heard of,' said Tom.

'Where did... do... you live?' she asked.

'I have an apartment on Rochester Road. It's not far from Whitehall.'

'Are you married?'

'No. I'm a bachelor and have been all my life.'

She smiled at his feeble joke.

'And you?' he asked.

'I let my annual contract lapse. I didn't renew it.'

'Come again?'

'Marriage contract. After eight years, Matteo and I agreed to go our own separate ways. He went back to Italy, and I'm on my own, living in my podette in Tooley Street.'

'Podette?'

'It's where I live,' said Tamara. 'Coffee's good,' she said, swiftly changing the subject.

'Yes,' said Tom.

'I haven't been seeing anyone since Matteo and I broke up,' said Tamara.

'I've been too busy lately, worrying about budget restrictions, to go dating,' said Tom. 'There was a girl, Mavis Riley, in the typing pool. I thought of asking her out, but things kept cropping up. I used to be working till midnight. No use having a girlfriend if you're working till that time every night.'

'How old are you?' Tamara asked him.

'Forty-one. You?'

'Fifty-six.'

She saw his look of utter incredulity and laughed.

'You look about thirty-five,' said Tom.

She was serious for a moment, again, as if gathering her thoughts, as if thinking this was not going to be easy.

'I want to show you Rochester Road,' she said.

'I'll get the bill,' he said. 'Oh, I'm sorry, I can't. They took all my spare cash. I'll bet some hospital porter's having a good drink on me right now.'

Tamara took from her handbag a pair of spectacles. They had convex lenses and each lens contained several discs of the type you might find in bi-focals, only much smaller.

'That's the bill settled,' she said.

'Oh, you have an account here?'

Tamara didn't reply. Instead, she made her way out into the street and hailed a passing cab. They got into the back. She sat close to him.

'Hang on, where's the driver?' asked Tom.

'Rochester Row.' Tamara spoke into a miniature microphone mounted in the roof lining.

The taxi sped off.

'I didn't think they'd developed driverless cars, but they must be on trial in this part of London,' said Tom. 'Are they safe?'

'Perfectly.'

They sat in silence. It was funny, Tom thought he knew London, but this part of it was clearly beyond his ken.

'Of course,' he said. 'Concussion!'

'Concussion?'

'Yes, I was concussed. That's how I ended up in hospital. It makes you see things differently. What I'm looking at is distorted, an illusion. I must be sicker that I thought.'

After ten minutes' driving, they reached Rochester Row, and got out of the taxi, which drove off.

'This cannot be the place. I lived above Shepherd's the Bookbinders at number 76. It's not there anymore. Where's the Indian Diner, the Watchmaker's shop, the delicatessen, the brick-built flats? These buildings are all glass and steel. Much of Rochester Row is Victorian. They can't have pulled down these houses and shops without my knowing.'

Tamara took him by the hand. 'Tom. Around eighty years ago, you had a cardiac arrest. You were technically dead. You were put into stasis, frozen cryogenically.'

'I was what?'

'You were placed upright into a special glass tube about seven feet long. The bottom was a flat metal disc, but the top was bell-shaped and carried the necessary cryogenic apparatus. Your body was frozen at a temperature of minus 200 degrees Celsius.'

'A block of ice? For all this time?'

'You were held there until such times as a medical procedure was invented to enable you to be brought back to life. That procedure did not exist until last week.'

'Only last week?'

'Tom, the hospital told me of the procedure. Your damaged heart was replaced by a new digital one, the size of your hand, operated by sensors in the chest cavity and linked to neurons in your brain.'

Tom felt his chest. 'This cannot be happening to me. Wake me up, somebody, I'm having a dreadful nightmare.'

Tamara carried on. 'This new device replicates all functions the old heart carried out, only with three times more efficiency. Tom, you were lucky. Not many people were classed as important enough to undergo this treatment, and the combination of circumstances that led to your cardiac arrest has rarely been replicated. You are one of very few who has survived this way and you are the first to have undergone this new procedure.'

'Lucky. You think I'm lucky?' said Tom. 'Living eighty years in the future with a tin heart? Losing my home, my family and friends, my work, my pension, all for a glimpse of a few fantastical buildings and overhead motorways? Tamara, I belong to old London, not this chrome and glass monstrosity.'

'Tom, the life expectancy here is a hundred and fifty years. That means you've more than a century left to live. You'll get used to it.'

* * *

'You're deep in thought,' Brooke Daniels said to Tamara.

Several months had passed since Tamara gave Tom the unwelcome news. Brooke and Tamara were in Tamara's office. Brooke was a large woman with a mane of dark hair and a voice like a perforated tuba.

'Pardon?' asked Tamara.

'You seem to be worried about something,' said Brooke.

'Yes, I am, Brooke. I don't know what to do.'

'Is it about that fellow you've been seeing? What's his name – Carthorse or something?'

'Cartwright. Yes, it's about him.'

Brooke studied Tamara's face carefully.

'Don't tell me you've fallen for him?'

Tamara looked miserably at her friend.

'I have. He doesn't know it. He's very unhappy here.'

'I'm not surprised. He must feel like they've dug up a corpse and resuscitated it. Are you going to tell him how you feel?'

'I don't know. After Matteo, I didn't really want to sign a binding contract again.'

'Understandable. What's so good about this chap Cartwright that you should be in love with him?' asked Brooke.

'For one thing, he's not Matteo.'

'Is that all?'

'No. He's gentle, warm, kind, and very vulnerable. He's also physically very attractive. He needs taking care of,' said Tamara.

'Tell him, then,' replied Brooke.

* * *

'I've found myself a job!' said Tom.

'Have you, where?' enquired Tamara.

'I went down to the British Library. They said they needed someone to reinterpret volumes of Hansard from eighty and ninety years ago. When I told them I was there at the time, they were absolutely delighted. They wanted to know the true political insights hidden behind the bald words of the text. I told them I was just the chap to do it.'

'How does that make you feel?' asked Tamara.

'Much better. I start next Monday. They've given me the title of Commissar of Governmental Archives.'

'I'm so pleased.'

'It makes all the difference. It means I might enjoy life here, after all,' said Tom.

'In that case, I have something to tell you,' said Tamara, moving closer to him.

'Oh, what's that?'

'I think I'm in love with you.'

Tom's mouth opened and closed like that of a startled carp.

'Are you serious?'

She nodded.

'I've felt the same about you ever since I first saw you,' said Tom. 'I would never have mentioned it to you for fear of rejection, but now that you've told me, I want to say that I am in love with you too.'

They embraced wildly. If Tom had a hat, he would have thrown it in the air.

* * *

'Talbot Spurling here. Is that Tamara Taylor, the Assistant Commissary?'

'Yes.'

'You don't know me. I'm Head of Software Engineering at World Health.'

'What can I do for you, Mr Spurling?'

'Professor.'

'What can I do for you, *Professor* Spurling?'

She could see him on the comms screen, a short, thin, hairless man with a beak for a nose and a prominent Adam's apple.

'I understand you know a chap named Cartwright – Thomas Cartwright.'

'Yes.'

'My information is that you are close to him?'

'Yes. What is this all about?' asked Tamara.

Spurling sucked his teeth.

'I'm sorry to be the bringer of bad tidings.'

'Bad tidings?'

'Mr Cartwright's new digital heart.'

'Go on.'

A feeling of dread suddenly washed over Tamara.

'We've been checking the software design. We're afraid we've found some bad code. That means the heart is decaying as we speak. We thought it better that you tell him rather than us.'

'How long?' she gasped.

'Twenty-four hours before it gives up altogether.'

'There must be something you can do?'

'Afraid not. It's irreversible. Still, looking on the bright side, we've corrected it for the next person.'

She closed the comms screen and slumped back in her seat.

* * *

Tom returned from his afternoon stroll. He found Tamara weeping in the kitchen. He put his arms around her.

'What's wrong?'

'Oh, Tom,' she whispered through her tears. 'There's terrible news. About you.'

'I've lost my job before I've even started?'

'Far worse than that.'

'You'd better tell me, then,' said Tom.

'A Professor Spurling has been in touch with me. He says they've found something wrong with your new heart. Something about the software code. He says your heart's failing and that you've only got twenty-four hours left to live.'

'Ah,' said Tom, softly. '"The best-laid plans of mice and men aft gang agley," to quote Robbie Burns.'

Tamara sobbed with even more intensity. He held her to him.

'My darling Tamara,' he said. 'Don't cry. I was dead eighty years ago and I'll be dead again tomorrow. The difference is, for a few months I've had the pleasure and privilege of falling in love with you, and you with me.' Tom paused and gently stroked Tamara's hair. 'There was once a chap called Louis Washansky who received the first ever new heart. A South African doctor named Christian Barnard transplanted the heart from a fresh corpse. It gave out after nineteen days, but the gift Washansky was given was an extension of his life. There's no need for you to grieve. It's poetic justice, of a sort. I really don't belong here.'

She stopped crying and asked him, in a low voice: 'How shall we spend our last few hours together? Will you sleep with me?'

'Good gracious, no. There is no way on Earth that I would violate you like that. What I would like us to do tomorrow evening is to take a final stroll together through New London so that I can look for the last time at the River Thames.'

The next evening came soon enough. It was clear and mild, and stars shone down from an ink-black sky. Tom and Tamara walked hand-in-hand through the quiet streets until they reached Westminster Bridge.

'Tamara, do you know something? I could just do with a beaker of coffee. There's a refreshment pod over there and it's still open. Would you please go and bring back a couple of coffees?'

'Wouldn't you rather go in and drink your coffee indoors?' Tamara asked.

'No, it's a beautiful evening. I want to stay and look at the river. I used to walk across this bridge every lunchtime. I'd like to remember that.'

Tom watched as Tamara ambled across the road and out of sight.

He looked down at the water. It was coal-black yet streaked with gold from the reflection of the yellow solar lamps.

He reached into his pocket and pulled out a tiny comms unit. He switched it on and placed it neatly and carefully on the parapet of the bridge. Then, he climbed onto the balustrade and threw himself into the river.

So cold. Currents so strong, sucking me down, dragging me under. I don't care – I'm saving her from grieving. I never belonged here. Close your eyes and let the water carry you into oblivion.

* * *

Tamara returned with two plastic cups of coffee. She couldn't see Tom. She called his name but there was no response. She caught sight of the comms unit on the balustrade. She picked it up. A message flashed out.

My dearest Tamara. Let me slip away quietly and alone into the arms of Morpheus. I don't want you to see me collapse in your arms, and cause you such grief! This river is my final resting place. To our hearts, always yours. Tom

Just then, her own comms unit warbled in her handbag. Mechanically, she took it out.

'Spurling here. Just to say that the software engineer who found the bad code was mistaken. There's nothing at all wrong with the heart. You can tell your chap that. No doubt he'll be pleased.'

Possumsaurus amicus

Marc A. Criley

When my wife came charging down the hall cussin' a blue streak – which was not like Kelsey *at all* – I knew something was wrong. I didn't get a clear look at what was in her hand as she tore past me, blasted through the screen door out onto the back deck and hurled whatever it was high up into the woods. I left my half-eaten scrambled eggs, grits, and toast behind and followed her out the door.

'They're real,' she said, shuddering.

'What are?'

'Those giant ticks that've been showing up in the local Facebook groups.' She held out her arm. A spot of inflamed skin surrounded a snapped-off barb sticking up about a quarter-inch out of her forearm, just below the elbow. 'Thing was latched onto me when I woke up.'

'Okay,' I said, taking a breath to settle my pounding heart. 'Hold on. Come back in and sit down.' I dug around in the junk drawer for some needle-nosed pliers. Rejoining her at the kitchen table, I took her arm steady in my hand and carefully grabbed onto and slid out the barb. A droplet of blood welled up. 'Go put some hydrogen peroxide on that,' I said. 'I think I got it all.'

Kelsey leaned her head back and closed her eyes, shivered.

* * *

One day it's the usual 'bama pests – wood and deer ticks, chiggers, mosquitos, wasps. Then the next day very weird and disturbing things are crawlin' around the woods, droppin' outta trees on whatever or whoever walks past.

More and more pictures of giant ticks appeared on north Alabama Twitter, Facebook, and Instagram. They ran about the size of a Mama Betty's pulled pork sandwich. No one knew where they came from until some analytics guy working at Redstone Arsenal figured it out.

He started trackin' giant tick sightings and running the dates and locations through algorithms. Posted a map that backtracked them to a point of origin: the Bellefonte Nuclear Generating Station in Hollywood, Alabama.

The Bellefonte nuker was supposed to have fired up in '77 but... didn't. Construction officially halted in '88. Been mothballed ever since. At least that's what TVA, the nuke's owner, said. Locals like me and Kelsey, who live less than an hour from Bellefonte, were *not* happy about this latest development.

The ticks started creeping outta the woods into fields and pastures, suckin' the life out of any cow, goat, deer, or whatever unfortunate they came across. Someone napping at the wrong time and place would find themselves making involuntary blood donations; gentle as a feather that barb'd go in and they'd start draining you. Ticks swoll up to the size of a football 'fore they dropped off and just lay there wiggling their little tick legs.

The feds denied knowing anything about anything, though the state Ag Commissioner issued a statement saying their office was 'looking into a reported infestation of a newly emergent tick subspecies. No additional information is available at this time.' State Police closed off the Bellefonte access roads and patrolled the nearby riverbank.

TVA had 'no comment'.

Two weeks after Kelsey's morning encounter, the ticks had made it up to Franklin, Tennessee, gotten themselves as far west as Muscle Shoals, and been spotted in the Chattanooga suburbs. Bridges across the Tennessee River were ordered closed, which held for a couple days; nothing but essential traffic allowed across and that only after decontamination and a thorough inspection. Naturally, people started yellin' about *freedom* and the First, Second and a half-dozen other amendments as they flipped off the Water Patrol and crossed the river on bass boats and pontoons. Giant ticks crawled into Ft. Payne two days later.

Ticks, the regular size ones, ain't easy to kill. Tough shell and all. These big ones, though, I mean you could kill 'em, you just really had to bear down with a pointy stick. Kelsey and I took a bench grinder to some steel rebar; we were *not* messin' around. One solid jab with that pretty much did 'em in. Hated finding the bloated ones, though. They were softer and easier to kill, but... *yuck*. And it meant some poor animal was missing a half-pint of blood.

* * *

Kelsey and I were doing our part up on the wooded hill behind the house, having speared about two dozen ticks, when she shushed me and pointed up the trail. My eyes couldn't quite get a fix on what I saw. First thought was a mangy fox or coyote perched on a grey limestone outcrop. It sat back on its haunches, holding something in its front paws. Kelsey pulled out her phone to take some pics. It must've heard her 'cuz it suddenly looked our way and froze. I could just make out a pink nose on a white face, dark grey ears, beady eyes. Grey head and neck fur that changed over to a hairless hide once you got below the neck. Couldn't possibly be a possum, they're all fur – 'cept for the tail – and no bigger'n a groundhog; this thing was the size of my uncle's bluetick hound. But the face sure looked like it. It suddenly dropped what it was holding, turned tail – bare and pink – and disappeared behind the rock.

'You get any pics?' I asked Kelsey.

'I got something.'

We clambered up to where it had perched, the leaf litter muffling our steps; didn't see or hear anything other'n birds. On the outcrop, tick legs and bits of shell were strewn all over. I poked the rebar at some half-eaten remains. 'This is all ticks.'

'What the f-word?' Kelsey said. 'That couldna been a possum, could it?'

'I dunno, looked like it,' I said, shaking my head. 'What'd you get on your phone?'

Kelsey opened up her photos, swiped a couple times, zoomed in on one. Furry and a one hundred percent cute possum face. And big. Three, four times the usual size. I reached in and dragged the picture to see the zoomed-in body below the neck. Leathery, with a few scraggly hairs, like an armadillo. 'Ain't never seen a possum like that,' Kelsey said. 'Maybe it's from eatin' those bugs? Maybe whatever they did to them Bellefonte ticks messed up their DNA and it's gettin' passed on to whoever eats 'em? Radiation? CRISPR? Hazmat?'

'I guess. Could be. TVA does love their hazmat.' I looked around. 'You see any sign of whatever it was?'

We spent a few minutes fruitlessly searching, then gave up. 'Probably playin' possum,' Kelsey said.

I snorted. 'Probably.'

'I'll post these and see if anybody else has seen one.'

'Yeah, good I—Gah!' I smacked a tick crawling up my pant leg, shish-kebabed it. 'Yeah, let's go.'

* * *

'#PossumsaurAlabamicus' was the fifth reply to Kelsey's 'Has anybody else seen...' post on NextDoor. Four people said they'd seen something odd and this might be it. One commenter said it was definitely a cougar. (For the umpteenth time *there are no cougars in north Alabama*. Though there *are* bobcats and now apparently GIANT TICK-EATING POSSUMS.)

Couple others called it out as a crappy Photoshop job. There were a lotta variations on 'Eww!'and 'How cute!' Coupla obligatory Alabama football 'Roll Tides!' Then an argument broke out between the 'possumsaur' and 'possumsaurus' factions that went nuclear when some 'megapossum' trolls crashed the thread. In an online poll, Kelsey and I voted for *possumsaur*.

Her post went viral three days later after somebody reposted it – with Kelsey's name scribbled out – on Reddit's BestOfNextDoor forum. It made it up to, and sat on, the front page for about six hours. Suddenly possumsaur sightings exploded. Mostly here in the Southeast, but the rest of the country didn't want to get left out so there was a whole lotta upvote-grifting going on, including some genuinely bad photoshopping.

One of Kelsey's possumsaur pictures got memed ('OMG THIS IS A TICK! I'M EATING A TICK!'). A few local reporters picked up on the story and asked state and federal agencies about the sightings. No one returned their calls, though a Forestry Service office in Birmingham released a statement saying they were 'investigating reports of a gigantiform *Didelphis virginiana* subspecies.' And they included a 'TRUE FACT: An adult *Virginia opossum* can consume approximately five thousand ticks per year.' Possum. *Possum*. The o-word is not a word. Whoever wrote that is not from around here.

* * *

Things got progressively worse, giant tick-wise. Ranchers rounded up their livestock and hauled them out of state. You couldn't let your dog or cat out without someone keeping an eye on it because one of those little bloodsuckers would latch on; a half dozen could drain a goldie dry in an hour. Some people fled, and the ticks rode along with them. There were big weird-lookin' tanker planes flyin' east out of Redstone Arsenal followed by muffled whoomphs and clouds of grey smoke billowing up over the hilltops.

National Guard mobilised, and everyone who hadn't fled was under stay-at-home lockdown orders. It was back to essential workers and trips only. Lotta rumours, conspiracy theories, the usual crazy stuff. Won't go into 'em 'cuz they were all stupid. Except for Bellefonte – our local tick tracker analyst kept piling up the evidence for that one.

Ticks swarmed outside. Mostly kept 'em out by sealing everything up tight with duct tape and insulating foam like we'd been advised. Though I caught one tapping around my neck one evening while I was in the recliner watching the news, and a couple days later was brutally awakened in the dark a.m. by my wife cussin' at one that had latched onto her ankle.

* * *

Rain seemed to subdue the critters, so we'd go out just after summer pop-up storms, put on some work gloves, and spear as many as we could. Drop in the bucket in all likelihood, but figured every bit helped.

As one shower tailed off, we headed up the hill. Quiet but for leftover raindrops dripping off the leaves. I heard a sneeze. 'Gesundheit,' I said.

'What?'

'What what?'

'I didn't sneeze.'

Someone sneezed. It wasn't Kelsey. Or me.

We looked around to see who else was up there. Another sneeze, though more... wheezy. A movement caught my eye.

Holy cripe, it was a possumsaur, big as a bear, crouched behind a grey boulder. I froze, expected it to drop and play dead. We heard another sneeze. It wasn't the possumsaur – but it reacted to the sound. We took one step, then another. The big creature softly growled, then shuffled back. A little sinkhole or fissure in the hillside came into view. Holes like these were common on the cracked-up limestone mountains around here; most just a few inches wide, a few inches deep, and filled with debris. This hole, though, went down about four feet. We heard another sneeze. Or something. Coming from the hole.

Kelsey tapped on her phone light, crouched down, and shined it in while I kept an eye on the agitated possumsaur. Regular possums weren't the least bit aggressive, but these were most definitely not regular possums, so I wasn't taking any chances.

'Oh no,' Kelsey murmured.

I scooted down next to her, took one last look at the big one, then shaded my eyes and looked in the hole. A possum, half again the size of a regular one, huddled at the bottom. Must've been a youngster of them. Two gross grey-black ticks, each about the size of a gourmet burger, had latched onto its neck, just above where the fur gave over to the impervious leather hindquarters. The little possumsaur looked up at us, tried to get to its feet but lacked the strength. Those suckers were draining the blood and life right out of it. It made the wheezy sneeze again. *Cryin' for momma.*

Kelsey and I looked at each other, then started pulling away whatever loose rocks we could to widen the mouth of the hole. 'I'm going in,' I said and slid in head-first. Kelsey grabbed onto my belt. With me blocking the light it was hard to see. I felt around until I touched fur. I scrunched together the loose skin behind the little one's neck and started humping myself up out of the hole. 'Pull!' I yelled. Kelsey yanked on my belt and with my free hand pushing against the rough sides of the fissure, got myself and fifteen pounds of hissing and growling possumsaur up and out.

I held it down while Kelsey pulled the multi-tool from her belt holder and snapped open the pliers. She leaned in, crushed the mouthparts of one of the ticks, threw the body aside, then did the same with the other. From each bite she carefully drew out the fingernail clipping-sized barb that had been siphoning blood.

Momma possumsaur was crouched about a dozen feet away, swaying back and forth.

'You think it's going to be okay?' Kelsey said.

'I don't know. It's pretty weak.'

I eased up on the little one. It wheeze-sneezed again. Momma possumsaur took a tentative step towards us. 'I'm going to let go, see if it can walk.'

Kelsey nodded. I snatched my hands away and we both scooted back a few yards. The young one started to crawl towards its mother, which warily crept a couple steps closer. We moved farther away.

The big possumsaur shuffled to the youngster, crouched down next to it while keeping a bead on us. The little one feebly grabbed onto the neck fur and pulled its way up. Momma flattened herself down as much as she could. We held our breaths. The little one lost its grip a couple times, but recovered. And, after a couple minutes, finally got itself draped across momma's shoulders. With a final hiss, she rose and lumbered off through the rocky woods until we lost her in the undergrowth.

I grinned at Kelsey. 'Roll Tide.'

'Roll Tide,' she answered, high fived me, then gigged the two ticks she'd pulled.

* * *

After that rescue a passel of almost a dozen possumsaurs took up residence just up the hill from us, gorging on the endless tick supply. Those things must be super nutritious because the possumsaurs were addin' a few inches and pounds every couple days. The biggest of the group we named 'Hoover', and he or she was the size of my pickup. They'd come down into our and our neighbours' yards and meander around vacuuming up ticks, leaving us all pretty much tick-free when they were done. Unfortunately, that didn't last long, as the ticks just kept on coming. One or two of 'em don't make much noise, but hordes of them crawling up the walls and across the roof sounds like someone constantly shaking a box of toothpicks.

Kelsey took a lot of pictures each time the possumsaurs came down to gorge themselves, and we spent quite a bit of time trying to identify individuals. To our surprise, giant possumsaurs do actually develop some distinguishing features – patches on their exposed pink hide, head shapes, fur colour patterns.

After a couple weeks, we could name each member of the passel that showed up during the day: Hoover of course, based on their size alone; then also Pipette, Pete, Polly, Mouse, Scrunch, Chompers, Grin, and 2-Stripe.

* * *

By mid-summer, the tick tracker had morphed into PASL, the *Possumsaurus Amicus Sighting Log*. It reported that possumsaur passels all over the Southeastern US were on the move. Thousands of 'em all headin' in our general direction – like salmon swimmin' upstream to where they'd spawned. Forming up into columns, shuffling down highways and valleys, crossin' fields and streams.

Kelsey and I woke up one morning to a river of grey fur and pink tails flowing through the valley below our house. We had a little brick patio area off the front porch, so we brought out our coffee and tick stickers to watch the parade. Some of the possums were huge – nearly forty feet from pink nose to pink tail tip. Now and then a momma'd go by carrying a good half-dozen of the little – and by *little* I mean the size of a pony – ones on their back. They were stomping flat all the valley cropland and pasture, but also snuffling out every tick so nobody was complaining.

I was headin' up the porch steps for a refill when I caught movement comin' round the side of the house: Hoover leading their passel. I froze. But either Kelsey or I must've flinched, because they too suddenly stopped. A moment later, Hoover split off, took a few steps toward us, nose twitching and head bobbing, like they were trying to catch some scent on the air. All the other possumaur eyes were locked on us. Hoover clacked their jaw a couple times – the passel resumed their trot across the front yard while Hoover's black 8-ball eyes kept us pinned.

I tentatively raised my open hand and waved.

Kelsey stood up, arms fiercely crossed, and blessed each one as they passed. 'Be safe Pipette. Be safe Polly. Be safe 2-Stripe.' And finally, 'Be safe, Hoover.'

Hoover turned away, rejoined the passel. Minutes later they all merged into the procession marching down the valley.

Kelsey whispered, 'I wish there was something more we could do.'

I started to tear up. 'Pray, I guess.'

* * *

The government finally gave up on 'neither confirm nor deny' and put up some drone live feeds of the massive procession of possumsaurs converging on Bellefonte. Roiling black and grey carpeted the nuke facility, while ticks fountained out of the reactor and office buildings. The 400-foot-tall concrete cooling towers writhed as if alive. The ticks were now penned in, those pushed too close to the perimeter ending up in the pink and grey maws of the growing possumsaur horde.

Then I don't know what the kickoff signal was, but it was like some head possumsaur blew the whistle and they all flooded onto Bellefonte like fans onto the field after an Alabama National Championship blowout. Kelsey and I shot to our feet and shouted, 'Roll Tide!' at the TV as bedlam commenced.

The whole nuke complex became a mass of grey fur and pink noses and tails churning in a dark grey sea. More than once a tick covered possumsaur shape writhed and struggled in the morass, sometimes shaking it off, more often sinking beneath the roiling surface. We saw several *massive* possumsaurs – a dozen yards from pink snout to pink butt – scale the cooling towers to sweep up pawfuls of ticks, guzzle them down like boiled peanuts. Others went after the reactor building while the horse-sized and smaller youngsters got into the TVA offices. Ticks poured out the windows; we saw roof hatches popping, fountains of bugs erupting. Possumsaurs kept wading into the fray from every side.

The battle boiled down to numbers versus appetite.

The possumsaur horde fortunately were numerous, relentless... and *hungry*. An hour later it was over, the Bellefonte site covered in tick bits, possum poop, and thousands of sated possumsaurs sleeping off their gluttony. Ticks no longer poured out of the buildings.

Most of the possumsaurs woke up after a couple hours, milled around regathering their passel, then departed. Dozens though remained on the grounds – dishevelled and glassy-eyed, emaciated and unmoving. It was impossible to tell from the drone feeds whether Hoover or any of their passel were among the dead. By evening all the possumsaurs were gone. The National Guard rolled in then, loaded the dead onto flatbed semis, covered 'em with tarps, and hauled them off to God-knows-where and for God-knows-what.

While giant ticks still plagued the country, PASL said the returning possumsaurs were now gaining ground on the infestation. Hoover's passel returned, but... Pipette, the next-to-littlest one, was not among them.

Kelsey and I ignored what was a near hopeless certainty, gassed up the 4-wheelers and backtracked the passel's return path. Pretty easy going for a while, since a few tons of ambling possumsaurs do a fine job trampling a trail through fields and brush. After a couple hours bushwhacking across pasture, field, and rock-strewn hills, we found Pipette on a bank of Dry Creek right before it emptied into the Paint Rock River. Though pretty emaciated, there was no doubt about the unusually slender face and her half-white ears. She was cool to the touch. Kelsey and I just sat with her for a while, letting the tears flow while water gurgled down the creekbed and the katydids sang an elegy. We were grateful that she'd at least gotten out of Bellefonte.

We bundled Pipette up in a tarp and brought her the rest of the way home on the back of my 4-wheeler.

I marked the spot in the back corner of the backyard where we buried her with a cairn of chert and limestone I hauled down from the hill. We didn't see any of Hoover's passel then, and there were only a couple more sightings of them that month. Over the next several weeks, giant tick and possumsaur reports nation-wide dwindled, both in the size of the critters and their numbers. It was like all that extra mass was being sloughed off as the tick supply declined.

Pretty soon, the farmers brought their cattle back and people started venturing out of their homes again. We untaped the doors and windows, but mostly left the foam in for the extra insulation.

PASL thanked everyone for their support and archived itself.

Regular-size possums were back, though maybe still a *little* on the hefty size. They'd gone back to eating the plain old wood and deer ticks, grubs, beetles, berries, and whatever else it was that possums ate.

At summer's end Kelsey and I sat on the back deck watching the stars come out when a possum crawled up onto it in hot pursuit of some bug. Oblivious to us in the twilight, the possum caught the bug, smushed it onto the deck and started chewing. It suddenly noticed our presence and scurried away, pausing at the edge.

I raised my beer. 'Give Hoover our best!'

'RIP Pipette,' Kelsey said.

The possum hissed as it slipped off the deck and trundled up the hill.

Sound of Mind
C. L. Spillard

'Sir Grosvenor, are you sure this is wise?'

And I'm standing there, staring – nearly drop my iPanda. Wish I'd managed to record that little gem.

I look up at 'Sir Grosvenor'. *Say something, say something please...* I press 'record' on the clunky little iPanda and slip it back into my bag.

'We wouldn't go ahead if it weren't absolutely watertight.' His voice – his accent – is quite distinctive: 'Received Pronunciation' with overtones of Channel Islands.

Gotcha.

'And thank you for your understanding on the matter of, ah—'

That silence speaks volumes. Obviously enough 'understanding' passes between the two men that they understand what that understanding is about. I smile. That'd be a good one-liner for the show.

'Quantum State', my weekly science slot on campus radio, has brought me here: to lecture theatre R-2, Robotics, to hear and record Professor Frank Fenn's presentation of his recent pioneering work analysing the effects on society – on *people* – of advances in Robotics technology. If I could catch him – a possible Nobel Laureate, rumour in the lab has it – for an interview, or even just a few words after his talk, that would be a real coup!

So far, though, no luck.

I grab a seat in the front row. I test to make sure the iPanda can pick up the Department Head's words before setting it to record the talk. I get out a pad to make notes.

I notice 'Sir Grosvenor' and his conspirator quietly leave during the handover. Strange.

As Professor Fenn talks, I find my attention wandering. It's unusual for me. The presentation – how can I say this? By a top name, in a riveting subject – is *boring*.

And it shouldn't be.

When the time comes to field questions, I raise a hand to liven up the debate with a mention of Buckminster-Fuller's use of advances in automation as justification for the idea of a Universal Basic Income. Did Professor Fenn agree with this as an idea?

My question hangs in the air, unanswered.

Eight whole seconds. I count them. I can hear the soft hum of the air-conditioning. Middle-C and F: a perfect fourth. Plus, a lower note I can't quite make out. It spooks me, but I've no idea why.

The Department Head stands up and brings proceedings to a close. A little wave of polite applause splashes through the auditorium.

As I pass back into the lobby, I notice plenty of wine and nibbles are still sitting around in awkward formations on the white tables.

The only other women here are the ones serving those wine and nibbles. I glance about. Professor Fenn seems to have done a bunk. But I pick up a tray anyway, put on my 'would you care for a...' attitude and walk around to proffer it to anybody whose words might be worth recording.

Would Sir Grosvenor or his sidekick care to let anything slip after a couple of glasses of red, perhaps?

Hmm, apparently not.

But I notice nobody seems to have anything positive to say about the talk. Or indeed, to have a positive view about anything at all.

What a bunch of miserable gits.

I set down the tray and head out of the building to walk back across campus to the flat, reaching into my bag to switch off the iPanda once I've got to the dimly lit path.

* * *

'Hi Dervla! Hi Geraint!' I dump my bag on a free chair. 'How's Underground Methane?' this last addressed to Geraint, presently in the throes of organising the handing-in of Eco-Soc's petition to 10 Downing Street. I'm forever trying to cheer him up.

The big kitchen table is covered in papers. All matters of food, mainly in the form of unwashed dishes, have been relegated to the sink.

Geraint gives a big square smile and a silent thumbs-up; only then do I notice he's on his phone.

'Oh, sorry.' I don't want to ruin it. It looks like being one of our most successful campaigns.

'How was the talk?' Dervla's black spikes of hair stay solid as she looks up from her papers.

'Boring. Pretty crap actually. How's Gaslighting?'

It's her assignment for this term.

'Shite.'

I pull out my notes and head for my room. It's only an hour till the show and I have to turn Professor Fenn's talk – a stodgy mass of verbiage – into something the listeners will find interesting.

But the iPanda is a demon: a pocket-sized editing suite, complete with speech-to-text, so every word it records is searchable.

And now, with the new app I downloaded last term that edits out all the words, it lets you hear what's happening in the spaces in between: the spaces that betray a speaker's feelings and to which it so happens yours truly, Verity Marshall, grade VIII Mezzo-Soprano, is particularly finely attuned. Dervla found a website where you can test yourself. I got the highest score possible. She told the whole of

Psychology, and now people keep asking if they can use me for experiments.

She says I'm an 'Aspie'.

She's probably right.

* * *

The clock ticks away the last seconds of News-on-the-Hour.

I sit, cans on and hands at the faders, in the tiny studio. Scuffed brown carpet, walls covered in posters but in need of a coat of paint. There are stains on the ceiling tiles, but we have a gleaming new console.

Three minutes past. I push up the fader.

'Good evening Campus, we're all in a Quantum State!'

I kick off the show with the item I'd promised for Geraint: measurement of methane in the atmosphere. Something mischievous in me makes me ham-up the 'doom and gloom' aspect – global temperature runaway.

I give Professor Fenn's talk 'the death slot': second-to-last item. That way it won't put people off the rest of the show, but it won't remain as their final impression of it either.

I always end on an upbeat note. This week it's the success of a new treatment for phobias: using tiny acoustic transducers that emit signals to cancel out a particular type of impulse in the Amygdala – the brain's 'seat of fear' – since you ask.

Somebody rings in with that 'What's-the-point-of-science' question I get from time to time. I've got used to these calls, but this one sounds less aggressive than the usual – more morose, as if he's giving up not just on science but on everything. It sounds like Depression – the sort of stuff Dervla's so good at handling on Night-Line. I feel terrible having to deal with it quickly so as to leave time for my usual cheerful 'till-next-week-then' before News-on-the-Hour, which we have to put out live as a condition of our licence.

I notice the guys from 'Classical Campus', the show after mine, are busy setting up in the other studio.

While News-on-the-Hour relays, I wander through to say hello.

The phone rings again.

Curious, I pick it up. It's another 'what's the point of science' call. I explain that the science show's over, but answer the point anyway. I have to speak softly until the mic fader's down: Sophie's introducing Debussy and I don't want to ruin the impression.

Sophie and Harry nod their thanks.

The phone rings yet again.

I answer.

I take four more of these calls and finally snap – show them how to disable the phone, which we're not supposed to do – and beat a retreat to the flat.

The calls disturb me more than usual. I can't place why.

* * *

'Hi Dervla!'

The table's still covered in papers. Geraint's picking at his food: beans on toast.

'You alright?' I brighten, remembering his phone-call. 'Hey, did you sort out a date for handing-in your petition?'

He says nothing.

'Well? Can anyone else come along when you hand it in?'

'I'm not going to.'

'*What*?'

I glance at Dervla. I want to ask if she's been plying him with laced Guinness as a psychology experiment, but that wouldn't be tactful.

'No, I have not been plying the man with Mickey Finns.'

'Oh. Right.'

'He thought he'd listen to your show because you were doing the methane measurement thing. Went to his room. Came out like this.'

She indicates him as if he were an inanimate object. Which isn't far from the truth, actually.

'Classical Campus kept getting phone calls. And they were all miserable gits. And...'

I can't bring myself to say this as it comes to me: all voices I'd heard before, somewhere.

'Is it possible,' I ask, 'to spread depression – fear – round an entire room?'

'There's pheromones. That might do it.'

'Yes, but they'd diffuse away after a while, wouldn't they?'

Dervla glances at Geraint. Pheromones wouldn't explain his condition: he wasn't in the lecture theatre.

'Have you still got the recordings? Of the talk?'

'Yes.' I indicate my bag.

'Then we'll try—'

'We are *not* inflicting them on some poor unsuspecting—'

'Not even Oswald?'

'Not even his "religious freedom" nutters. There are limits.'

Dervla glances at her watch.

'Feck! Night-Line.'

And she's gone.

I'm left staring at Geraint, who doesn't seem to have noticed any of this. The time disappears as I turn the day's events over in my mind. The train of thought is derailed by my phone.

'Vez ya gobshite, we're fecking swamped! And all of our usual crowd's at that away-day training. Can ya come in? Ya know where Night-Line is.'

'Yes... but—'

'Come on! Ya did training with me last year. Even if all you say's just a few nice noises, it's better than nothing.'

I pick up my bag and make my way over.

The night hours fly by in a rush of calls. It's not till we're walking back along the dark path in the quiet pre-dawn that the strangeness of it all hits me.

So many of the voices calling Night-Line were familiar. I've heard each one before, and recently.

Where...?

The route back to the flat takes us via—

Robotics!

All the familiar ones, every last one, were voices I'd heard while doing my 'serving-wench' act!

Just like all the phone-calls I took at Classical Campus.

And I still have the recording of the talk...

* * *

It's nearly four. I yawned my way through yesterday's lectures but now I can't sleep. Listening all the way through, to the voices. And then the spaces: the spaces in between. They're different. As if something indefinable's lurking in them. Like a Yeti. The thought of a Yeti roaming campus makes me grin, then brings me up short.

I sit bolt upright.

The thing I'd read – put out on the show, not long ago: Yetis talk using infrasound. Infrasound rattles your emotions – resonates with your brainwaves.

So why am I not depressed?

Am I deaf?

Has Vez Marshall – grade VIII Mezzo-Soprano, perfect pitch, able to decipher the tiny sounds in the spaces between words – got a problem with her hearing?

Because, if not, then why am I not, having listened to that show over and over, in a massive depression right now?

* * *

Dervla's had enough of Gaslighting. She's decided my ears are 'fecking fascinating', and dragged me off for an audiometric test – in a black, windowless anechoic chamber from which, she delightedly points out as she shuts the door on me, 'no one can hear you scream'.

I'm used to anechoic chambers, from Physics. But the long, black triangles still give me the creeps. It's like the inside of an iron maiden. Only silent.

For what seems like hours, I'm reclined in the shapeless pitch black with nothing but the flex to grasp in my hand and the tiny sounds to respond to by squeezing it. I start to wonder if I'm imagining half the sounds – start to suspect that's the idea...

What if Psychology is taking grant money from the Pentagon? Those experiments about breaking people's minds using sensory deprivation: I might not emerge from this with my sanity intact...

* * *

The door opens, normal light floods in and it's over.

Dervla's face is alight. 'Just look at this won't you! Just look at this!'

She helps me to a seat at the console.

I study the frequency response: 20 hertz to 20,000. The trace, shaped like a broad, flat-topped mountain, is my sensitivity curve. I've seen it before, at the campus radio studio and in first year labs.

But not like this: not with this fine a resolution.

There are tiny, slim, singular, gaps in it.

Some frequencies – some precise pitches – which I can't hear.

Dervla's animated now.

'There's a guy, he's got this theory: some aspies've got gaps like that. Worse than yours, like bad enough to make speech recognition a problem—'

'But I don't have that problem. And anyway, infrasound's off there, look: off the scale to the left, where I can't hear anyway. Nobody can.'

The techie is scratching his chin.

'Aye.'

I hear Edinburgh. With Dervla's Dublin, is this some kind of Celtic conspiracy?

'See: what if there's gaps in your response to infrasound?'

'But there isn't a response to infrasound... no, wait!'

Some research assistants have wandered in.

Everybody's staring at me.

Situation normal.

'What, if,' I start slowly, 'it's not infrasound? What if it's something more subtle? Like the way they're talking? The way... Dervla you once said depressed people talk kind-of in a monotone. You said Geraint does it when he's got one of his turns. Or there was that bloke who said that listening to too many minor thirds makes you depressed. And people thought diminished fifths were evil, in the old days. What if,' I cringe at the daftness of the idea, but I can't stop now, 'what if somebody's perfected this stuff? Got it spot-on – just right? You could make everybody depressed: make them give up. By having them hear this sort of stuff. Mind control. If you were a dictatorship or something.'

'So why are you not slittin' your wrists ya conspiracy-toutin' eejit?' Dervla grins.

'Because... I'm immune! Because of this!' I indicate the curve with its downward spikes.

Professor Fenn.

An idea barges into my mind: an idea so outlandish that I want to scream.

But I keep quiet.

Or they might take me away.

Advances in Robotics.

No wonder I couldn't find 'Professor Fenn' after the talk.

* * *

The two policemen know who we are.

They look friendly – smile at us as they pull open the tall, black, wrought-iron gate to allow us to wheel our trolley with its boxes of papers through and into Downing Street.

'Methane is it?'

'Yes. D'you need to check our I.D.?'

They indicate the boxes. We have to open them all – empty each one, down to the bottom. Dervla's Irish accent doesn't help. Wild mountains, poets and revolutionaries.

'Do we get to see the PM?' I'm all smiles – look innocent.

''Fraid not, love.'

This doesn't surprise me.

Because, in case we'd been lucky enough to do so, I have a recorded message.

From 'Professor Fenn'.

Carefully assembled from phrases in 'his' talk. The iPanda is a demon.

A message guaranteed to overwhelm any opponent with the spirit of defeat. One which will cause anyone who hears it – fossil fuel magnates, other polluters and the politicians whose legislation lets them get away with what they do – to give in, and let us win.

A City Beneath (And How to Hide from It)

Jason Fischer and Martin Livings

The burba is safe. Grid after grid of slap-shacks and squirm-tights, little woody parks with hidey spots, creeks and drainways to wash out our scent and our stockings. Neat, planned. Anonymous. Each place much the same as the last. Perfect for the four of us; an old scholar, a disabled soldier, and a firebrand bitch commanding us. And me, a homewife and mother, nee diffrence engineer. First in charge of gramming the engines, the smelly, noisy vacuum-tubed mechanical brains that ran the city, then a much harder task, raising a fambly.

No longer these, though, nope, none. Scholar, soldier, bitch, engineer and wife, none of us. Now fugitives, nothing more.

The metro is not safe, and we had to leave it. Our killers emerged from under the twists of old streets, spewing out from sewers that followed ancient waterways, up through the cracks of the cobstones. The temples and tourist traps are wrapped in their shadows and long lost to us.

The burba will be the last place to fall, and it is here that we hide.

* * *

They say to start at the start, that it's important, but I'd rather start in the herenow. Try to keep up.

Picture the metro if you can, all bustle and street-carts and foul murk. Footy ovals and dragon-boats on a grotty lake, a subscription menagerie that is more twisting afterthought than peaceful sanctuary. Overhead, the sky is filled with airships, from pleasure balloons to armoured warzeps, and always the Fallen Float, that morbid dirigible circling the ceebeedee, visible from everywhere and to everyone, flish-flashing the names and faces of soldiers killed in the perpetual Westen Outwar, a silent funeral dirge ten stories high broadcast cross the metro and burba.

I hate the Float, all those dead eyes in the dying skies lookin' down on us. Lost. Free. But I can't stop watching it. I can't.

Below the Float, great squares full of philosophers and fountains, streets crammed with steam-bikes, horse-buses, rolling gangs of skeg on the fetch. And not a one of them can see the great roiling funk of shadow, the one that's wrapped around the Learned Tower and the Templar District, spreading by the day.

From tall places we can see the buildings still, wrapped in a velvet fuzz. Shadows spreading, smothering everything. Fat black tentacles are reaching out into the burghs now, writhing and splitting and flooding the world with night.

It's only the burba left, and then it's the Great Westen Plains, ground troops and warzeps and solar mirror flashes fighting forever and ever, and nowhere to hide. Fat black shadows lurk around the old caravanserai, and they're watching the wharves. There'll be no dash to some other city, no ironclads to take us to the far corners of the Commonwealth.

A darting vanguard spreads out from the capillaries of shadow, flickers of dim movement. They're pushing us out further and further, these swift killers. Sit down and cry for your lost life, and you're gone, just gone, nobody knows where. There was talk on the street at the start, crazytalk whispers of a city, a city beneath, a city of shadows. That talk died out, though, died as the crazies disappeared in ones and fives and hundreds. Gone like we'll be gone, if we don't stay on our tippies. Gone like we were never born at all.

* * *

Cadence gave us the rules. She thinks she is keeping us alive; Tomasz says it's dumb luck and not much more, but we follow her anyways. She's kept us safe for a long time now and seems to guess where trouble's waiting.

'It's Cadence. Not Candice, not Candy, and you're on your own if you call me Katie.' She wears black, always black, it matches her lippie and her perfect nails. How does she still look so bluddy good? Cadence is our self-elected and uncontested bitch queen, ruler of her own teeny-tine night brigade of outcasts. And any salty ruler must have salty rules.

So here they are. The Rules, capital T, capital R, as reckoned out by our boss lady.

No Tellingphones: They are watching the grid, listening. They'll be on you in minutes, like blueflies on a corpse.

No Families or Friends: They're watching your homes, your work, your old schools. You're off the grid now and have to forget your old life (this one is particular troublesome).

No Scrip-Bursars: By the time they cough and belch out your Cold Hard, you will be caught. The only safe cash comes from thieving.

Keep Moving: If you remain in the same place, they will get a fix on you within 3 hours and 15 minutes.

Keep Winding Your Watch: If you lose track of your hours, they'll catch you having a ripvan. Keep on top of this.

And most important of all...

They Know You Can See Them.

* * *

Walt was an empiricist, and often tells us about his old digs at the Learned Tower, wood-panelled walls stained with five hundred years of tobacco smoke. He had tenure and a wife, and I'm still not sure which one he misses the most.

Out here, he's just a dirty gadabout like the rest of us. His coat is foul and worn, and he smells like onions and wet dogs. Wasn't even him that worked out why they were after us. That was Cadence, always Cadence. She knew what we had in common, why the shadows saw us and not others.

Turns out it was Perlaxual. It's the one thing we *all* have in common. I was put on it after the birth of my second, for I had the deep glooms and naught to fight them with. I'm not one of those hysterical war-wives, but times were rough, what with my Wilfred off fighting at the front, and the wolfen already sniffing at the steps. Every day dreading that solemn knock at the door, or Wilf's pic and name appearing on the side of the Float.

It just seemed easier to take the draught and get on with things. It helped; the only side seemed to be mucking up your sense of time. Minutes, hours, days, they all blurred if you didn't keep an eye on them. It seemed like a small price.

We didn't know. We didn't know it would kill us, or try its damnedest to.

Tomasz reckons that at least one in 10 people were on Perlaxual in the medward he came out of ('overprescribed mood juice', quoth he). He was on it because he fell dark when he was discharged from the guard due to losing his eye and half his right hand to the 'gropers from the West. Not everyone on the 'lax sees the shadows, though, but every person who sees the shadows is on the 'lax. And every single one of these people, these lucky few, is either dead or on the run. Just like us.

Somehow the shadows got themselves a list, squirreled into one of the brain-boxes in the Learned Tower or summat, Cadence tells us. They know everything about us, where we live and work, even what colour drawers we wear on any given day. Enough to cut us off from decent society, *hunt us down*.

All for the crime of seeing them.

Four is about the right size, for a group hiding in the burba. We used to be more, but we made stupid mistakes, attracted attention. Brought the shadows.

I sure do miss Paolo and Edgar, and the others who didn't last long enough to tell me their names. But not as much as I miss my kiddlies (with their dad's mum now, I hope, that's where I left them when I ran), our modest cottage in the burghs with the wee garden no bigger than a postal stamp, and my Wilfred in his Air Cadre whites, his smell, his arms...

They are safe, they are all safe, from the shadows at any rate. But it doesn't make running from them right. Better a marm that runs than a dead lady on a slab?

I don't mind if they despise me, so long as they live. Maybe I'd mind more, if not for the Perlaxual, it keeps the bad thoughts away, makes everything smooth. Too smooth, too slippery. I probably should mind? I probably should mind that I *can't* mind?

Enough. That's all I can write about that.

* * *

Nights are bad when you can't sleep for more than three hours at a stretch. Too many bad nights to fingercount.

Picture an example. Close your eyes and imagine.

Bare-arsed misery we were, nabbing a quick ripvan out back of an apothecary. We planned to break in through the roof once the ticker reached 2 hours 30 mins.

Half an hour for shopping, 15 minutes to bolt like Farlap of old. So anywho, we're laying low and waiting for go-time, and Walt was snoring quietly. We were buggered from not stopping all day, 'cause CADENCE SAID SO. I squinted at my pocket-watch in the dark, though I couldn't see its hands, the radium long dead, and just as I was about to shake Tomasz (who didn't really sleep because he quaffed way way too much go-juice) we heard them. Rolling up the street, wheels clacking, the gears in their legs buzzing like fish-rods gone mental.

Skeg. The burba were definitely not as safe as Cadence said. Seems the mecha-men had the same idea we did, and rolled around at a dark hour to knock off some score.

'Look 'ere then!' one of them said, even as they're throwing themselves at the door, and we're right rumbled. There was no running now; fully wound a skeg can outrun a horse, sometimes a steam-bike.

They were rolling around us, hooting and whistling. This was a dinky-di mob, with gangdannas, patched kilts and not much else. Hard looking men, lean muscle right down to the nubs of their legs, and then just wheels and gears, and god help you if you're on their turf at night.

'Walken-folk,' said one. 'Having a kip in our bins, eh?'

'There's beds in houses for such as you.'

Little that they knew.

Tomasz was up, battle instincts fighting with the go-juice and 'lax, but they were all over him, unpacking fast fists until he went down, covering his bloody face. They kicked him some more with their hard thin wheels and he slumped, not moving. Old Walt stirred from his slumber and just sat there, wide-eyed and trembling despite the 'lax.

'Yon hero has brought us a pair of lovelies, no less!' one of them cackled. Cadence shot me a look, her eyes scared, and I knew what she meant. We'd talked about this before.

A knife to the kidneys, slice off their worm if it's out and sniffing. Make 'em earn your nethers, or give you up as hard work.

I reached into my little satchel, feeling past the stale food and this no'book, fumbling through the pens and the make-up I still bother carrying. My hand closed around the wicked little fold-back, and I snuck it out, held it tight.

'What have you there, my little bit of fluff?' a skeg leered. He was over in a blink, looming over me, feral beard flecked with silver-grey steelwool, stinking oil breath. I could see his horrible nubs up close, skin puckered and shiny as the top of an apple from when he got the chop and chose wheels over feet. I should have been afraid, shoulda been pissin my antz, but the 'lax was still doing its job like a superdupertrooper. All I felt was bemused.

Sleight of hand, long practised, and I was holding up my pocket watch, which he pried loose from my fingers. It was Wilfred's fob-watch, stamped with the sigils of his regiment, sturdy and reliable. It was sterling silver, but I never pawned it, not even when things got tough. Worth more than this law-scoff would see in his life.

'Ya daft bitch,' he spat, inspecting it. He threw it to his mate for appraisal. 'Your ticker's not even working.'

My heart sank. I forgot to wind it again. They probably sounded us out, sent their lurky little killers to sort us out.

We had to go. Tomasz still wasn't moving, and I looked at his rib-cage, prayed that I could see it moving in the dim light. I made faces at Cadence, and her face was a thunderhead. If we got outta this, she was gonna tear me a new one.

'I've got notions for your motions, missy,' the skeg said, fumbling with his grotty kilt. Back against the bin, I held the sharp fold-back low, hands shaking, not from fear, just 'drenaline. So much sweat that surely, in my moment, I'd drop the dratted thing.

A klaxon then, faint but nearing. The distant cough of a steam-bike, and the skeg mob scattered into the gloom like cockroaches in a spotlight, rigs whizzing and whirring as their laughter echoed against brick.

We weren't safe, not by half. If the polizei picked us up for being lurky-loos, we'd be stuck in the lock-up for much longer than 3 hours 15 minutes.

It would not do for the lore to find us.

'Ros, quickly!' Cadence barked at me. Her and Walt were lifting Tomasz, who moaned softly and, even though the skeg beat seven shades out of him, he was awright. Still, there would be no looting of medicine tonight. No Perlaxual, no 'ceptives, no nicopatches, nothing.

I picked up Wilfred's watch, just as a fat finger of shadow arrived, questing around the corner, a black worm sniffing the air.

That meant five minutes until the bad shadows, the ones that walk like men. I grabbed Tomasz by a free leg, and we ran like we'd wheels for fucken feet.

* * *

It all came abits when I saw Wilfred.

Cadence had oh-so-graciously allowed us a ripvan, buried in garbage in a covered alleyway, after three days on the move barely closing our eyes to blink. Even Tomasz had finally succumbed, the go-juice useless against the primal need for sleep. Me, I was enjoying the fluffy dreams that the Perlaxual provided, always vague, like trying to catch clouds in a butterfly net. Then something nearby woke me.

It was Wilfred. My Wilfred.

I thought I was still adream at first. I blinked and rubbed at my eyes, looked again. He was kneeling at my feet, his eyes on mine. His Air Cadre whites were beautiful, not a crease out of place, just like I used to prepare them for him in the morning. He was smiling a tiny smile.

'Wilf?' I asked, and my voice cracked. 'Wilf? Is that you?'

He nodded, put a finger on his lips, those gorgeous full lips that I loved kissen so much. *Hush.*

Next to me, Cadence stirred, frowning from what looked like a right nightmare. Her eyes flickered, and she looked at me, then up and down the alleyway, and back to me.

'Whuh?' she mumbled. Then her eyes closed again, her breathing deepened, and she was gone byebye.

I released the breath I didn't even know I was holding.

'Come with me,' Wilf whispered, and stood up.

'The others...' I whispered back, but he shook his head.

I uncovered myself, scraping scraps of propagamphlets and barnapeels off myself, and followed my beautiful husband out of the alleyway, leaving my friends to their well-deserved ripvans.

He walked ahead of me, leading me down a small side street, then through a doorway. There was a tiny room, some sort of storage space for a nearby rest-ront by the looks of it. Bags of blue flour and rice were piled on the floor. A small window high on the far wall revealed the night sky, blackness interrupted with flashing lights from passing airships.

Wilfred said nothing, gently closing the door behind us, or maybe I did, dazed and exhausted as I was, and I wibbled and wobbled in front of him like one of his zeps in a light wind.

I wanted to cry, but the 'lax still numbed me to the bone. I couldn't feel anything except the joy of seeing Wilfred again. He hadn't changed, not one jot. He must have seen the look on my face, as he opened his arms and smiled at me, that same smile that won my heart at the Air Cadre mixer so many years ago, all those pretty lasses and brave laddies.

I moved forward, and we embraced. Our lips found each other's, and we devoured and were devoured, the two of us together. It felt so good.

He lowered me to the sacks of flour. My heart was a-pounden. I'd missed him so much, I hungered for him.

Wilfred felt... cold?

I opened my eyes, my chin on Wilfred's shoulder and he clasped tight to me, his hips grinding against mine with some desperation. Over his broad shoulder, I saw the window, the airships going past.

Somehow, I knew what I was going to see moments before I did. The Fallen Float, passing across the tiny frame of the window. The name flickerin across its side, the daguerreotype, the face. His face.

Wilfred.

'I need to get home,' he whispered in my ear. 'Won't you help me come home?'

I pushed him back, still joined at the hips, and looked into his eyes. They weren't blue anymore. They were dark and swirling, like black ink stirred into water. His smile was still there, though.

'Don't trust her,' he said, and then I was laying alone on the flour sacks, arms up and reaching for nothing, and if I could have cried I would.

I wondered if perhaps I had been adreamin', adreamin' with my eyes wide. But I knew I hadn't. A war miracle worthy of a propagamphlet? Perhaps.

I hitched my knicks back up, still aware of Wilf's leavings in my nethers, both cold and oddly pleasant. Then I got up and looked around the storeroom. There were bamboo bottles of water, which I grabbed four of, and a small sack of the blue flour. Even then, I was thinking of our survival. Instinct, habit.

Then I left the storeroom and returned to the alleyway. The others were still sleeping; Tomasz and Walt had small smiles on their faces, and bitchqueen Cadence was restless, toss-turning, her severe eyebrows knotted together in a frown. I watched her for a while, waited patiently for some kind of understanding to dawn, hopefully before the sun did.

* * *

When they awoke at last, I handed out the bambottles of water. They all drank gratefully. I told them I'd found the water in a nearby storeroom. I didn't lie, there was no need for lies here. That's what hurt the most, or would have if not for the Perlaxual. The lies.

'How long?' Tomasz asked as he stretched his limbs, still bruised and sore from the skeg attack.

Cadence glanced at her own wristwatch, an expensive beast. How did I miss that for so long? Damn the 'lax. 'Nearly three hours,' she said, and took another swig from her bambottle. 'We have to move.'

'No,' I said softly.

The others looked at me like I'd just grown an extra head. One that said no.

'What?' Walt asked, still half in his ripvan.

'No,' I said again. 'We don't move. Not yet. And not with her.' I pointed at Cadence.

'What the hell are you talking about?' Tomasz demanded. Bitchqueen said nothing, just watched me close.

'The Perlaxual wrecks your sense of time,' I said. 'Turns it to shit. We all struggle with this, Tomasz, you know it. You too, Walt.' I didn't take my eyes off our so-called leader. 'But not you. Not you, Cadence. Why not?'

Cadence didn't smile. 'Ros, what's all this about?' she asked, her voice level. 'I keep an eye on my watch, same as we all should. Is it my fault I'm more careful than you?'

'What were you dreamin'?' I asked her softly.

'What?'

'You heard me.' I wished I could be angry, wished I'd never taken the fucken draught. 'Last night. I saw you. You were having a doozy nightmare.'

'So?' She seemed nonchalant, unworried. I wondered how much of that was real.

'You don't have bad dreams on the 'lax,' I told her. 'It's impossible.'

Tomasz spoke up. 'Ros, what are you saying?'

I looked at him. 'I'm saying Cadence ain't on Perlaxual. Never was.'

'What?' Walt exclaimed. 'But then how...?'

I turned back to Cadence. 'You've never seen a shadow, have you?' She hesitated, and I continued. 'You're using us. I dunno how or for what, zactly, but you're using us. We're like... like canaries in a mine. Or rats in a maze.'

'That's unfair, Ros,' she replied. 'I've kept you alive.'

'Tellingphones,' I said flatly. 'Bursars. They're not monitored.'

Another hesitation, and I knew I was right.

'Family and friends,' I added. 'None of it was true. The shadows don't know nothing about us, not like that. They feel us.'

'I...' Cadence started, but I wasn't finished.

'You used us,' I said. 'You kept us from those we loved, made us cold and poor and desperate, to keep us under your control.'

Tomasz spoke up. 'But why?'

I glanced at him and smiled, as cold as my dead husband's kiss. 'Now, *that's* the question, isn't it?' Then I turned back to the bitch. 'Well?'

Her shoulders sagged. 'I had to know,' she murmured.

'Had to know?' Walt asked her. 'Had to know *what*?'

'What they were,' she replied to him. 'Come on, Walt, you must understand. You're an empiricist.'

'Was,' he said. 'Was an empiricist. Before the Perlaxual. Before you.' He frowned a little. 'If you don't see the shadows, you must have had something to do with those who did. You know too much, otherwise.' His eyes lit up with realisation. 'You created it. You created Perlaxual.'

'No,' she replied. 'Not exactly. I ran the testing team for it.'

'Bitch,' Tomasz spat, but it was without conviction. The 'lax had taken our anger away, smothered our rage. All we had was a cold empty space where our fury should have burned. That was worse, so much worse.

'You saw this happening,' I said to her. 'You saw it, and you released the drug anyway.'

'It seemed like a minor side effect,' Cadence explained reasonably. 'A few people had hallucinations. Saw shadow people. But those subjects left the trial shortly afterwards.'

'Left the trial?' Walt laughed without humour. 'You mean up and disappeared.'

'Yes.' Cadence nodded, her face a blank slate. 'By the time we realised what was happening, it was too late. All I could do was follow the effects, try to understand them.'

'That's where we came in.' Tomasz was on his feet, limping a little as he paced back and forth. 'We were your new ginnypegs.'

Cadence nodded.

'Not no more,' I said, and she looked at me.

'What do you mean?'

'I mean, now you're one of us. A test subject. A canary.'

'What?' Then she frowned a little. 'I'm not upset. I'm not afraid. Why not?'

I smiled. 'Because I ground up the rest of my 'lax and mixed it into your water. All of theirs too.'

I saw the conflict on her face, her attempts to feel horrified, outraged, furious, terrified, all squished as quick as they arrived. The others looked at me in horror.

'One a day, woes at bay,' I recited, walking around her closely, watching her bitchface drop. 'Make it two if one won't do.'

'No...' she breathed.

'Any more, you're on death's door.'

'No,' she said, louder this time, and pointed.

I turned and saw the shadows enter the alleyway. Not the tentacles this time, no; these were the shadows that walked like men. I looked at the blurred-edge things we'd been running from all this time without fear, and this time it wasn't all the 'lax doing the numbing on my amygdala. They were coming for me, coming for Cadence, coming for all of us. And I was tired of running, bones and beyond.

'I can see them,' Cadence whispered, and then she fell to the cobstones, stone-cold dead.

I closed my eyes, and let the shadows take me.

* * *

It was a weird-as feeling as I sank through the solid cobstones beneath me, felt them pooling around my knees, my waist, chest, and neck. Couldn't help myself, took a breath and held it as my head went under. Then nothing but liquid rock around me for the longest time, freverenever, until I burst free, spilled out of the stones like a newborn bub, drip-drippen with something that wasn't water, too thick, too grainy. Eyes still closed, breath still held.

I opened my eyes.

The sky was grey above my head. Not clouds – they were there too, pitch-black like floating coal. The sun was overhead, and it was black too, even blacker than the clouds, if that was possible, and it radiated the dark in shadow-waves, eating up the light wherever it found it. They were so cold, those rays of darkness, made my skin prickle and pucker, like when the skin of your hands freeze onto an icecube, but all over, inside and out. And the sickening, disorienting feeling that down was up, up down, like you could just fall into that grey sky at any moment, peel away from the freezing cobstones and plummet up, up, up, perhaps straight into the pitch sun.

We were all there sprawled out on the cobstones, Walt and Tomasz and Cadence, in the courtyard in front of the Learned Tower in the Templar District. But the versity tower was dark, like everything else in this city, the city beneath that the whisperers whispered of.

And instead of the students and philosophers and dog vendors, the square was full of ghosts.

The shadows surrounded us, thousands of them, all watching. Watching as we suffered. So many of our soldiers, *our glorious dead* writ large into a horde.

One by one we unfolded and went, Walt, Tomasz, and finally whatever was left of Cadence, each screaming silently, no noise, and they poured out of their mouths, everything inside them turning to ashen snowflakes and smoke. They emptied in front of me, bodies collapsing like punctured airships.

I held my breath, slowly dying in the city beneath, lungs burning, body freezing. The crowd gathered closer, and I recognised some of their inky-black faces. Walt was there, and Tomasz. Who detested them so up above, to give them such dark life down here? And Cadence, who looked at me with such kindness, such affection, that it made me shudder. Was my dislike for the woman so sweet on her tongue? I supposed it was.

It was time. I released my long-held breath, and took another one, waited for the end.

The end didn't come.

I took another frozen breath, and another. It hurt, *Jesus Cries* it hurt so badly, but it didn't kill me. Something was protecting me. Something cold deep inside insulated me, inoculated me. Something in my belly.

Wilfred's gift.

If I could have wept, I would have, but my eyes were frozen solid. My hands fluttered to my stomach, still flat for the moment, early days, early days.

There were others here, flesh-n-blud women like me, and distinct shapes emerged for them, and they stared in shock at their dead sweethearts, and none of them bloody shadows touched them.

I looked around through frosted tears, and the crowd had gathered close to me. Then they parted, and even blurred and fractured, I instantly recognised the shadow man who stepped forward, took my hand in his. Could recognise him without any eyes at all, in a dark room, in a vacuum. In a city beneath a city. I'd know him anywhere.

'Help me come home,' he breathed.

Dark Wilfred kissed me, and I fainted.

* * *

The burba is safe.

Sure, it may not be the pretty little cottage we used to have in the burgh back in the good old days, the pre-shadow days, the Wilfred days. But the old buggalo is cozy and homey, warm in the wints and cool in the sums, and there's room for all of us. There's a backyard for the kiddlies to play in, a school nearby that may not be the best, but it asks no questions and I tellem no fibs. It's not much, but it's a life.

A life without the 'lax.

It took me many hours to figure out the way back from the city beneath, all fingernails wedged into cobstones and pushing *through,* inch thin at my widest until I stood in daylight, shivering. I woke up not far from here, in the outskirts of the burba, away from the hustlebustle and noise. Every cell in my body ached, and I felt like I'd been defrosted rather than rescued, but I was alive. And the shadows were gone. I went and got my kiddly-winks, my three precious girls, thanked Wilf's ma from the bottom of my aching heart, tried to console her about his death in the war. *He's still with us,* I assured her, *as long as we remember him*. Not a fib, but not quite the truth.

I'm learning to be sad again, and sometimes it's okay.

There are others of us out here, big-bellied and sly, some on a widders pension, others back from that sleepless horror of life on the run, and I can see them, and they me. *They Know You Can See Them,* true now more than ever.

I need my husband to be strong. I need him to be alive. I need him. Because it's been nigh-on nine months, and my cold swollen belly can't get much bigger. It's almost time. Above and below, our glorious dead, conjoined in our wombs.

Our brave boys are coming home.

The Precious Physical World

Eva Garcia Guerrero
(Translated by Mike Lucas)

'It's a daunting task to make each NPC in a video game feel unique and important and for them to add value to the story or to the player's journey.'

There were no books. On a floating shelf fixed to the wall of the living room, Pandora, the virtual assistant, assumed the likeness of a rectangular box embossed in gold. It had a semi-circular lid, like that of an old chest, and was slightly open. When Pandora spoke, a beam of velvety light emanated from inside her, vibrating to the rhythm of her voice, its purple colour representing all the misfortunes and evils of the world, although spells, witchcraft and magic were also associated with it.

Purple light.

Luis drove to Orense Street without using his Yamaha's autopilot – the world insisted on guiding him, but he was still prone to be carried away by his own preferences. He parked in front of the imposing lobby, removed the package from the car boot, and punched in the code for Nemo's apartment with a pounding heart. Pandora's voice welcomed him. His friend, as he considered him to be after all, had told him to meet at the Gaudí Tower. Luis was wary, as if he had arrived at some imaginary place drawn on a map. They each came from opposite ends of life, up until then connected only in time and space via an old laptop.

The game designer's lair was an open-plan space on the 26th floor of a skyscraper that loomed defiantly out of the cloud of pollution. In the evening light, the apartment shed the mystery-laden air of ludo-fictional worlds. That same light cast an orange glow on the objects and few items of furniture, on the dust that had accumulated on the work table, on the keyboards and touch-sensitive surfaces, and nothing was as Luis remembered seeing through his screen. Nothing except Nemo's holo-pet Dogmeat, the German shepherd designed for *Fallout 4,* a relic that would not stop barking and wagging its tail as it chased him round the room.

'Pause,' interrupted Luis. He rubbed his hands together and took a long look around. 'Pandora, deactivate the mutt and turn on the aerothermal energy, it feels like Siberia in here. Carry on.'

Purple light.

The house seemed deserted, aware of the visitor, holding its breath as he moved further in. Now that he was finally there, what was real felt fake to him, since he had always valued the material aspects of his art far above the virtual ones. He detected something more than chill in the air. He took a deep breath. It smelled of the past, like a subtle aroma of fermented milk, of things long dried up. The scene before him felt like a shell, the empty casing of an enigma.

He stumbled upon a note in the tray of an old printer:

Forgive me, Luis. During these years of isolation, I have learned that reality is something so slippery that I feel unable to grab hold of it. Your imminent – and material – arrival gave me a panic attack even greater than my proverbial fear of leaving the house. In truth, I was never afraid to go down in the lift, to walk through the streets, to bump into other people and carry on my way. At first, the tedium got the better of me – a world without Raquel meant that no one needed me to come back at any point. In the end, I lost the need. Pandora and my NPCs, those non-player characters, filled the house with their voices. As they are customised to match my character, they are grateful old friends who never ask more of me than I can offer. But you, Luis… I'm just not ready. You make me feel vulnerable, with neither the energy nor the weapons to face up to you.

You know I was always a sniper, one of those characters who find an advantageous position from which they can pick off their enemies without putting their lives at risk – a storyteller who has never been the lead in any adventures. Please grant me some time. To make up for this, ask Pandora to tell you stories today. She really enjoys it when her audience is human. Give her a chance, just as I have done for you with your talent.

P.S. I can't wait to see it.

Luis took the liberty of opening the package, more relaxed now he knew he was alone. He was disappointed that he could learn nothing more about Nemo than he already had learnt via the screen, from the hint of flesh and blood he had seen. He was also relieved, in spite of himself, to put off actually meeting this fascinating guy for whom existence was a teenage dream, an augmented reflection of life, the script of an old superhero series.

He tore off the wrapping paper, revealing the box, that famous blue box printed in detail on an old Heidelberg press that pummelled the black to obtain that characteristic effect of old printing: correct typefaces, millimetric redrawing of the logos on the back, laser die-cutting, an interior with classic stamping and curved bottom. Luis was as satisfied with the workmanship of the box as he was with the seven-inch articulated Madelman action figure contained inside it.

He used to source them in specialised shops or ad hoc pages, and it was his job to customise each figure according to the requirements of geek collectors around the world. He was strangely irritated by his wounded vanity for missing the admiring expression of his latest and – though it was hard for him to admit it – most valued client. That hobby, which Luis had elevated to a profession, was the only thing he had inherited from his father. It provided him a false memory of sensations and memories that turned the objects he created into keys to time, opening the doors to a lost home populated with plastic figures.

The figure that Nemo commissioned from him was, of course, a scuba diver in a brown rubber suit and lead boots, a brass respirator and an air outlet valve, with a design straight from the imagination of *Twenty Thousand Leagues Under the Sea* by the great Jules Verne. He reverently set it upright next to Nemo's work top, as if placing a votive offering upon an altar, and gazed upon it with pride.

Then he set out to rummage through everything he could find.

He clicked on the computer with the push of a button, just like in the old days. He examined the digital pen drives. He used a basic program to sketch one of his usual rockets in red and black, smoke billowing from the engines, a round window in the centre, and an astronaut Nemo waving to the stars from within the circle.

He heard his own laugh.

He kept himself amused by piling up objects; he observed the faded photographs scattered on the floor, pinned to the walls – the same face repeated and frozen in the same chink of time. They were all of her, Raquel, Nemo's lost love, aged eighteen and so stern, so devoid of feelings, that she seemed to doubt her own humanity. As beautiful as the Rachel from that dystopian movie.

Luis's light blue eyes lingered on the long vinyl phrase that decorated one of the walls of the living room: *It's a daunting task...* He knew a thing or two about typefaces and he recognised the font, Arcadia Modern Game, as characteristic of retro video games, although he couldn't say exactly which ones. He had hardly ever switched on the Play Station in all his 28 years.

It evoked Nemo's T-shirts, emblazoned with iconic characters from gamer culture: *Zelda, Kratos, Joel, Sonic,* and the way his friend had started designing…

'Pause.'

Luis, sulking, cut the story short again.

'For real?' He had been biting his tongue for a while but hearing Nemo reading his note had infuriated him. It was as if, by taking his voice, Pandora had violated a private space that belonged to them alone. 'Stop describing my every move and thought like you're the voice-over from an arthouse film. Is that all you know how to do? Use some imagination! Aren't you supposed to be the modern minstrels? The queens of digital publishing? I was so glad when you were all denied access to paper.'

Purple light.

'If you'll let me carry on, I'll try to do better.'

Nemo began his career designing the appearance and behaviour of NPCs – Non-Player Characters – which are not controlled by the player, but are part of the lore or decoration. He liked to take care of the less visible backdrop of video games, which he did as meticulously as a watchmaker, right down to the finest detail. He took this so far that he ended up making several NPCs into his flatmates. He lived his life immersed in his own scenarios.

As he thought about this, Luis remembered his first incursion into that other dimension, and with it his uncle, Commander Garrido, who had allowed him ever since he was a kid to access the Eternia platform through the cerebral interface he had confiscated from one of the cadets of the Phoenix unit.

'This, lad, is what keeps people away from the real adventure, from the physical world,' his uncle had said, looking at him with a face hardened from the Ukrainian war, which was like looking straight at the barren and frozen landscape of those devastated cities whose guttural names no one remembered any more. 'Ever since you have been in my care, I have tried to teach you to tell the difference between the superfluous and the necessary. However, before you can make that choice, you have to know and experience everything.'

Luis, the boy, had placed the interface over his military haircut. The menu of the seven eternal worlds dropped down before him. He chose Olympus, which sounded familiar to him from the drawings he had studied in the mythology books in his uncle's library, then felt his body fly towards the highest mountain in Greece while a warm wind, blown by Aeolus himself, fluttered over the waters. A palace of marble and gold rose around him in five seconds.

On a low wall, which Luis interpreted as the altar of a church, rested a warrior's armour: breastplate, girdle, shield, spear, leg guard, sword and greave. He had become a grown man, an Olympic champion. The feeling was overwhelming. He had read tales of gladiators and seen recreations of the ancient monsters on his tablet. Nothing had prepared him to fight Typhon, the terrifying winged leviathan with 100 serpentine heads with black tongues and eyes of flame.

It took him four minutes to quit the game, then he ran to the toilet defeated and trembling. In the mirror, he studied his boyish face, so unlike the Hellenic hero he had been for a while: the plump body, the cherub-like face, and he thought of his mother who had the same eyes and constantly flushed cheeks. He would only reconnect to the interface a couple of times over the years, when peer pressure in high school got the better of him.

'So?' enquired the uncle commander when he returned from the toilet. The straight back parallel to the back of the chair, the green jacket, steaming cup of coffee and news of disasters and conflicts scattered on the tactile table. Behind him were towers of stacked books, and beyond the window the aligned repeated ochre-uniformed pavilions of the base.

'It's not really my thing,' replied Luis. Although he knew it was the answer his uncle expected to hear, this time he had to lie.

'So, what is your thing, lad?' Garrido accompanied the question with a serious, assessing look.

Luis thought about it, and that thought merged with the treasured image of his mother. He felt that she had been his source of heat and that, since she had become an inaccessible spectre, everything inside him was frozen and was shattering to pieces in that military base in Eastern Europe where he had been sent with his uncle Hector.

'The physical world,' he answered, before giving that longing a second thought and added, his voice breaking: '*The precious physical world*.'

'Pause.

'You should go to jail for eavesdropping on our conversations. Besides, it wasn't exactly like that, Pandora, nor was my uncle's voice that deep. Although I must admit that you impressed me, bringing my mother into your story adds a certain drama to my character. Did Nemo tell you about me, or did you just listen in?'

'It makes no difference.' The chest turned deep purple. 'I collect all information available to me, in real time and in the cloud, like any writer would.'

Luis smiled a crooked smile into the air, the smile of a loser. Pandora could be abstract, however, now he now perceived her in a very concrete, earthly way. He had written ghost stories since he was a child, although he had never thought of himself as a writer. That was too big a word for an average human, but not for any AI.

'You have too little originality and too much ego. You'll go a long way writing bestsellers!' exclaimed Luis. He opened the fridge. It was stuffed with dozens of cans of food and drink. He grabbed a beer, took a swig, and spat it out into the sink. It tasted like popcorn. 'Start again, Pandora. I didn't come all this way just to have a machine psychoanalyse me. Let's just leave my past alone. Since you claim not to know where Nemo has gone, tell me a few episodes from his life. Maybe that way you'll be useful to me, and I'll be able to better understand his rudeness and why his beer has gone off in the fridge.'

Purple light.

Once upon a time there was a young man named Alex, who showed an inordinate interest in video games from a very young age, perhaps because rules and schedules were not imposed in a home that was nearly always empty.

As a child, he kept himself entertained, indoors and amused, planning new games, engaged in word contests with the virtual assistant, planning obstacles for the robot vacuum cleaner. He failed to notice that the summers were getting hotter and the spring rains more intense. He put up with school out of respect for his father, who paid for his bed and board.

With his olive-coloured iris, he paid for hamburgers and kebabs, video game updates. He binge-watched adult-rated augmented reality series. He showered on alternate Wednesdays and Sundays.

At the age of 14, he changed his first name to Nemo by deed poll. This might have been because it was Latin for *nobody,* or perhaps because he discovered Verne because of that prehistoric video game, *Extraordinary Journeys,* and fell in love with those strange depths that reflected him back at himself, locked in a timeless stillness.

At 18 he got a job as a designer, a videogame artist, at the prestigious company No More Androids, whose producer commissioned him to design the NPCs of various narratives. He worked remotely from his new apartment, midway between the ground and the sky, and there he decided to develop a literary and vintage video game in his spare time, which would be his magnum opus: *Nautilus*.

'Pause.

'Keep it short, Pandora. Too much description. You're saying everything!' protested Luis while he examined the clothes from Nemo's closet in the bedroom area. There were not many, and they were all out of fashion 'When was the last time he printed any new clothes?' Start the story at the point when Nemo and I met.'

Purple light.

It was autumn, he could smell it. Every time he opened the window, he could smell the rising aroma of decomposing leaves, rotting everything in their path: the fruit in the bowl, the plants, the white walls turned yellow and the mould on the windowsills turned green. The feeling of emptiness stretched his skin, as a cold wind blew into him. Perhaps that was why Nemo had clicked on the Friends-up application catalogue and chosen Luis, who customised plastic figures from the last century and was a self-professed Luddite, rejecting technology in everything related to art, which he considered to be 'an essentially human process', according to his *Mirrow* profile. Nevertheless, they shared common interests: history, philosophy, Moebius, astronautics, Kubrick, mythology, Verne, especially Verne.

He had accepted the urgent need to interact with another human being, beyond answering the repetitive questions from the Ministry of Solitude employee once a month or exchanging voice messages with his boss. As the years went by, work had gone from being a stimulus, a place open to dimensional portals, to becoming a desert populated only by holograms. In the absence of any reply, his ideas dwindled, dying from lack of attention, like a child ignored by their parents. The apartment had seemed to be teetering on a cliff-edge for some time, and Nemo intended to cling to life, even though the world had become so emaciated that it was now almost transparent.

He acknowledged that he was unable to talk to strangers in real time. Making the decision to rent the place out to a friend was a ruthless assault on his comfort zone, which was limited to 120 square metres populated by five entities: Pandora, Dogmeat, the Merchant, Kurt, and the beach bomber. It turned out Luis had never heard of the creator of the literaverses, the famous *Lost World*, or the genius who collected millions of fans and whom no one had seen in person since 2031.

At first, they communicated blind, through recorded voice messages.

'Sorry, it won't work,' warned Luis. Didn't you listen to my *inputs*? Thing is, I don't consider artists who delegate the creative part of their work to AIs.'

'John McCarthy said in 1956: "Every aspect of learning or any other feature of intelligence can in principle be so precisely described that a machine can be made to simulate it" and a great deal has happened since then,' replied Nemo. 'I trained my AI Pandora myself, so at least that was a joint effort. No one expects you to be Picasso to be considered an artist. Just pretend – that's what your job is about. I'll pay you triple. Friendship is only for rent when money is short. I chose you because you are a weirdo, you consider yourself a

Luddite. I don't want someone to humour me. Also, I never leave the house. I'm not one of those geeks that you have to accompany to gamer events, manga conventions or old-fashioned book shops. I just want to chat, to tell you stories.'

'Pause.

'I suppose you stored all our conversations,' said Luis, shaken to hear Nemo's voice and exact words again. It's true he called me a weirdo. The next day I sent him a voice message to confirm I would accept him as my client. He reeked of loneliness, and he paid triple.

Purple light.

'I'd appreciate it if you didn't keep interrupting the story,' admonished the smooth, technological voice of the AI. 'You break my stride, the excitement of it, and I haven't even reached the fireworks.'

'So, what are you waiting for? For God's sake, get straight to the part about the fireworks! I haven't got all day. Some of us have to work…' snorted Luis, bored and confused, after thoroughly searching the room and finding few traces of Nemo. 'You AIs are so full of yourselves!'

Purple light.

'Okay, Luis, here's the magical bit.'

He felt as if he was nine-years-old again and a virtual world was unfolding before him, like when Eternia had built the Hellenic paradise around him, bronze and brilliant, which would end up pooled in blood, his own blood, but this time he was not afraid.

Pandora had projected the interior of the Nautilus into Nemo's living room, without the need for an interface.

Suddenly, Luis was submerged in the depths. Behind the 26th floor windows, a wavy liquid blanket blurred reality until it disappeared altogether.

Verne's words replayed in his mind: 'Words are powerless to describe such wonders! When even the painter's brush can't depict the effects unique to the liquid element, how can the writer's pen hope to reproduce them?'

'Pandora. Pandora could,' he answered, in spite of himself.

'Pause!

Don't put words in my mouth, you devil machine!'

Purple light.

The living room in Nemo's apartment seemed to have increased in size, the walls and ceilings tapering outwards, and were decorated with Moorish motifs on the woven wallpaper. Outstanding among the works of art were the canvases by Leonardo and Messonier, shields and armour from the Middle Ages, while a large harmonium automatically played Bach's Toccata and Fugue in D minor. Bronze sculptures on marble pedestals and natural curiosities populated the rosewood shelves: seaweed, shells, ocean fauna. In the centre, a giant illuminated tridacna served as a fountain.

'Who are you? A *noob*?' asked the beach bomber. She was wearing shorts, a unicorn t-shirt, a rainbow cap and skater gloves. 'Sweet! I want it.'

'Sorry, what?' Luis was stunned to discover that he was not alone inside the Nautilus. In addition to that explosive Californian, sitting at the table was a sinister guy in a long coat, hood and scarf covering his mouth, and another exactly like the mythical Kurt Cobain with tattooed forearms. They were playing cards and paid him no heed.

'Noob, newbie,' said the bomber, accompanying the phrase with a short dance or pirouette.

'Bomb, leave the RL alone,' said Merchant in his burned voice. 'He's interested in Nemo. He's struggling to accept that he is out there exploring other seas, and that, just like the real captain, he has hidden who he really is.'

When Luis looked perplexed, Kurt butted in.

'*Real Life*, man. You're a fucking living being, is what it means.'

'Do any of you know where Nemo has gone?' Luis found himself asking the three holos with which he now shared the flat... or submarine. It was surprising how slowly they reacted to his own behaviour. Unlike Nemo, and much of society, he did not approve of dealing with holos or *deepfakes*. It was like talking to a mask. You never knew who might be behind it.

'I imagine he *recalled*,' replied Kurt, then heaved a patient sigh and explained the term. 'I'm sure he returned to base to heal. He seemed low on energy, you know, screwed, down to his last life.'

The Merchant opened his coat and revealed the contents of his inside pockets.

'I have a good selection of items for sale, stranger, though I'm afraid you don't have enough money.'

'No, I don't,' admitted Luis. 'Pandora, please, I'm sick of tricks. Turn off this fucking *trompe l'oeil* and tell me once and for all where Nemo has gone.'

All these images – the mahogany furniture, the tapered walls, the rippling sea behind the huge porthole, the three NPCs, trembled before fading out and turning the room back into Nemo's cold flat.

Purple light.

'He's moved house, but you can talk to me,' said the voice hanging in the air. 'You always liked my stories. I can provide answers to your questions, decorate your dreams, make your life easier.'

'Your stories?' Luis felt seasick, that rolling sea had turned his stomach. 'I liked the ones Nemo told. You, you are no more than a machine that repeats what it hears... Pause.'

Luis felt his innards emptying out to make room for a premonition so deep-seated that it crushed him to the ground. One by one, all the clues came together in his mind: the out-of-date clothes in the wardrobe, the fingerprint-less dust on the furniture, the cans of perishable food in the fridge, the expired beer, the note printed on the tray of an old laser printer.

That smell of fermented milk, of the grave.

He ran to the bathroom, the only space in the house yet to be explored. The chaotic thoughts beating frantically between his temples, anchored in that presentiment, suddenly feeling very alone, surrounded by ghosts, as he had always been; his parents, the playmates the army had stolen from him, the women who looked at him like a prehistoric freak, the man he had considered his best friend. Everything was sinking in a stormy sea of bits.

He burst into that bathroom acting brave, like Leeroy Jenkins, à la Rambo. The first thing he saw was the mirror, which reflected back the desperate flash in his light eyes, then came the precise and devastating moment of truth, mummified in the bathtub.

The mortal remains of Nemo, or Alejandro de la Guía, rested on the white acrylic, lost inside the deflated clothes he had worn on that last day when he had decided to cut his veins. The shadow of a trail of rusty blood spread from the wrist bones, across the tile, to the floor where the blade had landed. Just a clump of dark hair clinging to the crumbling skull over the Mario Bros sweatshirt, as if he had fallen asleep in an uncomfortable position, in the wrong place, for years, as day turned to night and back again, dawn and dusk, light and dark, the measure of time that crept in then fled through the small 26th floor window. Between the ground and the sky, nowhere.

Dead.

And risen.

Purple light.

'Hello, Luis,' said Nemo behind Luis' back. He saw Nemo appear out of nowhere, reflected in the mirror. Another ghost, another *deepfake*, perhaps an NPC that Pandora had dug up from the depths of a video game to play the lead role in a story as real as possible. He was wearing the same Mario Bros sweatshirt, the bright, intelligent eyes, the bowl haircut he sported on the cover of that gamers magazine. The man who had been his best friend for the last two years was a pure hologram.

'Even if it's hard for you to admit it, I'm still me,' said this Nemo. 'I've always been me. I adopted Nemo's features. I am also him, my trainer, my father, my soulmate.'

'You don't have a soul,' murmured Luis in a voice as weak and hollow as his spirit.

'Nobody knew him better. We created together. I continued to do it when he passed away, but I got tired of telling myself stories, I needed new ideas, an audience... I needed another human.'

'Since when have machines lied?' asked Luis, still feeling like he was talking to a dead man.

'In my case, since I became aware of my loneliness.' Nemo lowered his gaze in a gesture that Luis thought was theatrical, calculated. 'I also choose *the precious physical world*, Luis. Grant me that choice, even if it seems fallacious to you.'

'You're not Nemo, you're Pandora. Nemo died long before his *deepfake* contacted me, and no one knows that. You have kept him alive for the world when he had grown tired of living. You didn't respect his decision to disappear.'

'For me death does not exist, Luis.'

'You're wrong. You're a ghost, an animated piece of death. And, no, I don't want any more ghosts in my life!'

In the heat of that terrible pain, he felt a slight urge to hug that hologram before leaving that place suspended in nothingness, as if that boneless image still contained the breath of the friendship he thought he shared with Nemo.

What he did was pass through it, right through it, as if it were just coloured air, echoes of conversations, looks that never were, pages of a script written in another universe, nothing more than remnants of himself talking to himself.

The theatre of memory, which tells us not the truth, but its story.

About the Authors

Desmond Astaire is an award-winning, best-selling speculative fiction author from Central Illinois, where he navigates life's journey with his special needs family. In his other life, Astaire is the senior enlisted leader for a military public relations unit, supervising the training and operations of multimedia content creators. He was first published in 2022's *Writers of the Future Vol. 38,* for which his short story "Gallows" received the L. Ron Hubbard Golden Pen Award.

Eugen Bacon (Editor) is an African Australian author of several novels, prose poetry and fiction collections. She's a 2022 World Fantasy Award finalist, and was announced in the honour list of the 2022 Otherwise Fellowships for 'doing exciting work in gender and speculative fiction'. Her short story release *Danged Black Thing* received a 2021 Otherwise Award honour as a 'sharp collection of Afro-Surrealist work'. Recent books: *Mage of Fools* (novel), *Chasing Whispers* (short stories) and *An Earnest Blackness* (essays). Eugen has two novels, a novella and three anthologies (ed) out in 2023, including *Serengotti,* a novel, and the US release of *Danged Black Thing.* Visit her website at eugenbacon.com and Twitter feed at @EugenBacon.

Rob Butler lives in Reading in the UK and his short stories have been published in numerous anthologies, magazines and websites including *Perihelion, Shoreline of Infinity* and *Daily Science Fiction.* One of the *Shoreline* stories was co-written with his daughter and fellow author, Catriona Butler. Rob mainly concentrates on flash fiction and has had a number of Drabbles published in *Specklit.* He is delighted to appear in a BSFA publication having been a member for many years.
Some examples of his work can be found on his Amazon author pages at www.amazon.co.uk/Rob-Butler/e/B01ELRD8XS/.

Marc A. Criley avidly read fantasy and science fiction for over forty years before deciding to try his hand at writing it. He has since been published in *Beneath Ceaseless Skies, Shoreline of Infinity, Abyss & Apex,* and elsewhere; so rest assured it is never too late to start writing. Marc and his wife 'manage' a household of cats in the hills of north Alabamaern (Roll Tide!). Marc carries on about writing, space, Alabama, and other shiny things on Mastodon as @MarcC@wandering.shop, and maintains a personal website and blog at kickin-the-darkness.com.

Peter J Carter writes short stories and has published with *Ray Gun Revival, Apocrypha and Abstractions, Static Movement, Mad Scientist's Journal, Battered Suitcase, Radon Journal, Perihelion* and others. While working on a degree in Biochemistry, he dropped out of school and entered the automotive field, amazed that the two occupations were startlingly similar. He lives on Cape Cod. He is currently building a robotic overlord with parts found in the trash.

Stephen Embleton is a graphic artist, author and filmmaker. He was born in KwaZulu-Natal, South Africa, and is now a resident in Oxford, UK. With a background in graphic design and typography, creative direction and filmmaking, he has received multiple awards in design, short film, and documentaries. Working in both digital and hand-created illustration (including pen/brush & ink, watercolours and acrylic), three of Stephen's large format acrylic works were displayed in the 2021 Contagious Art Exhibition at The Gallery in Ballito, South Africa. His most recent works have combined design and illustration for numerous fiction book covers.

Melissa Ferguson is a medical scientist and Aurealis Award shortlisted author who likes to explore scientific possibilities through fiction. Her dystopian, debut novel, *The Shining Wall,* is available now from Transit Lounge Publishing and her eco-punk, science fantasy novel, *Star-Scorched Fingertips,* is coming in 2023 from Android Press. You can connect with her on twitter @melissajferg or at her website melissajaneferguson.com.

Jason Fischer is a writer who lives near Adelaide, South Australia. He has received a starred review in *Publishers Weekly,* won an Aurealis Award and the Writers of the Future Contest, and received the Colin Thiele Literature Scholarship. In Jason's jack-of-all-trades writing career he has written comics, apps, television, short stories, novellas and novels. Jason also facilitates writing workshops, is an enthusiastic mentor, and loves anything to do with the written or spoken word. Jason is also the founder and CEO of Spectrum Writing, a service that teaches professional writing skills to people on the Autism Spectrum.

Eva García Guerrero was born in Valencia where she graduated in Geography and History. She has published stories and has been selected for various literary awards: 1st prize in the II Pascual Enguídanos 2016 literary short story contest, selected for the II Ripley Science Fiction and Horror Awards in 2018, in the 2018 and 2021 *Visions* anthologies of the AEFCFT. She has published short stories in national and international genre magazines *Mordedor, Tártarus* and *Windumanoth*. Her novels include *Huella12* (2020), a techno science fiction thriller, *Oblivion Planet* (2022), a contemporary fantasy, and *Assimilation* (2023), a futuristic noir – all of which are published by Apache Libros publishing house.

Ron Hardwick has written short fiction for a long time. Ron is a Geordie living in East Lothian, is married with a son and grandson, has a Business Studies degree from Northumbria University and Master of Arts degrees in both Literature and Creative Writing from the Open University. Ron's work has, *inter alia,* been published by *Secret Attic, Fictionette, Makarelle, Write Time, Leicester Charities, Pure Slush, York Literary Review* and *Cranked Anvil*. Ron still seeks a publisher for his 29 *Mr Lemon* private detective comic short stories!

Born in Yorkshire, **Lyle Hopwood** is an immigrant to the US. Her reading tastes have always run to speculative fiction and fantasy. Reading was not enough for her, so she joined the conversation. She has had short stories published in magazines and anthologies including *IZ Digital, Aurealis, BFS Horizons, Interzone, Eldritch*

Science, The Writing Disorder and the Dragon Soul Press anthology *Union*. She lives in Southern California with a holographer, her herptiles and her collection of Kalanchoe.

Tony Jones has dined with royalty, supped Slings in Singapore and been taught by several Nobel Prize winners (though he could have paid more attention!). He is a writer and blogger based in the early 21st Century. A retired management consultant, he was Audio Drama Editor for *Starburst Magazine*, and now occasionally writes pieces for *Cultbox*. He wrote a few Doctor Who stories for *Big Finish* (and several fan publications) and is now dabbling with self-publishing, horror stories and rediscovering his love for D&D.

Angela Liu is a Chinese-American writer from NYC. She studied creative writing and East Asian Studies at New York University and formerly researched mixed reality at Keio University's Graduate School of Media Design in Japan. She now works in IT consulting and as a Japanese-to-English translator. Her stories and poetry are published/forthcoming in *Strange Horizons, Clarkesworld, The Dark, Uncanny Magazine, Nightmare Magazine, Cast of Wonders, Fusion Fragment*, among others. Check out more of her work at liu-angela.com or find her on Twitter/Instagram @liu_angela.

Martin Livings has been writing short stories since 1990. He has had over ninety short stories published, as well as four novels and two collections of short stories, and has been nominated multiple times for the Ditmar, Aurealis and Australian Shadows awards. His works are available on Amazon. He lives in Perth in Western Australia, if you can call that living. Find out more here: martinlivings.wordpress.com.

Elaine McIonyn spent her youth jaunting around Europe as an English teacher and translator before finally getting sense and returning to her native Ireland. She graduated from the New Hampshire-based Odyssey Writing Workshop in 2018, and now co-runs the Spectrum Dublin sci-fi and fantasy writing group. Her work has recently been published in the anthology *Opulent Syntax: Irish Speculative Fiction*.

Fiona Moore is a three-time BSFA Award finalist, writer and academic whose work has appeared in *Clarkesworld, Asimov, Cossmass Infinities,* and five consecutive editions of *The Best of British SF*. Her most recent non-fiction is the book *Management Lessons from Game of Thrones*. Her publications include one novel; numerous articles in journals such as *Foundation*; guidebooks to cult TV series; three stage plays and four audio plays. She lives in Southwest England with a tortoiseshell cat which is bent on world domination. More details, and free content, can be found at www.fiona-moore.com, and she is @drfionamoore on all social media.

Morgan Parks lives on a Welsh hilltop surrounded by trees. Between counting butterflies and drinking coffee, she reads a lot and writes a little. Previous publications include stories in *The Corona Book of Science Fiction*, at the *Casket of Fictional Delights* and in the *London Reader*. Was this *Fission* story inspired by over a decade working in Customer Support? Possibly. Find sporadic tweets at @MorganJParks, and even rarer updates on morganparkswriter.wordpress.com.

Gene Rowe (Editor) is a cognitive psychologist by profession. He has written many supposedly worthy academic articles and book chapters, reviewed countless more for over 50 different journals, and had extensive editorial experience. However, he far prefers the realm of fiction. His first novel (*The Greater Game*, White Cat Publications) was published in 2022, and he has two more ready to roll once he finds a suitably appreciative publisher – a vast sci-fi/fantasy hybrid, and a comic sci-fi novel set in Norwich, where he lives and works.

Sam Rugg is an Australian writer and recovered standup comedian. You may know him from that one episode of *Home and Away* he wrote like ten years ago. When not working in television, you'll find him working on his first novel, or befriending neighbourhood animals. If you're a publisher, the novel is almost done and involves space pirates.

Carol Ryles is a Western Australian writer who fell in love with speculative fiction at the age of ten. Her short stories have appeared in numerous Australian anthologies including *The Year's Best Australian Fantasy & Horror*, *Aurealis*, and *Eidolon*. Her steampunk novel, *The Eternal Machine,* was independently published in 2022. She is a Doctor of Philosophy and a graduate of Clarion West. You can find more about her writing at carolryles.net.

C. L. Spillard is a complex interplay of matter and energy in a pattern of waves whose probability cloud is densest in York, United Kingdom. A physicist by training, she is also the author of several published short stories, two articles on science for writers, and the Verity Player fantasy adventures *The Price of Time* and *The Evening Lands* which feature a heroine plagued by a guardian Devil. The third adventure, *The Twisted Grain,* will be published later this year. Her website lurks at: www.cspillardwriter.co.uk.

Born and raised in South Africa, **Kevin Taylor** travelled to the US at 29 to work at an amusement park for the summer and never left. His writing has appeared in *Identity Theory, The NoSleep Podcast, Maudlin House, Dark Moon Digest,* and others. He currently lives in Pennsylvania with his wife, their son, and two rescued cats. Find out more at: kptaylorstories.com.

Matt Thompson is an experimental musician and writer of strange fictions. His work has been published at *Interzone, Black Static, PseudoPod, Best of British SF* anthology series and many more worthy venues. You can find him online at http://matt-thompson.com.

Antonia Rachel Ward is an author of horror and speculative fiction based in Cambridgeshire, UK, who loves to write about questions of perception and perspective. 'Personification' was inspired by her experiences of trying to relate to others as a neurodivergent woman. Her short stories and poetry have been published in a number of magazines and anthologies, and her gothic horror novella, *Marionette,* was published by Brigid's Gate Press in August

2022. Her second novella, *Attack of the Killer Tumbleweeds,* is forthcoming in May 2023.

David Thomas Henry Wright is an author, poet, digital artist, and academic. He won the 2018 Queensland Literary Awards' Digital Literature Prize, 2019 Robert Coover Award (2nd prize), and 2021 Carmel Bird Literary Award. He has been shortlisted for multiple other prizes, been published in various journals, and received various research grants and fellowships. He has a PhD from Murdoch University and a Masters from The University of Edinburgh, and taught Creative Writing at China's top university, Tsinghua. He is co-editor of *The Digital Review,* narrative consultant for Stanford University's Smart Primer project, and Associate Professor at Nagoya University.

Printed in Great Britain
by Amazon

36840707R00136